PRAISE FOR THE NOVELS OF

Emilie Richards

"Multilayered plot, vivid descriptions, and a keen sense of time and place."   —*Library Journal*

"Richards writes with rare honesty and compassion and has a keen eye for detail. This is a beautiful, heartwarming story that will find its way onto many shelves."

—*Romantic Times*

"Richards pieces together each woman's story as artfully as a quilter creates a quilt, with equally satisfying results, and her characterizations are transcendent, endowed with warmth and compassion."   —*Booklist*

"Richards's ability to portray compelling characters who grapple with challenging family issues is laudable, and this well-crafted tale should score well with fans of Luanne Rice and Kristin Hannah."   —*Publishers Weekly* (starred review)

"A flat-out page turner . . . reminiscent of the early Sidney Sheldon."   —*The Cleveland Plain Dealer*

"If you go for long, intense novels with multiple, unforgettable characters and complex relationships, run to your nearest bookstore and get ahold of *Beautiful Lies*. Put Emilie Richards on top of the bestseller list where she belongs."

—*The Romance Reader*

Blessed Is the Busybody

Emilie Richards

BERKLEY PRIME CRIME, NEW YORK

THE BERKLEY PUBLISHING GROUP
Published by the Penguin Group
Penguin Group (USA) Inc.
375 Hudson Street, New York, New York 10014, USA
Penguin Group (Canada), 90 Eglinton Avenue East, Suite 700, Toronto, Ontario M4P 2Y3, Canada
(a division of Pearson Penguin Canada Inc.)
Penguin Books Ltd., 80 Strand, London WC2R 0RL, England
Penguin Group Ireland, 25 St. Stephen's Green, Dublin 2, Ireland (a division of Penguin Books Ltd.)
Penguin Group (Australia), 250 Camberwell Road, Camberwell, Victoria 3124, Australia
(a division of Pearson Australia Group Pty. Ltd.)
Penguin Books India Pvt. Ltd., 11 Community Centre, Panchsheel Park, New Delhi—110 017, India
Penguin Group (NZ), Cnr. Airborne and Rosedale Roads, Albany, Auckland 1310, New Zealand
(a division of Pearson New Zealand Ltd.)
Penguin Books (South Africa) (Pty.) Ltd., 24 Sturdee Avenue, Rosebank, Johannesburg 2196,
South Africa

Penguin Books Ltd., Registered Offices: 80 Strand, London WC2R 0RL, England

This is a work of fiction. Names, characters, places, and incidents either are the product of the author's
imagination or are used fictitiously, and any resemblance to actual persons, living or dead, business es-
tablishments, events, or locales is entirely coincidental. The publisher does not have any control over
and does not assume any responsibility for author or third-party websites or their content.

BLESSED IS THE BUSYBODY

A Berkley Prime Crime Book / published by arrangement with the author

PRINTING HISTORY
Berkley Prime Crime mass-market edition / December 2005

Copyright © 2005 by Emilie McGee.
Cover illustration by Griesbach & Martucci.
Cover design by Rich Hasselberger.
Interior text design by Stacy Irwin.

ISBN: 0-425-20724-2

BERKLEY® PRIME CRIME
Berkley Prime Crime Books are published by The Berkley Publishing Group,
a division of Penguin Group (USA) Inc.,
375 Hudson Street, New York, New York 10014.
The name BERKLEY PRIME CRIME and the BERKLEY PRIME CRIME design are trademarks
belonging to Penguin Group (USA) Inc.

PRINTED IN THE UNITED STATES OF AMERICA

10 9 8 7 6 5 4 3 2 1

Acknowledgments

The author would like to thank Fran Bevis and the Wickliffe, Ohio, Service Department, particularly Larry, Dan, Stan, Lenny, and Joe for the excellent tour of those facilities. She also thanks Reverend Michael McGee for choosing such an interesting if occasionally harrowing profession, and the members of the six churches he has served for profoundly enriching her life.

1

Teddy was getting ready to bury the cat again, and old Moonpie, whose nine lives had been used up before he was fully weaned, was not protesting. Like me, Moonpie had given up hope that Teddy would quickly outgrow this phase of her development. Too old for protest but too feline for compliance, our silver tabby hung limply in my daughter's thin arms like a burlap sack loaded with buckshot. *Drag me off the picket line if you have to, Mr. Sheriff, but I'm not going to make it easy for you.*

"We've been over this," I told my solemn-faced child. "Just remember you can't bury a living cat. Even if you intend to dig him up again."

Teddy, tortoiseshell glasses pushed to the tip of her freckled nose, didn't blink.

"Well, I felt I had to say something," I added. Teddy's blank stare seemed to demand more. "Me being your mother, your moral compass, so to speak."

Ed came into the kitchen just in time to hear the last sentence. His reddish blond hair was rumpled and his eyes heavy-lidded. My husband always appears faintly bemused, as if there's some universal truth just out of reach, and if he only concentrates hard enough he'll finally be able to grasp it.

On this late summer Saturday morning, in jeans and an ancient Harvard sweatshirt, Ed looked more like someone the Consolidated Community Church had hired to dispose of the trash than the newest minister in an unfortunate lineup. He opened the refrigerator and stared inside. I think he hoped the orange juice would come to him.

"If Teddy doesn't have her own moral compass by now, she never will," he said.

The scent of a theological discussion was hanging thickly in the air, but we had been married for twelve years, and I could waft away this particular disagreeable odor without breaking a sweat. I put my arm around his waist and kissed his hairy cheek. Ed was mid-beard, an annual sprouting of red gold fuzz that only resolved itself when the hottest weather made a beard unbearable. Unfortunately, it was almost September and the weather had not cooperated. My lips tingled.

I stepped back and nudged the refrigerator door closed. Ed didn't notice. Outside I could hear birds singing sweetly and tires squealing on the small street that ran in front of our house. Summer noises in a small Ohio town where nothing ever happens.

"There are six new kitty graves in the backyard," I said, "and the Women's Society board is coming over in an hour to decide if we need professional help pruning the lilacs and forsythia."

"Pruning shrubs requires a visit?"

"Be glad they aren't deciding whether to buy us a new toilet seat. That took two visits. One to determine if the cracks could be repaired, and one to vote on the correct shade of white."

"They're never as bad as you make them sound, Aggie."

"And you're never around when they visit. If they came at midnight, you'd climb out the window in your bathrobe and claim you were making a pastoral call."

He sent me the eyelash lowered, "too bad the kids are in

the room" look that always turns my knees to jelly. "I could try to be as bad as you make me sound."

The kids were in the room, and I soldiered on. "Why don't you shepherd the ladies around the backyard? After you help Teddy fill in all her holes and change your shirt."

"There's nothing at the bottom of any of these holes I should know about?"

I shooed Teddy and Ed toward the door. Moonpie, still passively resisting in Teddy's arms, didn't even twitch his ragged tail. "You can give her some pointers on liturgy. Her funerals need work."

"I know all the words to 'Forward through the Ages,'" Teddy told her father.

I figured Teddy's rendition would get them through the job of filling in the ersatz kitty graves. I looked forward to the day our six-year-old daughter felt comfortable enough with death and funerals to move on to weddings or christenings, although I doubted Moonpie would stand for a long white dress.

Ed has been the minister of the Consolidated Community Church of Emerald Springs, Ohio, for a year. Just long enough, I know from experience, for the applause to die down and the whispers to begin.

We've done this before, Ed and I. Twice before, to be exact. Once in a medium-size church north of Boston, the spiritual home of Unitarian-Universalism—which is our chosen faith. Once in an urban church in Washington, D.C., with politicians and bureaucrats sitting on one side of the aisle and those who were suspicious of them on the other. That was my favorite, a culturally diverse, socially active congregation who stopped arguing frequently enough to perform a plethora of good works.

I was not pleased, after that stimulation, to come here to Emerald Springs, with its small, conservative congregation and buttoned-down rural charm. I was not happy, but I came anyway. I'm a coward. I'd rather be a resentful woman than the wife of a resentful man.

As Ed taught our daughter to sing "Nearer, My God to

Thee," I cleared off the kitchen table, stacking dishes in the sink and cereal boxes in the pantry. Then, on second thought, I took the dishes from the sink and stacked those in the pantry, too, behind the cereal boxes. There was only so much time before the invasion, and it was better not to trumpet the fact that a casual housekeeper had taken up residence in the Women's Society's beloved parsonage.

Although the house was held out to me as a bonus when Ed accepted this call, it's really anything but. Neither Ed nor I have wealthy families, and between us we're still paying off student loans that should have put one of us through medical school and on the road to a lucrative career. So buying a house won't be an option until our daughters have finished college. Not unless there's a mortgage company that takes down payments in sixties superhero comic books and Great Aunt Martha's willowware. We are stuck, it seems, with "bonuses" like this drafty Dutch Colonial and all the dust we can vacuum.

The vast majority of our first floor is taken up by that cavernous space realtors call a "country" kitchen and interior decorators call a "design error." Right now the counters, which lay at opposite ends of a twenty-foot space bisected by an eight-foot farmhouse table, were littered with mixing bowls, cookie sheets, and Aunt Martha's platter half filled with chocolate chip cookies.

I'd had the notion on waking that morning that I ought to serve refreshments as the Society board traipsed through our backyard discussing the perfect height and breadth of lilac bushes. Personally, I wanted my lilacs to look like an old-growth forest. I didn't want a view of the church across the alley since it already took up too many of my waking moments. But I suspected that when the Society board sat in the pews on Sunday morning, they wanted a view of the parsonage.

Just in case I had decided on a whim that week to paint the old frame house flamingo pink.

I gave the remaining dough a few slaps with a wooden spoon and checked to be sure the oven was still on. Then I opened a bag of walnut pieces so that my guests would have choices.

I doubted my culinary diplomacy was going to make much of an impression. Not a woman in the Women's Society would serve anything as ordinary as Toll House cookies to a gathering of this kind. Of course there isn't a woman in the society who still has young children, or a job, or a husband who works at home and trails papers and books through the house with the intensity of Hansel scattering bread crumbs. Most of the members of the board are thoughtful and forgiving. I'm young, of a generation not known for gracious entertaining until Martha Stewart reared her expensively shorn head. They will drink my Hawaiian Punch and ask for the recipe.

With the exception of Gelsey Falowell.

The ghostly enigma known within the confines of the parsonage as Lady Falowell followed me from counter to counter as I dropped the nut-studded dough on baking sheets that mysteriously darkened with every use.

Lady Falowell's baking sheets probably blinded the careless observer. Her baking sheets had probably been handed down through generations by women whose mission on earth was to keep dust, dirt, and baked-on grease from staining any of life's little surfaces. Aluminum monuments to the importance of appearances. *If* our Lady possesses anything as plebeian as a cookie sheet.

Gelsey Falowell is the chairperson of the Women's Society. In the odd year when she isn't the chairperson, she stands behind whatever pliant mannequin agreed to take the job and tells that unfortunate soul when to speak and how to move. Everyone knows Gelsey continues to run the Society, but if anyone minds, I'm none the wiser. In churches, some traditions are so deeply ingrained that logic—a quality on which we religious liberals pride ourselves—is lost in the whorls and grooves.

To say that *everyone* likes Gelsey would be incorrect. To say that *anyone* loves her is probably incorrect, too. Gelsey is like the furniture that's inevitably chosen for a pastor's study. Tasteful, awesomely formal, and so uncomfortable that no one who experiences it firsthand ever wants to linger.

Gelsey is ageless. Sometimes in the minutes before I fall

asleep at night I lay imaginary wagers. Seventy and not a year younger is my best guess, although I could be off by as much as a decade. She carries her tall body like a debutante and moves with the sure, rolling gait of a Tennessee Walker. Her hair is a striking blue silver and her eyes are nearly the same, both set off by the deep tan of a lifetime of tennis matches. I've seen young men trail her body with their eyes, halting ever so momentarily on a tight little rear that never, in the Lady's purpose-filled life, sat idly.

Gelsey is a woman of power and inbred good taste.

Gelsey is a woman whose bad side is a steep slope that leads to personal oblivion.

Gelsey despises my husband.

Ed doesn't believe this last part yet, and pointing it out results in questions about childhood trust issues and whether I'm having a particularly bad time with PMS. It's not that my husband isn't astute, but rather that he chooses to use his healthy intellect on questions like: "Why are we here?" And my personal favorite: "If salvation is only granted to a few, then why aren't the rest of us whooping it up?"

It's not that Ed believes everyone is good. Theoretically, of course, he believes we are born that way. But Ed is practical and experienced enough to know that things begin to change the moment that first 2:00 A.M. bottle is late or that first diaper drips unnoticed. He's seen the best and worst of people, an unfortunate hazard of his job. That he chooses not to see the truth about Gelsey is more a function of personal blinders than of a rosy worldview.

If Gelsey doesn't like Ed, then his life is going to become unbearably complicated. And Ed accepted the call to this nondescript church in this small, nondescript college town in this nondescript quadrant of the state of Ohio because he yearned for silence and simplicity.

Ed was, is, and always will be a scholar and *not* a politician.

I shoved a pan of cookies in the smoking oven. Noise echoed from upstairs now, an annoyed, ambiguous bleating, followed by my daughter Deena's shuffling feet. At eleven our oldest daughter moves everywhere as if she's slogging through mud flats on her way to an execution.

Deena's heading toward adolescence before I've had time to read up on it.

After the fulsome prelude, her arrival was a disappointment. In her father's flannel shirt and last year's gym shorts, she looked almost normal, almost happy—in its purest state an emotion I didn't expect to witness again for perhaps another ten years.

She pulled out a chair, making certain to scrape the floor as she did, and flopped down on it, resting her chin in cupped hands. Since she hadn't yet spoken, I figured we were off to a favorable start.

Time rode sweetly by. Through the window I watched Teddy and her father filling in the final hole. Moonpie was nowhere to be seen. I hoped for the best.

"I don't know why I have to get up," Deena said at last.

"I'd offer you a cookie, but you have to eat something healthier first." I pulled the sheet out of the oven and shoved the final one in its place.

"I'm going to strangle Teddy when she gets inside. I had the pillow over my head, and I could still hear her singing that stupid hymn."

"You'll need strength. She's a wiry little thing."

"How come I had to get up? Those ladies aren't going in my room." She lifted her head and looked at me with impossibly blue eyes. "Are they?"

I shrugged. Frankly, I was already suspicious the Society was conducting surreptitious inspections of the house when we were gone. A couple of times on returning from errands I'd found things out of place or once, odd impressions in my freshly waxed kitchen floor. At least if Gelsey and crew checked the house today, I'd be here for their tour.

Deena dropped her head again at my shrug. "Bogus. Why can't my father work for a bank or something?"

I tried to imagine Ed investing the funds of helpless old ladies. Taking breaks as the market crashed around him to

read new interpretations of Buber or the spiritual significance of cellular mitosis. I told her there was cereal in the
cupboard.

"Nothing I'd eat."

There was no chance Deena would starve. My softly
padded daughter has a healthy respect for food and a disdain
for Hollywood's skinny glamour girls. I'm not sure where
her positive self-image originates, but I'm sure not going to
root around in her psyche to find out.

Deena got up, chair riding comfortably in the grooves in
the floor, and went to the refrigerator. While I finished washing dishes she stood at the refrigerator and ate a carton of
blueberry yogurt, half a banana, and a chocolate chip muf-
fin I'd salvaged from Sunday's social hour. The minister's
salary might be small, but the parish house leftovers make
up for a lot.

Deena closed the door and faced me. This month her
strawberry blond hair falls straight to her shoulders. Hair we
take day by day, never knowing what the morrow might
bring. Her skin is still smooth and clear, her cheeks plump
and rose-tinted. Most of the time she is more interested in
cleaning out stalls at a country horse farm than in her image
in the mirror. This will change, I know, but for now I revel in
her disinterest.

"Do I have to put on different clothes?"

I recognized a challenge when I heard one. "Not if you
don't care what people think."

"Not people. The ladies' group."

"Last time I looked *they* were people. And it's the
Women's Society."

"Society women. Ladies." Her shrug said it all. "Is the
witch flying here on her broom?"

This particular metaphor was the first of its kind, but no
mystery. "Mrs. Falowell. And can the cute stuff, okay?"

"She acts like a witch." Deena picked at the edge of a
counter where the Wedgewood blue laminate was cracking.
Children, I discovered long ago, make it their sworn mission
to expose and highlight all flaws.

I couldn't blame my daughter for disliking Gelsey.

They'd a had an unfortunate run-in. Last month Lady Falowell had caught my daughter riding her bike across the church
lawn in a shortcut to the street. She had lectured Deena at
length on the expense of grass seed and fertilizer and respect
for church property. Deena, never easily intimidated, had
suggested that the Women's Society buy her a horse to replace the bike. The horse could keep the precious grass
mowed and fertilized. What a bargain.

Ed had heard every detail of that conversation from a
number of different sources, all of them female and post-
sixty. Luckily for us, most had been smiling as they recounted it.

I tried to calm the waters. "Sometimes when people live
alone, they get stuck on certain things that seem silly to the
rest of us."

"She doesn't have anything else going on in her life so
she picks on kids." Deena had been a PK—preacher's kid—
from birth. She knew the score.

Picks on kids. On ministers. On the partners of ministers.
"Something like that," I said.

"How long is she going to be here?"

As long as it took to drop hints that whatever we thought
of the Society's plans for pruning our yard didn't matter. Because the Reverend Edward Wilcox, his wife Agate Sloan-
Wilcox, and their two obnoxiously precocious daughters
wouldn't be living in Emerald Springs long enough to disap-
prove.

I scoured the counter and wondered why that thought
made me sad. Emerald Springs and I are not simpatico. The
town doesn't have a Chinese restaurant, for heaven's sake,
never mind Thai, Salvadoran, Ethiopian. The movies that
make their way to the local triplex in our one and only shopping mall routinely rate two thumbs down. Emerald Springs
is a one-horse town—or would have been if Gelsey had
acted on Deena's suggestion.

"I don't know how long she'll be here," I told my pouting
daughter as I tried not to think what that pout would do to
hormonal teenage boys in a year or two. "They're coming to
look at the yard. And you'll be on your best behavior."

Any argument was forestalled by Teddy and Ed's return. Moonpie streaked up the stairs, probably not to be seen or eulogized for the rest of the day.

Teddy joined her sister. They weren't peas in a pod, my darling daughters, but they clearly had the same father. Ed's reddish blond hair, Ed's dark blue eyes. Teddy was thin and athletic, the bane of every little boy on her soccer team, and the lusher Deena was on her way toward being a different sort of bane. But sisters they clearly were.

I, on the other hand, look only like myself. Ed once described me as "not quite." My eyes aren't quite brown, not quite hazel. My hair's not quite black. My body's not quite fashionably thin—I have boobs that make "dartless" clothing a joke.

I'm not quite pretty, although I suspect this never deterred a man, who only saw the boobs anyway. And in my opinion, this particular "not quite" was a blessing. I gave up trying to compete with other women once I realized I was not quite in the contest.

I developed other parts of myself. Parts that are clearly going to waste in Emerald Springs.

"I think I hear a car," Ed said.

In a rush I remembered everything I hadn't done. Taken out glasses and placed them on a tray. Filled them with ice. Opened cans of juice and poured them in a glass pitcher. Discovered the latest hiding place for our paper napkins. The board was early by more than ten minutes, but I should have expected that. Gelsey was the sort of woman who would try to catch Ed off guard.

"You greet, I'll finish here," I told my husband. "But change the shirt first."

He looked down as if trying to imagine what might be wrong. It said Harvard, after all. "Something with a collar," I prompted. "Something without writing on it."

He left for the master bedroom. I made my best guess on the napkins and celebrated a minor victory in the third drawer of an old maple cabinet in the corner. Deena grudgingly agreed to change her clothes, too, and left the room, and Teddy agreed to let the board in after they knocked.

Even Gelsey would have trouble finding fault with our Teddy in her beribboned pigtails and favorite denim jumper.

Motherhood is the best training for doing everything in double time. I finished piling cookies on the platters, got out the ice trays, and managed to open the juice cans. I was feeling on top of things, minimally in control of my destiny, when a scream from our front yard put an end to that.

"Teddy!" I knew the scream hadn't come from my daughter since it had clearly come from an older, hoarser throat, but I was determined to make sure the next one didn't come from Teddy, either.

I sprinted down our center hallway and arrived at the front door before Teddy could open it. Another scream followed the first. Louder and longer, ending on a wail that indicated another would begin as soon as the screamer drew a breath.

"Go upstairs and get your daddy," I told Teddy, barring the door with my body. I wasn't sure we needed Ed, but I was sure my daughter shouldn't be a party to whatever had happened outside.

Curious Teddy was less sure, trying to peer around my body and out the sidelights. Hands firmly on her shoulders, I turned her and sent her off to get her father. Teddy was on the landing and out of sight before I pulled open the heavy front door. A woman lay across our wide front porch, staring glassy-eyed at the sky blue tongue and groove ceiling.

It only took one horrified glance to see she was badly in need of one of Teddy's funerals. And clothing, for that matter. Except for the tattoo of a cobra with a skeleton's head curving around one ample breast, the dead woman, a hard-used blonde, was stark naked.

2

Between her third and fourth marriages, my mother the craftswoman took up needlework. Entire months passed unnoticed as she watched HBO and crocheted extravagant afghans for my two sisters and me. We, the Wilcox branch of the family, own three of that treasured collection. Now one of them, a granny square in hand-dyed earth tones, covered a body on my front porch. Another—a more upbeat turquoise basket weave—draped the trembling shoulders of Sally Berrigan.

"I don't usually scream like that," Sally said.

I perched beside her on the parsonage sofa, patting her shoulder with a hand that trembled, too. "That's okay. You don't usually find bodies."

Sally, who ran the public radio auction each spring, who ran three miles four times a week, and who'd run—unsuccessfully—for mayor of Emerald Springs during last fall's election, shuddered and fell silent again.

"We can certainly fall apart, or we can pull ourselves together and do whatever needs to be done," Gelsey said.

Gelsey's pronouncement had the ring, if not the humor,

of a church signboard. I tried to think of a response that wouldn't sizzle the parsonage air, but my brain was still caught up in the nightmare of a stranger lying naked on my front porch.

Ed came inside at that moment, as if sensing the need for his pastoral presence. "Jack just arrived. He'll wait outside for the police."

This meant Jack's job was to guard the body and make sure it didn't surprise anyone else. He was a hunky young man in his midtwenties, the son of Yvonne McAllister, who was perched on the other side of Sally, trying not to fly apart.

Jack was a first-year associate in a local law firm, enticed home with a promise that he could help with the firm's criminal cases. I suspected this body was as close to a criminal act as Jack had come since his return to Emerald Springs. Ed had called him because Jack and Yvonne lived only one street away.

"Why aren't the police here?" Gelsey demanded.

I wondered the same thing. Our small police department had a notoriously quick response time. I had expected them to beat Jack by minutes.

Ed's voice was deceptively calm. "There was a car accident on campus. They're on their way."

"We pay enough taxes to expect better service." Gelsey cracked consonants like whips, but her pallor belied the edge to her voice. Even Lady Falowell can't dictate to her circulatory system.

"The last tax levy failed," Sally pointed out. "We *don't* pay enough taxes. That was one of my platforms."

"And the reason you lost the election," Gelsey snapped.

Ed tried to distract them by addressing me. "Where are the girls?"

"Deena has Teddy in her room." Deena's room looked out over the backyard and the church next door. Not usually an asset, according to my daughter, but a genuine asset now.

"Did Teddy see anything?"

"No, thank God." And I had. Profusely.

"What was she doing there?" The question came from

Gelsey, and she *wasn't* asking about our youngest daughter.

"We don't know," Ed said. "Hopefully the police will shed some light on it."

Ed was beginning to sound comatose. Serenity was his response to stress, but sometimes his calm appeared to others as dispassion, or worse, disinterest. In Ed's family of origin, the only way to be heard was to speak quietly and politely. In my family that was a recipe for exclusion from every conversation.

"This is the parsonage, and *you* are the minister," Gelsey said.

"For Pete's sake, that doesn't mean he's responsible for everything that happens here," Yvonne said. She was one of the younger women in the Women's Society. Midfifties and as thin as a blade of grass, she chain-smoked whenever she was out of Gelsey's sight. Right now she looked like a woman who badly needed a cigarette.

"I think Reverend Wilcox might well be responsible for whatever happens in this house and on this property."

Gelsey turned to face my husband. She was dressed as casually as I'd ever seen her, in mulberry linen slacks, a matching knit shirt, and a diamond tennis bracelet heavy enough to affect her backhand. Gelsey owned extraordinary jewelry. Genuine stones and the purest precious metals. Heirlooms, she had told me once, as if that would have been perfectly obvious if I were just from a "certain" class.

"Who is that woman?" She paused. "Who *was* she?"

I fully expected Ed to shake his head. After all, how would he know? The dead woman was certainly not our average middle-class congregant. I had seen every inch of her. She was somewhere close to my age, but from appearances she had lived a harder, faster life. I'd glimpsed piercings to go with the tattoo, scars on one arm, coarse skin and short bleached hair, both of which were poorly cared for.

I also glimpsed surprisingly little blood, although clearly, even to my untutored eye, she had suffered a head injury. The close-cropped platinum hair had not hidden the bruises and one deep gash.

"Her name was Jennifer Marina," Ed said.

I caught his eye. "Ed, you knew her?"

"She stopped by the church office a couple of times."

"And why was she stopping by *this* morning?" Gelsey said.

I didn't like Gelsey's tone, but how unusual was that? At our first meeting Gelsey had looked me over carefully, and proceeded to interrogate me about my family background. I had failed on all fronts except one. I had not, despite all natural inclination, told Gelsey where she could stuff her evaluation.

Now Ed didn't tell her, either. He nodded, as if the question were perfectly reasonable. "I doubt she was stopping by today, Gelsey. I can promise each time she came to my office, she was fully clothed."

If Gelsey heard the vibrations of sarcasm, she didn't let on. "But you admit you knew her? What did she want?"

Ed didn't blink, but I could see he was losing his temper. His voice grew even softer. "I'm sorry, but it was private."

"Private?"

"Not everything that happens in the church is a matter of public record," I said, defending my husband, although I was curious, too. "I'm sure there's not a single church member who'd want everything they've said or done at Tri-C exposed."

"All that's a matter for the police," Ed said. And as if he whistled them out of thin air, brakes squealed and a police radio squawked from Church Street, just in front of our house.

"I'm sure the police will want statements from the three of you," Ed said, addressing the Society board as he headed for the front door. "Then I'm sure you'll be anxious to go home. Aggie will let you out the back way."

The door closed behind him. For a moment the room was ominously still. Then Gelsey said, "This church was founded in 1866, and in all the years since, we've never had a scandal to rival this one." She addressed the board, but her eyes flicked to me. "Not until Ed Wilcox took over our pulpit."

+   +   +

People twist facts during moments of crisis. Gelsey had twisted a few. Through the centuries, the Consolidated Community Church of Emerald Springs, Ohio, has suffered a number of scandals juicy enough to linger through generations in the hearts and minds of parishioners and more important, in the poorly kept church archives. I know, because I agreed to serve as historian this year.

Generally I don't take volunteer positions in the church. Who wants to go head-to-head with the people who sign your spouse's paycheck? But historian is a job I can do by myself. Just me and those ceased-pledging-and-breathing members whose secrets rest in scrapbooks and file cabinets and 8 mm movies of church picnics and ministerial installations. Call me crazy, but no one in the great unknown wants to fire my husband, paint the parsonage walls Ace Hardware puce, or give me advice on how my children should dress on Christmas Eve. Reindeer antlers, it seems, are not in the best of taste, particularly when teamed with a bulbous, electrified nose.

The archives are a wealth of information, and I've shared some teasers with the Women's Society board, along with my grandiose plans to put Tri-C's history in apple pie order and present it a la PowerPoint at the September meeting. True, dead blondes on the parsonage steps are a new twist in the life of the church, but we've had flaming love affairs, scandalous divorces, and once, during the Civil Rights era, a fiery cross on the front lawn. My presentation could turn out to be a real corker if Deena finishes helping me put all this on computer.

I thought of this as the room fell silent, because I didn't want to think about what Gelsey was really saying. Here was another excuse to fire Ed. All she needed were a few more facts.

Yvonne and Sally tried to cover Gelsey's words. They took me up on my offer of fruit juice and cookies and followed me into the kitchen while Gelsey remained in the living room. I suspected she wanted to be first in line when the police began questioning witnesses.

"Of course this isn't Ed's fault," Sally said. "Gelsey's

upset, and that's how she acts. You always see her at her worst. I'm sorry you don't see the same woman we do."

I stayed a mile away from that. "Everybody reacts to stress differently." By now the ice in the glasses had melted, and I poured the water in the sink and went to the freezer for more.

Sally dished out cookies on individual plates, although none of us were hungry. The batch with nuts had smoldered in the oven while I was busily discovering a body on my porch. The kitchen still smelled of smoke and cremated chocolate.

Sally set the plates on the table. "When I ran for mayor, Gelsey was the one who funded my campaign. She said I'd never win, but the town needed to hear what I had to say."

I nodded Buddha-like and breathed deeply.

Yvonne took her turn. "When my husband died, Gelsey was the one who took care of all the paperwork. I was in a fog for weeks, and when I came out of it, everything was in perfect order. And she made sure somebody in the church brought Jack and me dinner every single night until I could take care of things on my own."

At that moment I wanted to believe Gelsey performed these lovely acts simply to create a debt her friends could never repay. But I knew better. Gelsey did not like Ed, and she did not like me or our children. But no one inspired this kind of loyalty solely by manipulation. If emotional blackmail was the case, there would be resentment, too, and I heard none in their voices.

Sally lowered hers. "She's usually a help to the minister and his family. A support. I don't understand this. Everybody likes Ed. Everybody likes you."

"Everybody" was, of course, an exaggeration, but I liked the sound of it. Surely even the lone voice of a powerful woman couldn't silence the multitudes.

The conversation was cut short when Ed came into the kitchen, followed by Jack. Jack was dressed in cutoffs and a T-shirt that advertised Mud Wrestling Mondays at "Don't Go There," a particularly notorious bar on the western outskirts of town.

"This is what the enterprising young attorney wears?" I asked, giving him a quick hug. Jack is a love. Cute, sexy, intelligent. Sometimes I wish I had a daughter old enough for him, and sometimes I fantasize I'm ten years younger and minus one husband.

He pulled the shirt away from his chest. "The perfect crime scene wear. I'm a trendsetter." His smile wasn't steady.

Ed came over and dropped a comforting hand on my shoulder. "The police are securing the area. They've asked us to wait inside."

Even though I knew it was too early, I had to ask. "Do they know anything?"

"Well, now they know her name."

"Good thing you knew her. She wasn't exactly carrying identification."

I wished I could get Ed off to the side to ask what he knew about Jennifer Marina, what they had discussed, why she was living in Emerald Springs. But even if I'd been able to, there was an excellent chance he wouldn't tell me. Ed takes his role as a counselor seriously, and confidentiality is a large part of it.

"Would you like to check on the girls?" he asked. "I'll stay here."

I shot him a grateful smile. I wanted to tell our daughters what I could, to assuage the worst of their curiosity before it got the better of them.

When I left the kitchen Ed was pouring fruit juice over ice and asking his guests what they were feeling at the moment. Pastor to the core.

Deena's room is big enough for triplets, but that hasn't stopped her from filling the space. She has two desks. One for Ed's old computer, one to spread out books when she does homework. Her canopied double bed with a gingham and calico quilt and dust ruffle takes up one corner, and shelves take up another, filled with the Black Stallion, Harry Potter, and a musty, garage sale set of the Harvard Classics. She has a green striped beanbag chair against one wall, courtesy of my old college dorm room, and that's where she and

Teddy were cuddled right now. Deena was in full big sister mode, but I figured she was only good for another half hour tops.

"You two doing okay?" I stood in the doorway, waiting to be asked into the inner sanctum.

"What's going on?" Teddy didn't move. Deena's attention was so rare and mine so ordinary, she had clearly chosen her position based on relative value.

"May I come in?"

Deena waved a royal hand and I closed the door behind me.

"We've had a pretty bad shock," I said. "Somebody died."

"People die all the time," spoke the born PK. Deena, unlike her little sister, had already worked through the excess of memorial services and funerals in her father's line of work. To Deena, death was not an extraordinary occurrence, even in a congregation as small as this one.

"This was more unusual." I flopped down on the floor beside them. "Her body was—" I pictured them going blithely out the front door from this day forward. That was never going to happen if I told them exactly where the body had been found. "In front of our house," I finished. It wasn't exactly a lie.

"She died at our house?" Teddy looked curious, but not horrified.

"We don't know where she died. Probably not here. But she was discovered out front."

"By the ladies," Deena said. "One of them sure can scream."

"I told you it was a pretty bad shock. Not what you expect when you visit the minister."

"Who was it?" Teddy's forehead was wrinkled.

"Nobody I know."

"What's she look like?"

"Honey, I don't see why—"

"I might know her."

I considered that. I don't know my Teddy very well yet. She solemnly weighs the things that happen around her, much as her father does, and usually keeps her own counsel about them. I'm not always sure what's happening under those straight strawberry blond bangs.

I left out the tattoo and settled for the obvious. "She's about my age. Very short blond, almost white, hair. I've never seen her."

"I have," Teddy said.

"I really doubt it, honey. She's not a regular member. She—"

"I saw her yesterday. In the parking lot talking to Daddy."

I didn't know what to say.

"She and Daddy were fighting," Teddy continued.

"How could you know they were fighting if they were all the way back in the church parking lot?"

"I was outside, climbing our tree. She was waving her hands all around. Like this." Teddy gave a good imitation of a woman gesturing angrily and nearly socked her sister in the eye. "Besides, I heard her shouting."

I sat silently, wondering if I should ask what the woman had said. I didn't have to. Teddy finished on her own.

"She said: 'You can't tell me what I can do. I'll talk to anybody I want to, tell them anything I feel like telling them. I don't care who gets hurt!'"

I didn't doubt Teddy. The inflection was not my daughter's. She was imitating what she had heard and doing a chillingly fine job of it. I felt as if I'd just heard the dead woman's voice.

"Well, Daddy will tell the police everything he knows," I said, trying to sound reassuring and maternal. "Whatever was wrong with her, he'll be sure to tell them."

I wondered, though, if it were true.

3

Detective Kirkor Roussos was not exactly what I had expected. After the ethnic melting pot of Washington, Emerald Springs is Wonder Bread bland. Our most diverse citizens are third-generation Italians and Poles, with blocks and blocks of Anglo Saxons to water down that heady mixture. We have a small but vital African American community and just recently we've attracted a few Latinos. But Greeks, especially one who looked pure enough to be posing in a provocatively draped chiton, laurel wreath, and sandals, seem to be rare here.

Actually, the detective was wearing faded jeans, a black T-shirt, and a worn silk sportscoat. The last, I guessed by the wrinkles, had been pulled on in a hurry as he left to take this call.

He shook my hand as he introduced himself, but he assessed me, much as Gelsey always did. Thankfully, he seemed to find me less distasteful. He granted me one brief white smile, made more so against tanned olive skin, and asked me to take a seat in my living room.

"Call me Kirk," he said, dispensing with the formalities as he took a seat just across from me.

I guessed he was in his early forties, with black hair cut short and eyes nearly as dark. Surely there were entire fishing villages in the Aegean populated with men who stopped female hearts the way this one did.

I tried to make myself comfortable. "I'm Aggie."

He glanced down at a paper in his hand. "Short for Agate?"

"My mother polished rocks for a living the year I was born." Junie's rock-polishing stage had lasted long enough to include my baby sister, Obsidian, forever after known as Sid.

"How long have you lived here, Aggie?"

"Going on a year."

"In this house?"

"The whole time."

"Do you work outside the home?"

I assumed he was trying to put me at ease, but that question was destined not to. Lately I'd been feeling very Donna Reed and wishing I had some place to go in the mornings other than the supermarket.

"I'm a homemaker," I told him. "And mother."

He rested his notes on one knee and sat forward. "Tell me about your morning. What you did. Where you did it."

I left out waking next to Ed and the lovely things we had done immediately after. "I got up about seven thirty—"

"I'm sorry, does your bedroom face the street?"

"Yes."

"And you didn't hear any unusual noises while you were in bed?"

Just the ones Ed and I had made, but I couldn't say those were unusual. "Nothing out of the ordinary. I heard the newspaper hit the sidewalk at the usual time—"

"Which is?"

"A little before seven. It always wakes me up, but most of the time I go back to sleep for a while."

"What happened after you got up?"

"I took a shower, dressed, and went downstairs."

"Did you get the newspaper?"

"I made coffee first and got out milk and cereal for breakfast." I scoured my memory. How often was someone interested in the mundane details of my day? "I let the cat out the backdoor. Then I went out front for the paper."

"Did you see anything out of the ordinary?"

I wished I had. I wished I had the perfect detail to insert here, the winning lottery ticket in the murder investigation that would make this man's teeth flash again. But the morning had seemed like every other. The girls were still in bed. Ed was upstairs showering and getting ready for the day. Moonpie was stalking butterflies.

"Concentrate on what you saw," Detective Roussos said.

"The door was locked. I opened it and stepped on the porch." I shrugged. "No body. That I would remember."

"Go on."

"I reminded myself to water the planters. The petunias were drooping."

"They still are," he said.

I smiled a little. "You're a gardener?"

"Vegetables, some herbs. Go on."

"I walked down the front steps, not the ones on the side that go down to the driveway. The paper was lying halfway up the sidewalk. I got it, took it out of the plastic bag to scan the headlines, didn't like what I saw, and tucked it under my arm. Then I looked to see if anyone else was around."

He slid farther forward. "Were they?"

"Our street's not very busy that time of morning. I didn't see my next-door neighbors—"

He looked down. "Mr. and Mrs. Simon?"

"Right. An older couple. Usually I throw their paper up to the porch so they won't have to go up and down the stairs. But it was already gone."

I tried to picture the street that morning. We didn't have real neighbors on the other side of the parsonage, just a narrow alleyway leading to the church parking lot. The church proper sat beside the parish house and both backed up to the alley. "Sometimes the sexton is outside the church cleaning trash off the sidewalk or watering, but not this morning."

He looked blank, as if he wondered what bizarre rituals we performed inside the church walls and who performed them.

"A *sexton* is a janitor. Church janitor," I prompted.

He looked vaguely relieved. "Anyone else?"

I tried hard to remember. In every possible way the morning had been ordinary.

Every way but one.

"Well, there was a car parked in the driveway across the street, and now that I think about it, that's unusual. The house is for sale, and it's in bad shape so they aren't getting any movement on it. Lucy—my best friend—is a realtor, so she keeps me informed."

"Did you see anybody in it? Can you describe it?"

I tried to remember, even though I knew this was probably not much of a lead. "It was an SUV of some kind. I remember it sat up high, the way they do. You know, on big tires." I spread my arms to make my point. "One of the smaller ones. Dark green, maybe, I'm not sure."

"License plate?"

My arms fell to my sides. "I wasn't paying that much attention."

"Would you notice out of state tags?"

I considered. "I'm not sure."

He grimaced. "And occupants?"

"I didn't see anybody. The car was just parked there. Maybe somebody had gone inside to do repairs or cleaning. It was probably too early for potential buyers, and besides, the SUV wasn't the kind of car a realtor drives. Too casual. A little beat-up."

"Anything else?"

"Nope. The cat came around front, and we went back inside, and I made breakfast. My youngest daughter came down and ate cereal, then she took the cat outside again to bury him."

His face said it all. I explained until he relaxed. Gardener *and* animal lover. A back to the land kind of guy. Roussos would like my father.

I told him about Ed joining us, about his going outside to

help Teddy fill in the other holes she'd dug that week, about the cookies and the Women's Society board and Deena's arrival. I was out of breath by the time I finished, and his eyes had glazed over.

"During any of that time did you hear any unusual noises? Did you look outside at any point after you came inside from getting the paper?"

I tried to remember. "I stayed in the back of the house. We're protected from the street and don't get much noise, even with the windows open. I did hear tires squealing out front."

"Do you remember when?"

I did the math. "Between eight thirty and nine." I realized the squeals might well have come from the car that had dropped the body on our doorstep. The timing was certainly right.

"We were inside. All of us." I shivered. I was glad Teddy hadn't gotten up earlier. What kind of murderer waited until broad daylight to dispose of a corpse? It didn't make sense. A murderer could have been shielded from our neighbors by the tall evergreen hedge planted halfway down to the road on the other side of our driveway, and shielded from Church Street by a silver maple anchoring the corner of our porch. He might have backed in, taken the side steps, left the body, and screeched away.

But what if one of us had been close to a front window and gone out to see who had come to visit?

"If we showed you photos of SUVs, would you be able to pick out the make and model?"

I knew this was the place where I said "sure," and found the car on my first try. Impressing this man would be heady.

"No," I said sadly.

"Luggage rack? Bike rack? Clean? Dirty?"

I scrunched my eyes closed and willed myself to remember. I had barely glanced at it. "Just an impression that it wasn't brand new or all that well taken care of."

"Did you recognize the victim?" he asked.

I opened my eyes and shook my head. "I've never seen her before." I didn't tell him Teddy had. Ed would have to report the conversation in the church parking lot from his own perspective.

He stood, and I did, too. We were finished, but I had a question. "You know, I watch enough *Law and Order* to remember that head wounds bleed a lot. Hers didn't."

"Not by the time you saw it."

"She'd been dead awhile?"

He shrugged.

Dead and cleaned up and undressed. Although who knows when that last item had happened in the sequence of events. "Do you have any idea why somebody would do this? Maybe a serial killer who hasn't made it into the *Flow?*" The *Flow* was our local daily. *Emerald Springs Flow,* somebody's idea of clever.

"I don't have a thing I can tell you. But thanks for your help." He shoved his hand in my direction. I took it for a brief, hard shake, but I didn't let go when he started to withdraw.

"I have two young daughters," I said. "I'd like to know if we're in danger. Please don't be evasive." Then I dropped his hand.

"This is the first murder we've had in Emerald Springs this year. As far as I know we've never had one that looks anything like this."

"And statewide no one's dumping bodies on the porches of random ministers?"

"Not to my knowledge. But we'll know more as we go along."

"Will you tell us if we have anything to worry about?"

"You'll be the first to know."

Judging from his carefully schooled expression I wasn't reassured.

◆   ◆   ◆

Lucy Jacobs was waiting in my kitchen when I returned from talking to Detective Roussos. The yard was swarming with cops, half the Emerald Springs force seemed to be somewhere on the property, but Lucy had found her way inside without a word from anyone.

"So . . ." she breathed. "So, Aggie. This is too amazing for words. . . ."

"How did you get in?" Ed was gone. Between his interview and mine he had told me he was taking the girls to stay with the Frankels, church members who had daughters near the ages of ours. He wanted them out of the house until the police departed.

"I darted from lilac to lilac, then made one final sprint for the kitchen door."

"I guess the lilacs really do need to be trimmed."

"What—is—going—on?"

I'm still not sure how Lucy and I became friends. We aren't neighbors. She lives on the other side of Emerald Springs, an ambitious career woman with no children. She's not a member of our church. She's a Reform Jew who would sooner attend a hanging than any house of worship. But we met six months ago in a long line at Krogers. By the time the clerk got to Lucy the ice cream had melted and we were bosom buddies. Sometimes life works out the way it's supposed to.

I love a million things about Luce. She's funny. She has a smile that nudges her ears and wild red Orphan Annie hair. Best of all, she worries about all the things I forget to. Between us, the universe is basically covered.

"Do you know if the owner of the house across the street has authorized any repairs?" I asked.

"Aggie! Tell me what's going on!"

I did, succinctly. Lucy's a great audience. Her green eyes get as big as tennis balls when she's excited, which is most of the time. Her mother named her for Lucille Ball, and it's hard to say if her mother was on to something or the name influenced Lucy. But sometimes when we're together I feel like Desi should be practicing conga drums in the next room.

"You don't mean it." She sobered a moment. "That poor woman. What a terrible thing."

I told her about seeing the SUV. "So, do you know anything about the house? Can you find out?"

"Are the police using your phone?" She went to the wall phone and picked up the receiver. Disappointment scrunched

her features. "No, darn it." Clearly she had hoped to pick
up some tidbit from their conversation. "Hand me my Palm
Pilot."

I searched through a purse as large as a briefcase, found
and flipped open the organizer for her. She punched in a
name and squinted as she committed the resulting phone
number to memory.

I sat back and watched the master of information gathering.

Lucy leaned against the counter. "Sarah? How-are-you-
this-is-Lucy. I'd love to show the house on Church Street tomorrow, but I hear they're doing repairs. Can you tell me
what? Will it interfere?"

She listened, all eyes and coiling shoulder-length curls.
She gestured excitedly at me as the other realtor spoke. "Re-
ally? You mean I heard wrong? Maybe it was the owners then.
Someone saw a car parked in the driveway early this morn-
ing." She gestured again. "They're on vacation in Colorado?
How odd. And I'm sure no one was showing it that early. . . ."
She covered the receiver. "Do you want her to come over and
take us through the house? Or shall we go alone?"

I wasn't sure how things had gotten to this point. Wasn't
this a job for the police? On the other hand, what kind of
lead did they have? I'd seen an SUV in the driveway. Roussos hadn't been impressed. How long would it take before
someone got around to checking inside the house?

How about forever?

Lucy didn't wait for my reply. "Well, I think I'll just
check it out before I take my clients. They're not much of a
bet, so don't get your hopes up." She listened, said her good-
byes, and hung up. "She'll be so-o-o-o pissed when she finds
out what happened over here. She'll know I was lying." She
didn't sound concerned.

"Lucy, we can't march through the front yard and across
the street. Someone will notice."

"I'm parked in the church lot. We'll get the car and drive
to the house. It's perfectly legitimate, Aggie. I'm a realtor.
The house is for sale. There's a lockbox. If the police want to
come, too, let them."

Curiosity has always been my downfall. As a young child I was the fearless middle sister who climbed the forbidden backyard maple to spy on neighbor children. And later that same day as I waited for my X-ray, I was the one who followed suspicious noises and found my doctor and nurse conducting a private anatomy class. The other occasions when I've let my curiosity get out of hand are too numerous to mention. Rarely have they turned out well.

"Is this one of those minister's wife hang-ups?" Lucy said. "Are you afraid someone might think bad things about you?"

"If value judgments are being made, they have to do with a certain body on our porch."

"So?"

I was sure we weren't in danger. Whoever had dumped poor Jennifer Marina was probably in Pennsylvania or West Virginia by now. But it would be wonderful just to peek at the house, to see if there was any reason to summon the police and not wait for them to get around to a visit on their own.

I got to my feet. "Let's go."

I don't remember sneaking out of my own yard since I was a teenager. It was heady. I felt sixteen again, with all of life's decisions just ahead of me and Johnny Vincuzzo, the class bad boy, waiting on the corner.

Lucy drives American. This year it's a cherry red Chrysler Concorde with sandstone leather trim. According to Lucy she trades up as soon as the new car smell begins to disappear. No one eats chocolate chip cookies or peanut butter in Lucy's car. No one drips ice cream cones or picks up stray dogs. When she takes my girls on shopping trips or shows houses to clients with children, Lucy borrows her mother's Chevy or my minivan.

I gave the Concorde the sniff test, and it passed. This car would be around for months. I was glad. It was a pretty thing that cheerfully screamed Lucy's arrival, so I always had a moment to take a breath and prepare.

"Just what are we going to be looking for?" I asked. "Because I don't want more of what I found this morning."

"I'm sure that was awful." She paused. "Nothing like that ever happens to me."

I knew Lucy was genuinely sorry a woman had died. But if someone had to die, she was sorry it hadn't been on her watch. She was an adrenaline junky. A murder was fuel enough to drive her for weeks.

"Well, I wish it hadn't happened to *me*." I peeked at my house as we turned the corner. The body was gone now, but yellow crime scene tape fluttered from the railing of my porch. Clumps of police officers still chatted in the yard. "I wish it hadn't happened to *her*."

"And you never met her?"

I hadn't told Lucy about Ed's relationship with Jennifer Marina, or Teddy's version of the argument in the church parking lot. "A total stranger."

Lucy pulled into the driveway of the house and cut the engine before she reached for her listings book. "Okay, we'll just wander through. I was here last week. I think I'll notice if anything is really out of place."

"Out of place? It's furnished?"

"The owners rented it out for a few months, and they left the renters all the junk they didn't want in their new house. That's one of the reasons it hasn't sold. It's not a bad old place, but it takes imagination with all that stuff lying around."

We got out. I didn't look at my house, but I wondered if Detective Roussos was one of the men lingering on my lawn.

The house was standard issue in Emerald Springs. Built sometime in the first half of the twentieth century with a porch that had been enclosed sometime in the second, the house had dull green aluminum siding, trim that needed paint, a narrow front yard with overgrown rhododendrons, and an oak that menaced Church Street.

"The backyard is lovely." Lucy was in realtor mode. "It extends all the way back to the park. The inside trim is oak, and so are the floors. They redid the bathrooms not long ago. Nicely, too. Real tile. A double sink upstairs."

I followed her up to the porch and inside to the main door. "You don't have to convince me. I have a house. I live in the barn across the street, remember?"

"One of the prettiest houses in Emerald Springs."

I guess at times the parsonage does have a certain charm. Maybe I'm just afraid to fall in love with it. If Gelsey has her way, our occupancy will be limited.

I watched Lucy fiddle with the lockbox. "Let's get inside quickly, okay? I have a feeling we won't be alone for long."

Lucy was frowning at the box. "This is relatively new to me. Be patient. We've just gone to this system."

The lockbox was a new one, more mini-computer than padlock. Lucy inserted what looked like a credit card into the bottom, punched a series of buttons a second time, squinting as she did, then tried once more, cursing under her breath. This time the key storage compartment at the top opened. She retrieved the key and inserted it in the locks. There were two that looked brand new and no-nonsense, a doorknob and a dead bolt. Neither went quietly. After a lot of jiggling, the door swung open. She left it unlocked so getting out would be easier than getting in.

"I can pick a lot of locks if I have to," Lucy said. "You'd be amazed what being a realtor has taught me. But these two would be next to impossible. The lock on the knob's an expensive one with a deadlocking latch, which means no one can get in with a pocket or putty knife. They'd have to kick the door or pry it open. Then there's the deadlock. See, it has a steel shank here." She pointed. "And it automatically double latches."

I wasn't sure I wanted to know just how she had learned all this. I suspect a lot of locks had been picked on this quest for knowledge. I followed her inside, glancing behind me as I did to see if we'd attracted the attention of the men in front of my house. No one was sprinting across Church Street. That seemed promising.

We stopped in the entryway and gazed around. The living room was to my right, the kitchen straight ahead, just past a stairwell curving to the left. Lucy had been right about the lovely woodwork and the mess. The house smelled like mildew and looked like the final day of Tri-C's annual rummage sale.

"Don't say it," Lucy said. "Every realtor in town has tried

to get the owners to clean it out. We've even found people to do it for them, but they're odd ducks. They think it's a bargain just the way it is."

"It's such a mess how can you tell if anything's been moved?" I wandered forward. A window table with a dying fern sat beside the stairwell. I'd already passed a piano with most of the ivory missing.

Lucy followed me into the kitchen. Mismatched wooden chairs sat around a tile-top table with all of the grout worn away. "Nothing's different so far," Lucy said. "Except the smell is worse. Let's open a window." She opened one beside the table. "The basement needs waterproofing or a new sump pump. That's where the smell's coming from."

I could see possibilities here. Lots of them. With new countertops and new hardware on the cabinet doors, the kitchen would be improved drastically. A little paint, a little paper . . .

"You have a gleam in your eye," Lucy said.

"A little window dressing and this would be habitable."

Lucy leaned against a counter. "What would you do?"

I told her and added a few touches for good measure. "The floors aren't bad. I bet they could be scrubbed clean with Spic And Span and sealed. A couple of cheerful throw rugs, and this would be welcoming. Even homey. I grew up in rental houses. One right after another, and Junie, my mother, was a pro at making them come to life without spending much money." Ed and I have lived in enough old apartments to assure me I've inherited Junie's abilities.

We wandered through the rest of the downstairs. I told Lucy what I would do if the house were mine. I was making conversation simply to keep my mind off our real purpose. But as I talked, I searched, looking for something to place the murderers here this morning.

"Nothing different?" I asked after we'd made a circle and ended up at the stairs again.

"I don't think so." Lucy was peering up the stairwell. "Upstairs next? Or the basement?"

I prefer to take my chances in rooms with windows. I

climbed out of dozens in my misspent youth; I was confident I could make a quick escape from the second floor. I pointed toward heaven. "Who goes first?"

We climbed side by side. On the landing we peered into the second-floor hallway. Floors that needed finishing. Walls that needed painting. Nothing sinister.

Four bedrooms lined the hallway and a large bathroom sat at the end. We started on our right. The bedrooms were small and mercifully clear of most furniture. Overhead light fixtures illuminated the corners that sunlight didn't. The rooms were unkempt but undisturbed.

Except for the final one. This was the largest of the four with the closest access to the bathroom. There was another smaller room off of it with no hallway entry, which might well have been intended as a nursery or, perhaps, a study. The smaller room was lined with windows overlooking the spacious backyard. When the larger room revealed nothing extraordinary, I strolled into the smaller one.

The windows were filmed by grime, except for one which looked as if it had been recently washed. Very recently. The room smelled like Windex. "Lucy?"

Lucy was testing the plumbing in the bathroom. I heard the toilet flush. I strolled closer to the window, searching every inch of floor as I moved. The floor slanted just enough that an office chair would not be a good idea here. Gravity would always win.

The floor seemed cleaner beneath the window. I stooped and ran my finger along floorboards. My fingertip came up clean. Not so a few feet away where a fine dust coated it immediately.

I backed away, trying to judge how large an area had been washed. The wall might be cleaner under the windows, too, although I wasn't sure. The institutional green paint was old and faded.

"Lucy?"

This time she joined me. "Find something?"

I showed her. She frowned, studying the area. "What, maybe four feet by four feet of the floor? A window. And I think you're right about the wall under the window, too."

"Why would anybody clean this one area only, unless they were trying to erase signs of something?"

I knelt, then carefully and thoroughly I began to sweep my palms over the floor. Inch by inch. I saved fingertips for the cracks between boards. One crack that was larger than the others was still damp where water had pooled and hadn't yet evaporated. We hadn't been wrong.

"And the listing agent claimed that no one was here this morning?" I said.

"Aggie, Sarah would have an orgasm if she could get a cleaning crew in here. She'd still be bragging about her powers of persuasion."

I scooted back on my haunches and felt the next section. "Well, someone cleaned up for free. It's still damp." I continued my search, moving slowly toward the window. I could feel the slant of the floor as I moved closer. I pitched forward slightly. Another sweep and I was nearly at the wall.

I'm not sure I would have seen the glint of gold if I hadn't been so close. I know I wouldn't have felt anything out of the ordinary. But summer sunshine flooded the floor just in front of me, and caught the object wedged low between the wall and floorboards. It was so tiny I could see why our mysterious Mr. Clean had missed it.

"Look." I knelt and leaned forward. "Do you have a tissue?"

Lucy rummaged through the purse of all purses and handed me one that was still neatly folded.

I used it to dig for the object. When I was finished, I held it out to her.

"An earring?" I was disappointed. I had hoped for something more exciting. The object was shaped like a crescent moon, with a large gold ball on one end. The other end appeared to be threaded and the wire was thicker than I'd expected.

Lucy leaned closer. "That never saw an earlobe. Haven't you ever thought about piercing some more interesting part of your anatomy?"

I looked up. "Like?"

"Nipples? Belly button? Something only Ed would see?"

I had witnessed the hole in Jennifer Marina's nose and the multiple holes in the cartilage of her ear. I had missed the tattoo and body piercing craze by a number of years, and for this I have always been grateful. We had been about the same age, the poor dead woman and I, but Jennifer hadn't let age stop her from pursuit of fashion.

"It's called a barbell," Lucy explained. "My little sister has one in her right nostril, only hers is straight. This is the kind that goes in other places. Maybe just an eyebrow if the wearer isn't too daring, or maybe genitals. They pierce things now that our mothers didn't even have names for."

I got to my feet, still holding the barbell on Lucy's tissue. "We ought to tell the police. I noticed holes in the victim's ear and nose. This could be hers."

"You're a perceptive woman," said a voice behind us. A male voice. "Unfortunately, something tells me you're also too nosy for your own good. And maybe for mine."

✦ ✦ ✦

Ed and I like good wine, but we drink the cheap stuff. We like to pretend we've discovered secret stores of premium vintages, misbottled and sold for less than a sawbuck. It's easier to imagine when we've had too many glasses, which rarely happens, since that's expensive, too, in all sorts of ways.

Tonight I poured both of us a second glass and suspected that even Ed's Temperance Society foremothers would understand. It had been that kind of day.

I rolled my glass back and forth in my hands and gazed at it as if I were performing some esoteric pagan rite. "You know when you took the girls over to the Frankels' house?"

"Uh huh." We were cozied up together on the living room sofa, and he was finishing a book for Sunday's sermon. Judging from the small print and the twenty-word title, I hoped he planned to insert a vocabulary list and definitions in the order of service.

I stopped rolling and sipped before I went on. "Well, Lucy came to see what was going on."

"Lucy has a police radio in her kitchen?"

"She didn't need one today. The word was all over town."

"And she talked you into going with her to search the house across the street."

"Ed!" I knocked the book out of his hand. "Who told you?"

"Who didn't? I fielded phone calls all afternoon. People wanted to know what you were doing."

"Well, you could have asked me about it."

"I was just waiting to see how long it would take you to tell me. So what did you find?"

I recapped briefly and ended with the bad news. "Unfortunately, we were caught red-handed."

"Roussos?"

"The very one. He wasn't happy. He claimed we probably destroyed evidence, but I don't think the police would even have gone over if he hadn't seen us. A dozen realtors could have trooped through before they got there. Now Roussos is that much further ahead."

"What makes you think so?"

"Either Jennifer was killed in that house or at least she was there today before her body ended up on our doorstep."

"Does Roussos think so?"

"You think he'd tell me?" I snuggled against him. "Every man I know keeps secrets. Like the one I'm married to. You never told me anything about that woman."

"There wasn't anything to tell." Ed put his arm around me. "She came in for counseling. Nothing she said can be repeated."

I debated whether to tell him about my conversation with Teddy and decided there was no point in keeping it a secret. "Teddy saw you fighting with Jennifer Marina in the church parking lot. She mimicked the whole conversation like a pro. It's too bad vaudeville's dead. We could have gotten our daughter a gig on the Orpheum circuit."

He saw through me. "Jennifer Marina was a troubled woman. She asked my advice and I gave it. She didn't like what she heard."

I knew that was all I was going to get out of him. Jennifer

might be dead, but Ed took his job seriously. Whatever secrets she'd had would die with her. I just hoped those same
secrets hadn't killed her.

I sat up straight, because a terrible thing had just occurred
to me. "Ed, did she tell you something somebody else wants
to know? Are you in any danger?"

"You've been watching *The Sopranos,* haven't you?"

"No, really. Look, if someone killed her for something
she knew—"

"We don't know why she was killed."

"But they put her here, on our doorstep. On *your* doorstep.
Maybe it was a warning. Keep your mouth shut, or you'll be
next."

"I'm not worried, Aggie, and you don't need to worry, either. Nothing Jennifer told me would have gotten her killed.
You'll just have to trust me on that." He picked up his book
and found his page. In a moment he was immersed again.

I got up and checked all the locks on our doors, and for
good measure all the downstairs windows, too.

4

Sunday is the most chaotic day of the week for a minister's family, and sometimes I'm tempted to strike it from our calendar. Then at some point between the opening prelude of our morning service and Ed's final words, my blood pressure drops, my blessings parade in Technicolor, and I'm ready to face another week.

Not today. Today, after yesterday's events and a gush of last-minute crises, I needed that still, small moment of the soul more than usual. Instead, as the bombastic whoosh and toot of Tri-C's ancient tracker organ filled the sanctuary, I found myself surveying our parishioners, one by one, for signs of guilt. Who looked tired this morning, as if he—or she—hadn't gotten a good night's sleep? Who looked repentant, smug? Who, besides me, was unobtrusively searching the room?

Through the years of Ed's ministry I've become the mistress of snap judgments. I know what trouble looks like, and I know the members with whom I can really be myself. I'm afraid my accuracy is somewhere in the ninetieth percentile. Today as I assessed the familiar faces, those dear to me *and* those like Gelsey Falowell whose fondest wish was to empty the parsonage, I could not, in good conscience, believe any of them to be a murderer.

Gelsey, Sally, and Yvonne sat together in the row just in front of me. Sally and Yvonne to soak up whatever comfort they could from Ed's sermon, Gelsey to find more ammunition in her battle to rid the church of Ed's presence.

No matter what I thought of Gelsey, I couldn't believe any of these women would ever resort to violence. Every year Sally makes certain our church recognizes and shows its support for the United Nations. Yvonne is a pacifist and vegetarian who routinely splits her time between protests at Wright-Patterson Air Force base in Dayton and the fur department of the Beachwood Neiman Marcus.

And Gelsey, for all her behind-the-scenes maneuvering, is a pillar of Emerald Springs society who would die before jeopardizing her community standing. After all, it's Gelsey's sworn duty to show the rest of us how we should live.

I invented similar personality alibis for the other eighty or so parishioners listening raptly to my husband. Jack, who practiced the law and had too much invested in his future to break it. May and Simon Frankel, psychologists who teach conflict resolution through peer mediation at Emerald High.

The principal of our middle school, three of our best elementary school teachers, a juvenile court judge, our mailman, Emerald College staff and professors, the county agricultural agent, the president of the local food bank, two restaurant owners, two members of the city council. The list went on, each member, to my knowledge, a normal, responsible citizen who believes in discussion and the democratic way.

Not murder.

The music built and ended with a final crash. Esther, our organist, has played the old tracker organ for so many years she knows how to attack each key, stop, and pedal to get maximum volume. One Sunday a decade ago she tired of people chatting during her preludes. No one tries it now.

This morning Ed wore a black robe with a stole highlighting each of the major world religions. He looks particularly imposing in the pulpit. Ed is tall and broad-shouldered, and

he strikes a fine balance between father figure and honored
son. Thankfully he has no pretensions to be either, which
adds a welcome note of modesty.

Usually there's a buzz after the prelude, as if every
thought suppressed during Esther's fusillade must be ex-
pressed before settling down for the rest of the service. Today there was only an expectant hush. The woman sitting
beside me dropped her key chain, and poor Sally slapped her
hand over her heart in response.

Ed recited his opening words, and the board president
stepped up to the dais. Tom Jeffrey is a math professor at
Emerald College, middle-aged, nondescript, and a voice of
logic and reason. He lit our chalice—symbolizing the light
of truth. Then Ed stepped down and came to the front. The
church is small enough that he doesn't need a microphone.
Ed likes intimacy when he has a particularly important message to deliver.

"Before I begin, I want to address the events of yesterday." He swept the room with his gaze, as if trying to pull all
of us together. "As many of you know, a woman was found
dead on the porch of our parsonage. She was not a member
of this church, and to my knowledge, she has never attended
a service here. But she did come to my office several times
to ask for guidance."

He folded his hands at his waist. "I didn't know Jennifer
Marina well, and I certainly don't know why anyone would
want her dead. I do know she was very much alone in Emerald Springs, and because she was, I ask you to be her family
today. Please offer what prayers you feel comfortable with
during our prayer and meditation moments before the offer-
tory. And please pray with me now."

I closed my eyes, glad to have a chance, even briefly, to
mourn the loss of the mysterious young woman. But the last
thing I saw before I lowered my lashes was Gelsey staring
furiously at my husband.

◆   ◆   ◆

"I don't know why Gelsey dislikes Ed so much," May
Frankel told me after the service. The Frankel girls, Hillary,

six, and Maddie, eleven, had run ahead with my daughters to make sandwiches in the parsonage kitchen. May and I were walking slower, catching up on conversation.

I probed a little. "Sally says she's been a help to your other ministers."

May walks a perfect line between nurturing and confrontational. She's a petite, sweet-faced blonde who settles for attractive. May is the friend I consult when I need a sounding board on church matters.

"Sally isn't the best judge," May said. "She's intensely loyal. Gelsey tolerated our last minister, but only because he followed her orders."

Tri-C's last minister, a man at the tail end of a long, distinguished career, had warned Ed about Gelsey. He hoped, for Ed's sake, that Gelsey decided to take over a charity or serve on the local hospital board. The more she did outside the church, the easier Ed's job would be.

Unfortunately, Gelsey is very much at loose ends.

I decided not to pussyfoot around. "So Gelsey has a history of making trouble for the ministers?"

"She's one of the major reasons we've had four over a fifteen-year time span."

"It's a small church. Most ministers want to move on to bigger and better things."

"Particularly after a few years of going head-to-head with Gelsey."

I didn't smile, but in a crisis it's always nice to know the misery has been shared.

We paused at the backdoor. Inside I heard the sound of dishes clanking and Teddy exhorting the others to better behavior. "The thing is, May, Ed doesn't want to move up. He had a chance to do that, and he turned it down. He wants to do research. He wants to write."

"And we're lucky to have him. We know it. After training new seminary graduates or watching ministers serve out their final years, someone with Ed's energy and experience is a real breath of fresh air."

"Too bad Gelsey doesn't think so."

May took and squeezed my hand. "She has influence, but

she can't dictate. I hope it won't come to a fight, but if it does, Ed will have support."

I tried to put my uneasiness into words. "The thing is, it may come to a head sooner than you think. The death of that poor woman seems to have increased her anger. I have a feeling that for some reason, she blames Ed. As if he had any control over where the corpse was disposed of."

"He did a lot today to diffuse gossip. Don't borrow trouble. You're bound to be upset about things right now. That's natural. Try not to let your imagination work overtime."

But my imagination was already flying free. And as it turned out, it was no competition for the events that transpired next.

✦ ✦ ✦

Ed didn't come home until dinnertime. I wasn't worried, since I knew he had meetings after church and two people in the hospital to visit. By the time he dragged himself back to the parsonage, he was barely conscious. He flopped down at the kitchen table and rested his head in his hands.

I positioned myself behind him and massaged his neck. "Totaled?"

"Gar Johnson had another heart attack. They don't think he'll make it through the night." Gar was in his nineties, had lived a productive life, and had children and grandchildren to rally around him.

I dug my fingers into muscles as elaborately knotted as one of my mother's macrame wall hangings. "Are you going back to the hospital?"

"No, he's in a coma. The family asked me to stop by again in the morning."

"How about iced tea and a snack? Dinner won't be ready for another hour."

He covered my hand, but he didn't look up. "Tell me again why I accepted the call to this church?"

"You wanted a small, peaceful congregation that would let you pursue your academic research. This one has been around long enough to have a sizeable endowment, and therefore they can afford to pay you a living—just barely—wage."

"And you went along with it?"

I flopped down beside him and made him look at me. "This isn't about Gar, is it? You knew he was dying. He's been ready."

"The board called a special meeting tonight to discuss terminating my contract."

"You're kidding!" I couldn't believe the board had acted so quickly. After all, these were the same people who had taken weeks to decide whether to have the sanctuary carpet steam cleaned after the living manger scene went astray on Christmas Eve.

"Tonight." He made a stab at a grin, but it failed. "When I'm absolutely at my best."

"The board can't terminate you, can they?"

"No; Tom says he's trying to avoid a congregational meeting. He wants the people with complaints to air them now, to see if we can come to some sort of resolution before things get any worse."

"People? Or Gelsey Falowell?"

"People led by Gelsey. A few major players she's corralled to support her. She's using Jennifer Marina as her excuse. She claims I had something to do with her murder."

"They think you would kill the woman, hide her body, then sneak out of the house in the morning and drop it on your own front porch where your daughters could find it?"

"Logic has no place in this."

I sat back. "What are you going to do?"

"I'm going to tell them what I can, which isn't much more than I told them in the service. Then I'm going to hope they see reason."

As I had for the last thirty-six hours, I wondered just what Jennifer had told my husband that he had to protect with such vigor.

Ed labored to his feet. "I'm going to take a shower and maybe a nap before dinner. Will you be all right without me?"

"I'm coming to the meeting."

"You know that's not a good idea."

"But I want to know what they say!"

"I can tell you. But you shouldn't be there. You'll get angry, and you won't stay quiet. If you come to my defense, that will only make things worse."

I hate it when Ed is right. I fumed as I finished uninspired dinner preparations. This month we're vegetarians. From experience, I know we'll lapse. Bacon is the culprit, of course. In dreams I smell it sizzling in my kitchen.

The phone rang just as I finished chopping a pile of mushrooms, and I grabbed it before it could bother Ed. He was exhausted, and I wasn't letting anyone through to him, not even the search committee for a major metropolitan church.

Well, maybe just that one call. . . .

The voice on the other end of the line wasn't familiar. The man sounded older, with the raspy throat of a heavy smoker. And wonder of wonders, he wanted to talk to me.

I hung up afterwards, glad that one thing had turned out well that day. And when the family gathered around the table I told them all my good news.

"I have a job."

Ed looked up from a mound of brown rice and vegetables. "Job?"

I preened a little. "I applied for a job at the new bookstore that's opening down on Sparrow Street. Book Gems."

"Emerald Springs with a real bookstore? Wow, what's next? High-speed Internet?" Deena picked green peppers out of the stir-fry with awesome precision.

"I just did it on a whim," I told Ed, "but the owner called this afternoon. I'll be working part-time while the girls are in school. It's perfect."

Teddy stared at me as if I'd grown a more interesting head. "Work? You?"

I passed her a bowl of applesauce. "Amazing concept, isn't it? A mother who does something besides bake brownies for the P.T.A. and go on field trips."

"You never told me you applied," Ed said. "You never mentioned it."

"Well, if I didn't get the job, I would have hated to admit I'd lost out to some cute little coed."

Ed was staring into space now.

I waved my hand in his face. "Ed, I'm not starting a new law practice. I'm not running for Congress or sending the kids off to boarding school. I'm opening cartons and punching in credit card info. For twelve hours a week, tops. It will get me out of the house. Is there a problem?"

"I guess I didn't mention the other reason for that meeting tonight."

I was genuinely puzzled. We seemed to have segued back into an old conversation, when I'd thought that this new one would cheer him. After all, at least now, if he was fired, we'd have the security of my fifty-odd dollars take-home pay.

"That other issue wasn't enough?" I asked. With the girls sitting at the table I didn't want to repeat details of the movement to fire their father.

Ed's voice grew softer, and I knew we were in trouble. "Book Gems plans to have an adults-only room in the back. Half the ministers in town are up in arms. Tri-C has been called on to join them."

✦   ✦   ✦

Lucy called after Ed's departure, and the moment she heard my tone, she promised to waltz over bearing good Irish whiskey and a carton of whipping cream. I made the coffee, Luce made it Irish. Strong Irish. Enough to nibble the edge off my depression.

"Well, the good news is that Gelsey and her friends will have trouble figuring out who to dislike more," I told Lucy. "I sell porn, and Ed attracts naked bodies to our porch."

"You don't have to take the job," Lucy said. Tonight she wore denim overalls cut to the panty line, over a rose colored T-shirt that owed more to spandex than jersey. Once upon a time I had dressed to provoke. Now I was too tired, or too content. I wore faded jeans.

"It's going to be a classy place," I told her. "One of the other booksellers showed me the plans when I applied. Heather-toned carpets and polished oak shelves. Plush armchairs with reading lamps in most of the aisles. An eclectic mixture of genres. A coffee bar. It's costing the owner a fortune, and it's just what the town needs."

"Except for that little ole room in the back."

After the conversation at our dinner table I had called Book Gems' owner, Bob Knowles, and asked point-blank about the adults-only room. He hadn't minced words.

"It's not kiddy porn," I told Lucy. "*Penthouse* and *Playboy,* and maybe *Hustler* behind the counter. Some erotic novels, but classy ones. Gay love stories. He claims he's trying to appeal to everyone except the lowest common denominator. Which in this case is probably the Emerald Springs Moral Majority. They don't have any idea what he's really doing, just that there's sex involved. I don't know how these people multiply."

"Aggie, you know I don't have a problem with this, but how's it going to look, you working there?"

"Maybe sexy books will pale in significance to murder. You think?"

"You must want the job pretty badly."

I did want the job. I have a bachelor's degree in humanities and all the course work for a master's degree in eighteenth-century philosophy. I met Ed before I started my thesis, and by then, I had already realized there wasn't a college professor hiding inside me.

I tried to explain. "Before the girls came along I held a new job every place we lived. I have no clerical skills and an education that prepared me to stare at my navel. Right now this bookstore is as good as it's going to get, and the hours are perfect."

"You could sell real estate."

"I'm busy on Sundays, remember?"

Lucy fell silent, and I went upstairs to make sure lights were off in my daughters' bedrooms.

The girls were asleep. School started next week and I was trying to get them in bed earlier each night to prepare. I went back downstairs to find that while I was gone Lucy had made us each another Irish coffee. The caffeine and the alcohol were at war, and she was hoping one or the other would declare a victory.

Lucy brought my second cup back to the table. "I talked to Sarah about the house across the street."

"What more could she say?"

"Well, I just wondered if anyone besides the owner might have a key."

I had vowed I was going to leave this matter alone. Being caught in the act of snooping by Emerald Springs' hottest detective had been highly humiliating. Now I realized how easily vows can be broken. "And?"

"She did some checking for the police, so she already knew. Two people have keys to the backdoor, with locks, by the way, that are first cousin to the ones at Fort Knox. For a house with nothing to steal, this one is well secured. Picking them would be a real challenge."

I headed her off before she got the bright idea to try, just for the heck of it. "She didn't tell you who has the keys, did she?" I asked. Lucy knew everyone in town.

"She *did*." Lucy plunked down beside me, Medusa curls clawing the air around her head.

"You're going to tell me, right?"

"I am *so* good at making you wait."

I pretended nonchalance. "Have I told you about Deena's last dentist appointment? The yearly line-up for my book discussion group? Ed's sermon schedule for the fall?"

"Yvonne McAllister for one."

I didn't know what to say.

Lucy filled in the silence. "Her brother lives next door to the owners, to their *new* house, that is. Yvonne knows them slightly, and she promised she'd look in on the old house once in a while when she was on her way to or from church. She has key number one."

This was news. It was in character for Yvonne to help even the remotest acquaintance, but her tie to the house was surprising.

I tried to bring some reason to our gossip. "We don't

know Jennifer was murdered there, or even if she was ever there dead or alive. Besides, any realtor with access to the lockbox could have gotten in."

"Not between nine in the evening and nine in the morning. Everyone is locked out. That's the way it's programmed. Plus with this system, we can tell if and when any realtor enters, by their codes. It's all recorded. And maybe a really good locksmith could get inside without a key, but it would take a talented pro."

I whistled. I hadn't known the logistics. And dollars to doughnuts, that was the very time period during which poor Jennifer, in one form or the other, had visited.

Lucy preened. "Don't worry, I can't see good old Yvonne in killer mode. But depending on where she keeps her key, someone else might have gotten hold of it, right? That good-looking son of hers? A friend?"

I waved the part about Jack away. "Who has the second one?"

She dragged out her words. "You're really going to like this."

"Did I ever tell you the story of Teddy's first swimming lesson?"

"The mayor." Lucy sat back, eyes glistening.

"You're kidding!"

"Browning Kefauver the Third has the other key."

"Why?"

"Remember I told you the owners rented out the house for a while? That's why they left the old furniture behind? Well, Brownie's half brother and his wife were the renters. They were moving to Dallas, and they sold their house sooner than they'd expected. So they put most of their stuff in storage and rented the house across the street for a couple of months until it was time to head south."

"This must have happened before we came. I don't remember anyone living there since we moved in."

"Before they left they gave their key to Brownie so he could supervise the movers and make sure all their stuff went to Dallas and the owners' junk stayed behind."

"And he never gave back the key?"

"Get this. He claims he lost it," Lucy finished triumphantly.

The idea of Emerald Springs' anal-retentive mayor having anything to do with Jennifer Marina's murder was intriguing.

"He doesn't drive a green SUV by any chance, does he?" I figured Lucy would know. Lucy has sources at City Hall and can find out anything.

"A cream-colored Lincoln."

We had sipped and talked our way to ten o'clock. I knew the meeting at church should be ending soon. Emerald Springs was an early to bed kind of place. Former farm towns often are.

"I'll walk you to your car." I rose and cleared away our cups. One more mug of Irish coffee and Lucy was going to be sleeping in our guest room. "You're okay to drive?"

"I went light on mine. You needed the extra shot. And I parked at the church. Some bozo was blocking your driveway."

"That happens all the time. The prevailing theory is that the minister and family have no life and therefore no need to use our car."

Outside the sky was clear and the stars were spectacular. In the parking lot we said good-bye, and I watched Lucy drive away. The girls are sound sleepers, and I'd locked the house tight so I had a few minutes of freedom. The lights were on in the parish house, and I saw movement in the foyer, although the light in Ed's study was off. Since this probably meant the meeting had broken up and people were lingering over good-byes, I decided to go inside. Ed hadn't wanted me at the meeting, but he hadn't said a word about the farewell party.

The foyer, where our secretary's desk is located, is open and modern, with nothing more than a low brick planter heavy on philodendron separating his desk from the coat closet and reception area.

I expected to see a dozen or more people but only found two. Simone Jeffrey, the board president's wife, and her teenage son Ron, a lanky, dark-haired boy who, judging from behavior at monthly potlucks, routinely consumed enough calories to fuel a football team.

"I thought the meeting was over," I told Simone after a brief greeting. "You, too?"

"Tom told me to pick him up at ten. He's an optimist."

I didn't know what else to say. Simone is a nice enough woman, who attends most services and social events and lays low otherwise. But gossiping about the possible outcome of the meeting was inappropriate.

I chatted with Ron instead, asking whether he was looking forward to his senior year at Emerald High and a plethora of the other questions adolescents find repugnant. Silently I asked his forgiveness.

Ron was about to strangle me when the door to the meeting room behind the secretary's desk flew open.

My immediate impression was of a flock of geese flying in V formation. Gelsey was the leader, with the gaggle in formation behind her. I know too much about geese. Last year I helped Deena research a report on the Canada variety. As geese fly their wings create an uplift, and by sticking together they boost their flying power about 70 percent. Those who want to fly solo feel an uncomfortable resistance and usually return.

This particular gaggle consisted of five people. With the exception of Gelsey, most of them were relative strangers. I recognized Fern and Samuel Booth, longtime members who rarely attend but continue to give generously. The couple behind them had been pointed out to me at the beginning of Ed's ministry, but I couldn't remember their names or significance.

"After everything we have done for this church, to be ignored and ridiculed!" Gelsey swept out the door, her neck extended purposefully and gooselike.

"Gelsey . . ." Tom Jeffrey tried to squeeze past the others. "Nobody is—"

Gelsey didn't even look over her shoulder. "I know what you're trying to do. You've discounted everything I said. I know when I'm being placated. I won't have it."

Tom succeeded in his task and caught up with her,

momentarily destroying the gaggle's alignment. "No one is trying to placate you. You know we—"

Gelsey stopped and spun to face him. Her eyes were blazing. I doubt that she'd seen me or Tom's family standing open-mouthed beside me. She was as angry as I'd ever seen anyone, and for a moment I wondered if I should separate them. I had the oddest feeling Tom was in danger.

"Don't try to tell me you respect me!" Gelsey lifted her hand but she only used it to reinforce her words, chopping the air in front of her. "You didn't even listen to what I had to say."

Tom tried reason. "We gave you five full minutes to state your concerns."

"My concerns? Mine? I'm concerned for this church. I have supported it with every fiber of my being and with a sizeable amount of cash. And when I die Tri-C's endowment will grow substantially!"

"Everyone is grateful for all you've done."

"Not grateful enough. Not nearly grateful enough."

Samuel Booth, an older man with a potbelly that would ground a gander, put his hand on Gelsey's shoulder, whether to comfort or restrain her, I couldn't tell. Gelsey shook it off angrily.

Tom tried one more time. "Gelsey, why don't we—"

"I know when I no longer have the respect or consideration I've earned! And if you won't listen to those who know this church best and have its welfare truly at heart, then I can't trust this board with my money, can I? Well, maybe you won't have to worry about spending any more of it. I'm canceling my pledge, and as soon as my attorney can see me I'm changing my will!"

Tom didn't grovel as she probably expected. He stepped away from the formation. "Respect and consideration can't be bought. You have both, no strings attached. But so do the other members of the congregation who are represented by this board. And it's the board's decision not to call a congregational meeting at this time. Your concerns have been logged and noted."

Gelsey ignored him and started forward again, and that's

when she saw me. She stared as if I were part of a conspiracy that intended to rob Tri-C of its soul. Emerald Springs' own little Village Church of the Damned.

She drew herself up again, and I waited, breath halting in my chest.

"Ask your husband what he was doing with that woman on Wednesday night," she said, stabbing the air with a finger. "Even if your husband refuses to discuss it, they were seen, you know, at Don't Go There. You ask him, then maybe you can convince me he's completely innocent of that murder. It's the quiet ones we have to fear, isn't it?"

Not one word that crossed my mind could be uttered by a minister's wife. I stepped aside to let the gaggle pass. Then I waited until the air they had churned up was calm again.

Silently and alone, I found my way home.

5

Of course Ed refused to tell me what he'd been doing with Jennifer Marina in the city's most notorious bar, although he did admit to seeing the son of one of our Women's Society members, an Emerald College senior, there that night, hence Gelsey's information.

I explained that the seal of confession was a concept dating from the twelfth century or earlier—a historical period not known for enlightened thinking—that we were Unitarians in case he'd forgotten, and that even our good friend Father Greg wouldn't make a case for a bar stool at Don't Go There as a substitute for the confessional booth.

Of course, I should know better than to argue theology with Ed. My brain didn't function normally again until the next morning.

The odds were against the old neurons firing then, as well, considering what came next. After breakfast Deena conducted a ghost tour of the grounds for her best friends, eight of them, at least.

I'm not sure how my daughter became the center of a group of girls who can only be described by that dreaded word *popular*. I hope she's conducting a private sociological study complete with statistical analysis and charts, but I'm beginning to fear the worst.

The girls call themselves the Green Meanies, a name that came with them, fortunately, and was not a product of Deena's vivid imagination. The title is more or less appropriate. Most of them are good kids, but a couple are borderline psychopaths—or possibly just a few months ahead of Deena in the hormone game.

At this point Deena doesn't seem to care that these are the girls who in middle school will ask her to do things my best friends only read about in purloined copies of Jacqueline Susann's novels. These are the high school cheerleaders who will choose the alpha males of their graduating class to father their children, then divorce them when better providers appear. These are the future society matrons who will star in our biannual "Broadway" show to benefit Emerald Springs General, who will chair the Christmas dance at Meadowlands Country Club, who will follow Deena's career as a world-famous anthropologist or a specialist in rare tropical diseases, and wonder why she didn't marry Quentin Quarterback and settle into life in Emerald Estates.

And, of course, I am not projecting. I am not terrified.

I served orange juice and doughnuts after the tour, watching helplessly as the girls streamed through my kitchen door chattering about dead bodies. I counted the uses of *gross* and *creepy* and noted who was showing off newly developing breasts and who was wishing.

Carlene O'Grady was the first to address me. She looked at the platter of doughnuts and pitcher of orange juice as if these were the weapons that had killed poor Jennifer Marina.

"Carbs. Wow, that's more carbs than I've seen in one place before." Carlene giggled. I'll try to omit the giggling from this point on. It's standard punctuation for eleven-year-old girls.

Carlene is rail thin. Her mother, Crystal, is thinner. I've gotten evil looks from Crystal for serving carrot and celery sticks and herbal tea when she and the other Green Meanie mothers visit. Crystal will only be happy when I serve air and spring water with a flourish.

I put two doughnuts on a plate and handed them to Carlene with a brimming glass of juice. "I've read this particular combination promotes a healthy complexion."

Carlene shook her blond head—her mother is blonder—as she grabbed the plate. "My mother says you're a free spirit."

This was possibly the kindest thing Crystal had ever said about me. To forestall less pleasant revelations, I mingled and chatted with the other girls as I passed out the carbs.

Next to Maddie Frankel, who was out of town today, Tara Norton is my favorite Meanie. She and Deena are in gifted classes together, and Tara keeps Deena on her intellectual toes. Like Deena, I'm not quite sure how Tara got into the group. Her dark hair is a mass of dense, frizzy curls. She wears glasses with black cat's-eye frames, which sit on a nose she may yet grow into. Her body is short-waisted and compact, and that will probably only intensify with age. It's a testament to the better qualities of Meaniehood that the girls see Tara's intelligence, keen sense of humor, and remarkable smile. Apparently there's hope for them after all.

"You must have been scared to death when you found that body," Tara said.

"It wasn't what I was expecting." I held out the doughnut platter and hoped she got the last one with chocolate icing before Betsy Slavonik, always ravenous, made a grab for it.

She took a plain glazed and broke it into tiny bits, popping the first into her mouth and chewing thoughtfully. "I bet you're trying to figure out why the body ended up at your house, aren't you? And who killed her."

I wanted to deny it, but honesty is the least I can do to speed the Meanies on the road to maturity. "I'm certainly curious."

"You'd be good at solving crimes. I bet you'll figure it out."

"Why do you think I'd be good at it?"

"You pay attention to everything. What is Shannon wearing? Don't turn around."

Shannon Forester was somewhere behind me, but that was no problem. I'd taken note already. "A purple sweatshirt that says 'Go for the Grape,' faded blue jeans, tennis shoes that need to be replaced, and gold clips in her hair."

"The shoes are her brother's. He wore them when he scored the winning basket against Wellington last year. She thinks they're cool."

I made a note that Shannon's feet must be ultralarge and growing, in case I ever noticed giant footprints outside our windows.

"The *police* need to find the killer," I said, trying for virtue. "I bet you were brought up on old Nancy Drew mysteries."

"Agatha Christie. I like Miss Marple best. Hercule Poirot is an egotist, and there are too many of those in the world." She leaned forward. "Half of them in this room."

I wanted to giggle.

The Meanies vanished after a time. You can always tell when the Meanies are gone. Not only by the silence, but by the torrent of oxygen rushing back into the room. I took a few deep breaths and considered whether I should do what I'd contemplated through long, sleepless hours of the night.

The struggle didn't last. I dialed my own best friend.

"Ed has a meeting tonight," I told Lucy without preamble. "And Jennifer Marina was waiting tables at Don't Go There before she took up residence on my front porch."

Lucy didn't need an explanation. "What time do you want to go?"

I did the math. "If I can get Stephanie to babysit . . . let's say eight. We might even beat Ed back home."

"You're not going to tell him?"

"I think I'll forget to mention it."

I hung up, and while I gathered sticky juice glasses and brushed away doughnut crumbs, I asked myself why I was snooping where I didn't belong.

The answer came down to this. I *felt* like I belonged. The body was deposited on my front porch. My husband knew the victim and was still protecting her secrets. Gelsey's honking over Ed's involvement in Jennifer's death was getting louder and louder. I no longer felt safe in my own house and worried about my children. Tara, one of the smartest eleven-year-olds I know, thinks I have something to bring to this investigation.

And, last but certainly not least, I am terminally curious. Make that exceptionally curious. *Terminally* has a ring I'm not crazy about just now.

+ + +

By seven fifteen Ed was on his way to the parish house for what promised to be the kind of finance committee meeting where a change of clothes and a toothbrush are required. Over vegetable lasagna with soy cheese he'd told me not to wait up for him.

Not a problem.

By seven forty-five, fifteen-year-old Stephanie Blakely was nodding off as I gave last-minute instructions. I knew she would perk up the moment she had access to the television and telephone, plus half a dozen leftover doughnuts.

Stephanie is a good babysitter. Once when the pilot light on our old gas stove went off, she noticed the smell and opened all the kitchen windows. Then she took the girls to stay at her house until her father could come back and re-light it. She knows first aid and CPR, and she lets Teddy pick any book in the house for her bedtime story. Of course, that was before Teddy chose our ancient set of World Book Encyclopedias and insisted Stephanie begin with Volume A.

By eight, Stephanie, Deena, and Teddy were watching our well-worn DVD of *Aladdin,* and Stephanie was promising to style Teddy's hair like Princess Jasmine's. I was good to go. Lucy arrived with a gift, something appropriately addictive and noisy called "Bop It," guaranteeing that the girls would not sleep again until the next millennium.

We took Luce's Concorde since she refused to show up at a place like Don't Go There in my Nissan Quest. Lucy seemed to think a minivan was a sign we were not serious barflies. As if my patchwork jacket—my mother's latest work—and neatly pressed khakis weren't proof enough.

Don't Go There sits on the outskirts of Emerald Springs like a pimple on the cheek of a Norman Rockwell bride. The town itself is admittedly picturesque, dressed up in its best finery and waiting for something important to happen. Unfortunately, Emerald Springs has been waiting at the altar for a very long time.

Don't Go There makes no pretense of waiting for anything, nor does it yearn to be picturesque, at least not judging by the overflowing dumpster within spitting distance of the front door.

This section of our fair city is called Weezeltown, for reasons nobody questions. The button factory, which anchored it and subsidized blocks of homes crowded on to narrow lots, closed years ago. The houses, covered in asphalt siding or painted dreary earth tones, are slowly being condemned and torn down. There's talk of turning the factory into an upscale shopping mall, the surrounding landscape into a ritzy subdivision. Now if they can just find enough rich folks in this dreary economy willing to live or shop here.

We pulled slowly into the parking lot. Missing letters in the bar's neon sign had turned the name into Don Go here, and from the pickups and motorcycles in the lot, any number of Dons had taken the invitation to heart.

With the Dons in mind, Lucy parked at the edge of the lot, hoping to avoid becoming the target of any form of bodily elimination. Tonight she was dressed modestly. Brown skirt close enough to her knees to nod in recognition. Camel-colored sweater loose enough to slide a nail file between the sweater and her midriff. Shoes with sensible three-inch heels.

All right, the shoes were not sensible, unless we needed a weapon.

Considering where we were, the shoes were sensible.

Lucy pulled her keys from the ignition and zipped them securely in her purse before she turned to me. "Just how did Gelsey Falowell know Ed was out here talking to Jennifer before she was killed? You don't suppose Gelsey's a regular, do you?"

"Apparently one of our college students is a regular," I said. "And he wasn't afraid to admit it."

She wiggled her eyebrows at her reflection in the rearview mirror, clearly some sort of facial aerobics I needed to

investigate. "And Ed didn't tell you ahead of time that someone might have seen them together?"

"Torture the man and he'd die mute. All the world's a
secret."

Lucy, apparently pleased with her forehead's admirable
flexibility, bounced a couple of cherry red curls into place
and started to get out of the car. I held on to her sleeve for all
I was worth.

"Luce, we stay in the shadows and we don't step on toes,
literally or figuratively. No scenes, okay? If Ed has to post
bail for me, that will be the last straw at Tri-C."

"It's got to be hard to be Aggie Sloan-Wilcox. Always
torn between dancing on the table and singing hymns." She
pulled loose and got out.

Since it was now too late to reconsider, I joined her.

Halfway to the door Lucy stepped carefully between a
condom wrapper and a puddle that made me glad we had
parked farther away. A trio of motorcycles at the other edge
of the lot had drawn a small crowd arguing about ape hang-
ers and buckhorns, but nobody paid any attention to us.

"I always wondered what this place looked like inside,"
Lucy said.

"I can tell you. Smoke so thick you can cure a slab of
pork while you wait for your brewski. Peanut shells on the
floor. Vinyl-covered bar stools patched with duct tape. A
jukebox that's too loud, a pool table where balls follow the
tracks of a thousand missed shots, men in interchangeable
flannel shirts or black leather. Tattoos, missing teeth,
chains."

"You haven't been here, have you?"

"On those rare occasions when Ray leaves Camp Vigilance, this is the kind of place he favors." Ray is my father.
Camp Vigilance is his very own compound. Some fathers
own farms or condos. Ray's compound has ten-foot concrete
block walls to keep out whatever bad guys define the moment.

"Ray took you places like this?"

"Part of my training. He thinks the folks who frequent
these places are real men, the kind he wanted me to know,

which simply means that if so moved, these guys can and will shoot anything that breathes."

"My father took me to the opera."

"At the compound we live our own melodramas."

As nutty as it seems, Ray's a good guy, and some of his friends aren't so bad. But Ray lost a screw or two in Vietnam, and now survivalism is second nature. I clarified. "Ray's very responsible. When we visit, he locks up his guns and shaves off his beard. That's how much he loves my girls."

"A prince among men."

Actually, I thought Lucy might like Ray. But so far my father wasn't certain that the route to Emerald Springs from the compound in Indiana was either land mine or guerilla free. So regretfully, he had stayed away. I consoled myself with the knowledge that there was a better chance of his visiting Ohio than our last home in D.C.

Lucy is not one to hesitate. She pushed open the door and strode right in, and I followed in her wake.

My description had been way off base. The room was smoky, yes, but larger than it appeared from the outside. Someone had paid attention to lighting. There were no dark corners for clandestine meetings or drug buys. Stainless steel chandeliers with low-wattage bulbs hung over nearly every table, and a long strip of lights adorned the back side of the bar. Alan Jackson serenaded us from a modest jukebox in one corner, but at a moderate level, so conversation was still possible. There were no peanut shells on the floor and more amazing, no trash. The floor itself was battleship gray tile that looked almost new. The beige laminate tables were either occupied or clear.

Since I knew about Mudwrestling Mondays here, I wasn't surprised at the low stage that ran from one corner in the back to the other. I *was* surprised at the four women in matching baby doll pajamas who approximated a chorus line as Jackson wailed "Don't Rock the Jukebox." Two of them carried teddy bears. Two sucked their thumbs.

Lucy was transfixed and momentarily mute.

I wondered who had performed the night Ed came here to see Jennifer. "Live entertainment," I said. "The hallmark of a classy joint." I looked for a seat out of sight and far away from a seventy-something drooler whose hands were busy under his table.

"Somebody needs to talk to that second dancer from the right. With that complexion she shouldn't wear pink." Without consultation Lucy chose a table right in the center of things and dropped into a ladder-back chair. "I need a drink."

Modest drinker that I am, I thought that sounded like a fine idea. So did a buxom brunette dressed in a royal blue satin wrapper and feathered high-heeled mules. She had napkins on our table along with a basket of pretzels before I could point out the too-close-for-comfort drooler to Lucy.

"What's with the nightwear?" Lucy leaned closer to look at the brunette's name tag, which rode the woman's right breast like a surfer at the apex of the perfect wave. "Keely."

Keely had a Jersey accent. Or maybe Brooklyn. "Pajama party. Didn't ya know?"

"I sleep in the buff," Lucy said.

"Oh, that's too bad. Gordy don't allow nudity here."

I for one was glad Gordy—whoever he was—had standards.

"Who are the dancers?" Lucy asked.

"Dunno. Some ladies from town. There's a talent contest."

She took our order and left. I leaned over the table. "If I look closely, will I recognize anybody?"

"One of the dancers looks a lot like a woman I sold a house to last month."

I glanced up at the stage, averted my eyes, then glanced again. None of the Green Meanie moms were there. I'd been hoping, at the very least, to catch a brand new side of Crystal O'Grady.

"No one from the church," I said. For this blessing, I said a silent thank you.

"I think they're having fun."

Before Lucy could begin planning "our" act, I headed her off. "What's the best way to find out about Jennifer, do you think?"

"We could try Keely. She must have known her."

"It's daunting to discuss murder with a woman who's dressed like a film noir mistress."

"What do you think she has on under the robe?"

"I don't know, but I hope she doesn't get close enough to the old guy over there for us to find out."

"You mean the old guy petting his dog?"

For a moment I thought this was a brand-new euphemism, then I glanced around and saw that indeed, the head of a golden retriever was peeking out from under the drooler's table.

"You allow pets?" Lucy asked, when Keely returned with a sex on the beach for Lucy and a glass of red wine for me.

"Dave's dog, you mean? Just him, that's all. Bud's like our mascot, you know? Nobody complains. Dave and Bud don't stay long. Drink one beer, watch the show, and leave. They don't hurt nobody."

I was feeling better about the place. They were kind to animals. There was only a one drink minimum. "Keely, we were wondering if you have a little time to talk?"

"Sure. What about?"

"Jennifer Marina."

Keely had a kewpie doll mouth, which was a match for slicked down black hair and wide blue eyes. "You know Jenny?"

I wasn't sure how I felt about the nickname. *Jennifer* had been one thing. *Jenny* brought the body back to life. Jennifer had been a woman with friends who had shortened her name to something perky and hopeful.

"I'm the one who found the body," I said.

"Oh . . ." Keely plopped down next to Lucy and leaned over. "How did she look? I mean, Jenny was real careful about that. She always wanted to look a certain way, you know?"

I considered my options. *Pale. Naked. Dead.* "Sad." It

was the best I could do. "Like she didn't deserve to be there."

"She didn't. I won't say she was nice, like somebody who went out of their way for you, you know? But Jenny wasn't the worst, either. She was fair. She didn't cop tips that didn't belong to her. She did her share."

I felt my way. "Did you get to know her? Did she tell you much about her life?"

"Why do you want to know?"

It was a fair question. "I'm just trying to understand. Trying to put the whole thing in some sort of perspective."

That seemed to make sense to her. "She did talk a little. I guess nothing was a secret. She wasn't from here. She hadn't been here that long. I think she didn't plan to stay long, either. She was just here to make a little money. She had kids."

"Kids?" Lucy said. "Here? What happened to them after, you know . . ." Lucy, who swore she was never going to have children of her own, sounded fiercely maternal.

"Oh, they're not here," Keely said. "They're in foster care. Jenny told me they were in Pennsylvania or some place like that. Funny thing is, she was a foster kid, too. In Pennsylvania or some place like that."

Somehow Jennifer's children and her need to make money were connected in Keely's mind. I probed. "Was she sending the foster family money? Is that why she needed this job?"

"She was saving up so she could get the kids back. She went to jail and lost custody, then she couldn't show the courts she had a way to take care of them, once she got out. So she was working here. Sometimes she danced, too, for extra tips."

I wasn't sure a judge would think dancing at Don't Go There was a route to model parenthood, but it was a little late to test my theory. "Do you know why she chose Emerald Springs as a place to earn money?"

Keely shrugged and for one terrible moment I was sure the satin wrapper was going to slip off her shoulders. "She never said. But Sax'll know. Why don't you ask him?"

"Who's Sax?"

She inclined her head toward the bar. "The bartender. Jenny was living with him. He got her the job."

I hadn't paid attention to anyone on that side of the room. Now I turned and saw the man in question. "Sax?"

"Sax Dubinsky." Keely got to her feet. "Just don't talk to him while he's busy."

That last part had the ring of "Don't pet the rottweiler while he's eating." Sax was at least six foot four, and nearly as broad. He had more hair than Rip Van Winkle after his nap, and even from a distance I could see his tattooed arms were in plain view and extraordinary.

Lucy thanked Keely, who nearly stopped my heart with another careless shrug. When we were alone again, Lucy raised one perfectly exercised brow. "How do we gauge when he's not busy?"

"We don't, at least not from here."

"Get your drink." Lucy stood and started toward the bar. I yearned for a disguise.

Sax was not dressed for the pajama party, and my gratitude was unbounding. A white tank top that bared the artwork on his arms and clung to a paunch the size of Cleveland was bad enough. I couldn't imagine what the man slept in, or box springs sturdy enough to hold him.

I insisted on the end of the bar farthest from the stage and closest to the door. We perched on stools side by side, and I tried to look like somebody else.

By the time Sax got to us, Lucy had finished her drink. Up close he was even more formidable. He had bushy graying hair tied at the nape with a leather shoelace and half covered with a red bandanna. He didn't have a full beard, rather long twin corkscrew curls sprouting from each side of a cleft in his chin. I imagined them rolled and tied in rags at night, the way the sisters tied their hair in *Little Women*. Amy, in particular, would be proud of Sax.

"You want another?" he asked Lucy. "Sex on the beach, right?"

For a moment Lucy looked as if she wished she'd asked

for a Manhattan or cosmopolitan. Something about the way
Sax said the words made my skin crawl, too.

Lucy produced a smile. "Yes, and another glass of wine
for my friend."

My glass was half full, but if we were going to wait until
Sax wasn't busy, I guess I needed an excuse. It would only
take one sweep of his tattooed arm to clear off our stools to
make room for heavier drinkers.

Sax returned a few minutes later, and surprisingly, he lin-
gered. "You here to perform in the show?"

I had been afraid that my new quilted jacket looked at
first glance like a bathrobe. "No, just to have a few drinks."
Before I could think of a way to say, "And find out about Jennifer Marina," Lucy did it for me.

"And we were hoping you could fill in some blanks for
us," she said with another manufactured smile.

"What sort of blanks?"

"Jennifer blanks," I said. "I found her body."

Sax didn't say anything. His sneer peeked out under a
sweeping reddish brown mustache. I'm sure his eyes were as
big as eyes are supposed to be, but for some reason they
seemed at least one size too small.

"So what do you know?" he asked at last.

"Somebody killed her and left her on my porch. She was
in town trying to earn money to put her family back together.
She lived with you."

He produced a cloth that had been marginally anchored
in the pocket of dark blue jeans and began to wipe the
counter. "Sounds like you know enough to pry your little Ivy
League ass off that stool and send it home again."

"It would pry a little faster if I knew why Jennifer was in
Emerald Springs in the first place." When he looked up I
turned up my hands in a plea. "Thing is, I'd just feel safer if
I knew this didn't have anything to do with my family."

"I answered that last question, it would sound like I was
the one that put her on your porch. And that never happened."

This man could have killed Jennifer with one blow. My
gaze flicked to his biceps, then back to his face. I'd discovered

something. "Jennifer had the same tattoo." I pointed to the tattoo of a cobra with a skeleton's head snaking up his arm, but I made sure to snatch my finger back immediately.

His eyes narrowed further. "How d'you know that?"

"Because I saw a lot more of her than I wanted to."

"Yeah, so?"

"Is that like, ummm . . . a lover's tattoo? Some kind of twist on a heart with 'Puff Daddy loves JLo' inside? That kind of thing?"

He snorted. I think this was Sax's take on laughter. "You ever hear of the Cobras?"

"It's a motorcycle gang," Lucy said. "Gets in the news every once in a while."

"Good to know somebody reads." He hung the rag from his pocket again and started to move away.

"You're saying you and Jennifer Marina were in the same gang? That's how you got to be . . . friends?" I asked.

He stopped and stared at me as if I needed an IQ transplant.

"Was her husband a Cobra, too?" Lucy asked. "The father of her kids?"

This snort was more pointed. "Rico Marina on a bike?"

"I guess he lives in Pennsylvania near their children," I said.

"He don't have nothing to do with those kids. He went to jail for beating Jenny. Now he don't live nowhere. Rico's like snot. He oozes here, oozes there, and you can't get rid of him no matter how many times you blow."

Our Sax was a bit of a poet. It's hard not to admire a man with a gift for imagery.

"Do you think he oozed over here to Emerald Springs and killed his wife?" I asked. I wondered if this was the secret Jennifer had shared with my husband, a fear of dying at the hands of her estranged husband. But surely Ed would have passed that on to the police immediately.

Sax's gaze flicked to the door and his sneer hardened into something more dangerous. "Well, why don't you ask him?"

Now, when somebody says those words, the subtext is this: *The man in question is now in the room. The man in question is moving in your direction. The man in question will just* love *being asked up close and personal if he is a murderer.*

Since I read subtext well, I was off the stool and backing away before Sax spit on the floor in emphasis. Lucy followed my example and right there between us was a hole wide enough for the furious Rico Marina to plug.

Rico was dark-haired with deep olive skin and a wiry build that was at least a hundred pounds lighter than Sax's. He ignored Lucy and me, like the middle-class, slumming-for-the-night busybodies we were. He leaned over the counter and grabbed Sax by his tank top.

"You killed my wife!" The obscenities that followed ran together into one word long enough to appear in the *Guinness Book of Records*.

I heard the end of the newly coined oath from ten yards away. By the time Rico had drawn a breath and Sax had shoved him into the table closest to the bar, I was almost at the door.

Unfortunately Lucy was on the other side of the melee, and it took her longer to skirt the edges of the room. By now the whole place was in disarray. The baby doll chorus line had been replaced by a hefty woman in a flowered bikini and sarong singing lullabies in Hawaiian, but apparently our Maui Mama headed back to the islands at the first sign of trouble. A lonely ukelele was the only sign she'd ever been there.

A table was overturned as patrons got into the spirit. Lucy was halfway around when a big guy in black leather bumped into her, then tried the same thing again because it had worked so well the first time. I went to help.

There are multiple advantages to having spent every summer of my childhood with Ray Sloan. When I whacked Black Leather on the shoulder with my purse, he whirled and I ducked, grabbing Lucy by her arm and pulling her to safety just as the guy behind me slammed into Black Leather. Ray says self-defense is all about timing.

We dodged and jumped. Once I pulled Lucy nearly to the floor as glasses crashed into the wall behind us. We reached the door unscathed and bolted into the parking lot just as two of Emerald Springs' finest joined us there.

I jerked Lucy into the shadows, and we skulked behind cars and under trees at the rim of the lot, watching as the cops jumped out of their cars—one from each—and sprinted toward the door. We were in the Concorde pulling out of the lot when another car passed us. This one was a dark sedan with a flashing light on top, the magnetic kind that rides in a glove compartment or backseat most of the time.

I was torn between turning my head and straining to see who it was.

My eyes met those of Detective Roussos.

No surprise there. I'm beginning to think that my fate and his fate are inextricably entwined.

6

In Emerald Springs the school year begins on the Thursday before Labor Day. I'm never quite sure how these decisions are made. I envision the throwing of the I-Ching in the school board conference room, the consulting of horoscopes, the consumption of multiple bags of fortune cookies.

Whatever the reason, Thursday morning the girls were up by seven. Today was a milestone for both. Deena assembled brand-new collections of notebooks and pens and rearranged them in her backpack for her first day at the middle school. Teddy, who was starting first grade, fought internal battles over whether to try the school's lunches or bring hers in her brand-new Shrek lunch box, which matched her green jumper. Five minutes before we needed to leave she decided on peanut butter sandwiches and Shrek.

At least she wouldn't lecture the cafeteria workers on the evils of hamburger on her very first day.

"You look comfortable," I told Deena when she came down for breakfast, wearing new flared jeans and a salmon colored T-shirt. Since breakfast is mandatory in our household she ate a slice of whole wheat sunflower seed toast with cream cheese and grumbled inaudibly.

"Are you looking forward to being at a new school?" I asked, hoping to stimulate her brain waves into activity.

"All my friends are dorks."

"The Meanies are dorks?"

"I'm not just friends with the Meanies." She rolled her eyes.

"Dorkness is even more global than that?"

"It's all clothes and boys. I'm going to be bored for the rest of my life."

And *I* was going to be bone-deep grateful.

Ed and I are responsible friends of the earth and proponents of zero population growth. Still, as I dropped Deena at the middle school, then a few minutes later watched Teddy stride purposefully through the front doors of Grant Elementary, my biological clock started ticking forty seconds to the minute. I wanted to rush home, grab Ed, and haul him back to the parsonage bedroom.

Instead I went to Jennifer Marina's funeral.

Actually, Ed was not grabbable. He was on his way to Columbus for a monthly meeting of Unitarian ministers. And since Ed was in charge of the program, he had no choice but to go. Not that anyone had asked him to perform the funeral. According to the announcement in the paper it was strictly a cut-rate affair at the local funeral home, but even at that, I wondered who was paying for it.

Why did I go? I suppose for the same reasons I went to Don't Go There Tuesday night. Plus something more. Someone needed to see Jennifer off. Someone needed to say genuine prayers on her behalf.

I was not convinced that anyone else would be there to see this woman laid to rest. Having viewed two of the men in her sad, truncated life, I could not picture weeping and wailing and tributes to the departed. A brawl, perhaps, an endless string of profanity, but no one to help speed poor Jennifer on her journey to who-knows-where-or-what. (Unitarians are not precise or focused on this particular subject.)

By ten I was sitting in the smallest visitation room at the Weiss–Bitman Funeral Home staring at a rectangular pine casket. A *closed* casket, for which I was enormously grateful, since I had seen far too much of Jennifer already.

Weiss–Bitman resides in one of the town's historic homes on Wren Street, not far from the parsonage. Built in the 1850s by a young couple expecting to fill the many rooms with children, it stood nearly empty for four generations as couple after couple tried and failed to provide the house with the patter of tiny feet. When rumors of a curse became so serious that no one else would try, the Weiss and Bitman families bought the house and turned it into the town's premiere funeral home. The patter of tiny feet would never again be an issue. The house has been devoted to the dead ever since.

The room where Jennifer was secluded was paneled in walnut with one lonely window draped in heavy red velvet. An upright player piano in the corner spewed forth an endless plinking honky-tonk of Christian standards.

I was alone with Jennifer. I let my mind drift and considered the path of her life. To the strains of "The Old Rugged Cross" and "Onward Christian Soldiers" I imagined the crossroads she had come to and the directions she had not heeded. I prayed that whatever awaited her was better than what had come before, and I prayed for peace for her soul. I wondered if anyone would provide a formal good-bye to Jennifer in Pennsylvania where her children lived, so that they could publically mourn their mother.

Five minutes before the brief service was to begin, two other people joined me. I recognized them both. Keely, from Don't Go There, and Rico Marina.

Rico and Keely didn't come in together. Rico entered first and took a seat on the other side of the aisle in the back. Keely came in a minute later and sat beside me.

Rico was dressed in a black T-shirt and black jeans, but I suspected black was for show. It helped play down the bruises and swelling on his jaw and along both cheekbones. One eye was swollen shut, and Rico was limping as he found his seat. I knew from the brief account in the *Flow* that he and Sax had been jailed for disturbing the peace. I had hoped the two men were sequestered in separate cells, and here was living proof. Now I hoped Sax didn't arrive in another minute to alter the "living" part.

Keely wore a yellow buttoned shirt with tails tied under her breasts and low-riding blue jeans with sequined flip-flops. Since this outfit beat the heck out of her blue satin wrapper, I was delighted.

"You been here long?" she asked.

"Long enough to say good-bye."

"You didn't even know her except when she was already dead."

"I'm glad *you* came. I'm glad she had a friend."

"She did?"

I wasn't sure if Keely just wasn't too bright, or if she was preoccupied. She kept turning to glance at Rico.

For the first time I was grateful for the noise of the piano, which effectively masked anything we said. "I'm sure this is hard for her husband."

"He shouldn't ought to be here. He was a bad husband and a bad father."

"Maybe he'll learn to be a better one and get custody of his kids."

"Rico? You wish! He don't care nothing about them. He'll give them to the state for real now."

I suspected the children would be better off in state custody. Perhaps now they could be adopted by someone who would treasure them.

"Jenny, now, she was a good mom," Keely went on. "At least she wanted to be, that is."

"You said she was saving money so she could get custody again?"

"That's right."

"I don't mean to be rude, but does Don't Go There pay that well? It doesn't look like the kind of place where the tips are huge, even if you do a little dancing."

Keely didn't seem to take offense. "Heck no. I can barely pay the rent unless I make a little something on the side."

I did *not* want to know how she accomplished that. I scrambled silently to change the subject.

"See, I paint birdhouses," she said, before I could open my mouth. "To look like people's houses, you know? I go through town and draw pictures, then I take plain old wooden birdhouses from the craft store or build them myself and paint them so they match. I add little touches, you know, then I give them to the owners for whatever they want to pay me."

"Oh." I figured I would need at least fifteen minutes meditation time to ask forgiveness.

"Jennifer had some problems with a customer or two, so her tips weren't that great," Keely said. "But she had options."

I prayed that the Weiss–Bitman director would continue to cater to the more affluent mourners in the other room. "Options?"

"Last week she told me things were looking up. Pretty soon she'd have the money she needed, then she was going back east, get some kind of office job to make the people at child welfare happy, and get her kids back."

"That sounds pretty sudden."

"Yeah. I asked her, and she said it was some kinda inheritance. The money was practically in her bank account. She said she damned well deserved it, too." She lowered her voice. "Of course, she didn't want Rico to know. She said he'd get his hands on it somehow. Too bad she didn't live to get the money, isn't it?" Keely's baby blues widened sadly, and it was clear that a connection between the money and Jennifer's death had never occurred to her.

It certainly occurred to me.

The assistant to the assistant funeral director came in to conduct what passed for a service. At lightning speed he read from the Bible, raced through two prayers, asked if anyone had anything to say, then sped on to the benediction before anyone could draw a breath. Jennifer's send-off was accomplished in record time.

Keely and I stood, and I glanced in Rico's direction, but he was already gone. Since Jennifer was scheduled for cremation, there was to be no graveside service.

"Gordy couldn't come. We're still closed, on account of

the fight. The place got pretty wrecked. Sax, he didn't want to come," Keely said. "Says funerals are stupid."

"Sax is a bit of a philosopher."

"I don't want to end up like Jennifer, you know? Nobody here to say good-bye to me, except strangers and a man who beat up on me."

I felt a wave of sympathy. "I live over behind the Consolidated Community Church. If you paint a birdhouse, I'll be happy to buy it. You come, and we'll have coffee."

Keely smiled, but I doubted I would ever see her on my doorstep.

✦   ✦   ✦

This was a day of new beginnings. At noon, Bob Knowles, the owner of Book Gems, picked me up at the parsonage to drive to Cleveland to attend a children's book trade show. My very first day as a bookseller.

Bob only got the bright idea to include me when he remembered I had kids. Yesterday he had started his telephone pitch with "trade show," morphing belatedly into "children's books" in time to cut short my impending panic attack. I don't think Bob needs help choosing literature for the "little room" that's upsetting so many of the Emerald Springs citizenry, but I was relieved to find I would be spending *my* afternoon with Lemony Snicket and Captain Underpants.

Although, let's face it, if that last title wasn't already taken, some X-rated author could have a field day with it.

When I got into the car Bob was smoking what must have been one of a long line of cigarettes. Smog billowed out to greet me. He's a big guy, with a unhealthy grayish complexion and prominent incisors. The combination gives him a Dracula-at-sunrise sort of look. He thoughtfully opened his window and tossed the latest butt into the street as I fastened my seat belt.

"I'm a smoker," he said needlessly. "Do you mind?"

" 'Fraid so," I told him.

"Then we'll leave the windows down."

It was not yet Labor Day, but the air was cool enough that ten minutes into the drive I was chilled. Not so Bob, who had his own little firesticks to keep him warm. After the next cigarette I asked how the preparations were going.

"So, the paint's all done, the shelves are in, the carpet's installed. We're going to be stocking the shelves after Labor Day, and cranking up the cappuccino machine. You'll be ready to start work?"

"All ready."

"I hired two women besides you, and two guys. All part-time."

I was sure we would all stay that way. I bet Bob didn't want to pay benefits. "You'll be barraged at first," I predicted. "I don't know why the chains never targeted Emerald Springs, but the town needs something more than what the college bookstore can offer."

"Yeah? The way some people are attacking me, you'd think I was opening a peep show."

"You could dispense with the adults only room."

"You know, most booksellers keep all this stuff under the counter. Every reader knows they can get it if they ask. So I'm just putting it out where people can look and find what they want. Nothing crude. Good stuff. I just don't get it. No kids will be going back there."

Clearly he *didn't* get it.

"Where did you live before you came here?" I asked. It seemed relevant.

"L.A., Chicago. Detroit for a few years."

"City people have different expectations. They don't see every store as an extension of community values."

"The people doing the complaining are a bunch of hypocrites. The same ones kicking up the sand will be sneaking to the back of the store next month to check out my stock."

I was sure he was angry, but I wasn't sure he was right. At the very least, he didn't seem to understand the people to whom he would be selling books. I tried again. "Why Emerald Springs?"

"I used to have family here. I visited as a boy and liked it. I was tired of cities after I retired from my job at IBM. I thought I'd give Emerald Springs a chance and see if I want to live here. But I'm too young to twiddle my thumbs."

I was beginning to wonder how long my job at Book Gems would last. The idea was solid. The choice of location was excellent. But I doubted Bob had the experience or insight he needed to make a go of this.

"Why books?" I figured I needed all the bad news up front.

"Because I read all the time. My second wife left me because I read so much. I don't know anything the way I know books."

This, at least, was in our favor.

We were fifty miles and three cigarettes closer to Cleveland before the conversation turned back to the prudery of the good folks of Emerald Springs.

"You know, I'm skating on the edge with the store," Bob said. "I thought I'd have a lot more money to put into it. Then the stock market took a dive, but I was already committed. So I started with less than I expected. Now this tempest in a teapot is going to cost me."

"It means that much to you to include an adult room? You could just do what everybody else does and keep the stock the protestors object to out of sight."

"I'm not going to let those right-wing, Moral Majority bigots dictate to me. We have freedom of speech in this country."

I thought there might be other compromises Bob could make that would satisfy everybody, but I knew better than to suggest it. On this subject he was sure he was right.

"Church people are bad enough, but it's really the fault of that bozo Frank Carlisle and politicians just like him," Bob continued. "Not to mention Brownie Kefauver and half the city council. They feed on these kind of issues. They come out of nowhere, put their finger to the wind to see which way it blows, then they cash right in."

Frank Carlisle is one of Ohio's thirty-three state senators, and unfortunately, he belongs to Bob and me and the 329,998 other people he represents in our large, rural district. He used to be one of our representatives in Washington, but he retired from that job about six years ago in his early sixties, preferring, he said, to work on a smaller scale and a more personal level.

In my mind, every time a politician moves down of his own accord, it means there's a scandal he's trying to avoid, but what do I know? Anyway, it's a toss-up which position was worse for Ohio. Do we want people like Carlisle ambushing American ideals and Ohio's reputation on a national level? Or do we want to keep that blessing closer to home?

"Has Carlisle or Kefauver jumped into the fray?" I asked. "Or are you speaking generally?"

"Generally, for the moment. Kefauver's trying to figure out which position will get him the most votes in the next election. Carlisle's trumpeting American values so loudly his listeners think they've been recruited to picket anybody that moves, chews, or has an opinion. But he'll be making it personal soon enough. You know he's coming to town, right?"

I could see why he was frothing at the mouth. That wasn't going to make things better.

He saw me shake my head. "To dedicate the new service center. The one they're building out on Gleason Road?"

I knew about the service center since it was a big deal in a small community, but only vaguely. "When's that?"

"I don't know, a couple of weeks I think. Maybe a little sooner. And who knows, he gets wind of what's going on with my store, he'll drop by to add his two cents' worth before the dedication. No stone left unturned. You wait and see."

"Maybe he won't bother. Maybe this issue is too small."

"It's not small to me. I already had to refinance my house. And by the way, just make a list of anything you see today that you think we should carry. I'll have to work out the costs before we order a single book."

I wondered if Keely needed help marketing her birdhouses. I suspected I was going to be at loose ends very soon.

By the time we arrived at the trade show and parked, Bob was in a better mood. He'd smoked three more cigarettes to lift his spirits while I vowed silently never to set foot in a car with him again.

We separated at the door so we could each cover half the room. The exhibition hall was huge, and Bob had promised I would be home in time for dinner. Ed was getting back from Columbus in time to pick up the girls and make his specialty spaghetti sauce.

I wandered, entranced. I love books, and I started reading to my daughters the moment they emerged from my womb. Even now that Deena reads to entertain herself and Teddy is sounding out words in simple chapter books, I still read to them every night. I'm not sure which is more fun, the girls or the books themselves. Sometimes I wonder if we have children because our own childhoods aren't long enough.

As I looked I wrote down some promising titles, skipping those about subjects so gloomy they would deaden young readers to the evils of the world or turn them into insomniacs. That left me with a plethora of books, but I was careful and only wrote down the best to save poor Bob from embarrassment.

Thumbing through picture books on one publisher's revolving display rack, I pondered why most of the celebrities in America thought they could write simplistic moral tales, when their own personal lives were a total mess. Someone tapped me on the shoulder. I turned, expecting to find Bob.

"Aggie, what are you doing here?"

Joan Barstow is the head librarian at Teddy's new school, and a member of our congregation. She's plump and gray haired, and she has perpetual laugh lines at the corner of her lips, the kind of librarian a child feels comfortable asking for help. Better yet, under that friendly librarian exterior beats an adventurous heart. Joan is a former champion in the calf roping division of what is now Women's Professional Rodeo, and she has a small farm outside of town where she trains half a dozen quarter horses. Deena worships her.

I explained about Book Gems and told her I was here with Bob.

"You drove with him? How did you stand the smoke?" she asked.

"You wouldn't be driving home in an hour or two, would you?"

Joan grinned. "I'll take you back."

"I'll muck out stalls for a week in gratitude."

"Don't worry, Deena and her friend Tara keep them clean as a whistle."

We wandered rows together, stopping at promising booths. Joan pointed out authors her elementary readers enjoyed, and we found a few new ones who seemed promising. I wrote down a few carefully chosen titles and Joan made notes, as well. We picked up enough calendars, bookmarks, and key chains to fill a piano crate. Our canvas bags sporting the show's logo were piled high with catalogs and advance reading copies.

"Bob's generating a lot of heat," Joan said as we neared the middle of the room where I expected to run into my employer. "But I guess he can afford it."

"I'm not sure," I said carefully. "A business needs all the customers it can entice."

"Well, he's probably banking on the fuss going away. And with his family fortune, I'm sure he doesn't need any real money from the store. I suspect it's more of a hobby."

I didn't think she was probing. Joan seemed sure of herself.

I did the probing. "Family fortune?"

"Don't you know? His mother's family owns two of Cleveland's salt mines. I'm sure that's why he settled in Emerald Springs. The Springs used to be their family home. And Bob's probably going to inherit the mines someday, so he'll want to be close by to run them. There's other family money, too, I think, but the salt mines are the biggest part. I'm sure he must own enough shares to keep going."

The fact that Cleveland had salt mines surprised me as much as the fact that Bob had plead poverty to me. "Salt mines?"

"The residue from an ancient sea. It's supposed to be more than fifty feet thick. Most of the road salt for the northern states is mined right here. No one knew about the mines until the 1950s, then they discovered there's a deep warren of underground rooms leading miles out into the center of Lake Erie."

Like any good librarian, Joan had the facts at her fingertips. "I had no idea," I said.

"There's a tour you can take, or at least there used to be. Maybe Bob could get you in. You take an elevator way down a shaft into total darkness."

"I'd rather have my teeth pulled, thanks."

She laughed. "Anyway, Bob should come into a bundle unless somebody discovers a cheaper, more effective way to deice the roads."

Either Bob didn't expect this windfall anytime soon, or like a true cheapskate he had exaggerated his financial burdens so I wouldn't ask for a raise in the next decade.

By the time we met up with him, I had scribbled the names of six dozen more books. I figured despite everything he had told me, Bob could afford them.

7

I'll confess that when I agreed to do a presentation for the Women's Society on church history, I had an ulterior motive. I am, at heart, a Luddite, a disciple of good ole Ned Ludd, whose nineteenth-century followers took axes and sledgehammers to what was then high technology, hoping to slow the advance of the industrial age. I don't understand computers, cell phones, VCRs, or Palm Pilots. Anything with a computer chip self-destructs when I walk into a room. Q has been known to abandon his celluloid frames when I buy tickets to the latest James Bond movie.

I am not Ray Sloan and Junie Bluebird's daughter for nothing.

Unfortunately, I'm a Luddite in need of reformation. Someday I may need a real job, so for the past year I have purchased every technology-specific Dummies book in print. My latest purchase explains the mysteries of Microsoft PowerPoint, and I promptly won the bid for an ancient version of the program on eBay.

Actually, I had Deena bid for me, since we now have a set of pots and pans from a dealer in Tucson in lieu of the picture frames I was certain I had purchased.

PowerPoint is the reason I volunteered for the presentation. Using Ed's laptop computer, Deena's superior knowledge, and a Dummies book, I set out to construct a slide show that would wow the Society, prove I've given up my Luddite ways, and establish myself as a valued member of the church community.

So, okay, the presentation was also to show how mature and forgiving I can be when my husband's under fire. When my father thinks he's under attack, Ray cleans his gun collection and stockpiles ammunition. My mother smiles her most brilliant smile and shames onlookers with her natural, ethereal radiance.

The ammo dump is my fallback position.

While Deena was home on summer vacation to supervise, I scanned almost one hundred prime photographs from the archives into our home computer. Step by miserable step I designed charts of founding members and the descendants who still grace Tri-C's hallways. I made tables of membership information starting in 1855, when the church was founded, right up until today. Of course, I included the happy fact that the church had experienced a growth surge in the early months of Ed's ministry.

Can we say "self-serving"?

I created titles and bulleted lists, enhanced everything with clip art, photos, sound effects, captivating transitions, music, and even animation. All in all it was Luddite immersion therapy. By the time I had a flawless thirty-five-minute presentation saved on the computer, I had rocketed into the 1990s.

On Tuesday I was getting dressed for the presentation when Ed wandered into the bedroom and sat down on our queen-sized bed to observe. I waited for him to comment on my new Victoria's Secret bra or the extra pound that had settled on my hips as payback for eating barbecued ribs, potato salad, and brownies at the Frankels' Labor Day party. So okay, yesterday I fell off the vegetarian wagon after clinging to it by my fingernails for weeks. Ed himself never stepped more than three yards from the grill, although he swears he only inhaled.

He gave the requisite wolf whistle, though his heart wasn't in it. "I was just chastised by e-mail. Did you know it's a long-standing tradition for the minister to host a Labor Day party for the board at the parsonage?"

"I know. But it was between the Frankels' swimming pool or our murder site. See my point?"

"You're sure you want to brave this presentation today?"

I had an inkling of the way Daniel had felt approaching the lion's den, but I didn't want to worry Ed. "It's one of the few jobs I can do for the church."

"Nobody says you have to do a thing," Ed said.

"You're afraid I'm going to screw this up, aren't you?"

He grinned and set my heart speeding. "Absolutely."

"Don't worry. Deena and I went over everything last night. I've borrowed a top-of-the-line digital projector from Jack's law office. I saved the presentation to two separate diskettes before I loaded it on your laptop. I memorized the troubleshooting section of the how-to guide."

"I don't know why you do this to yourself. You have so many other talents."

I was already dressed in my best dark skirt and red cashmere twin set—a gift from my preppy baby sister Sid—so I didn't wink and ask what talents he was referring to. I fluffed my "not-quite" curly hair, which falls not-quite to my shoulders.

"Earrings," I muttered and fumbled for the modest pearl studs that Nan, Ed's mother, had reluctantly presented to me on my wedding day.

Ed got up, lifted my hair off my nape, and kissed it. Then he put his arms around my waist and rested his cheek against my hair. "No matter what she says, don't let Lady Falowell get to you."

"She will be blinded by my competence."

"She'll find something to criticize. Don't take it personally."

I contemplated this as I made the trip to the parish house to set up the projector. Our Women's Society is a throwback to another time. If the Society hoped for more members, they would change their meeting time to evening and drop "Women's" from their name, thereby more than doubling their potential. But insular as the Society is, it serves a real purpose. The women watch out for each other. Some are widows, some are childless; some have never married. My generation may find its sense of community in a more inclusive way, but it won't necessarily be stronger.

The Society meets in the lounge, furnished through the years by bake sales, spring teas, and craft bazaars. The walls are lined with comfortable sofas and chairs and adorned with art treasures culled from rummage sale donations. It's a welcoming room, with its apple green rug and peach-toned walls. The Emerald Springs Oval is just across the street and the wood blinds are usually open for a view of ancient trees. This week the trees are just beginning to contemplate autumn.

When members began trickling in, I had the projector in place and handouts ready.

Yvonne McAllister was the first to arrive. She looked as if she was gaining weight, and I wondered if she had finally quit smoking. If so, I wanted her to talk to Bob.

"You're brave to do this," she said softly. "David against Goliath."

"I purposely left my slingshot at home."

"I'm sure Gelsey will be on her best behavior in public."

If Gelsey's friends were worried, this did not bode well.

Gelsey herself arrived at ten on the dot. She bustled in wearing a turquoise blazer, a skirt of subtle houndstooth check, a cream-colored silk blouse, and a rope of pearls which had undoubtedly been pried from real South Sea oysters. My mother-in-law would adore Gelsey.

Gelsey spoke to several people as she approached the lectern our sexton had set up for the meeting. The microphone was unnecessary since even a whisper could be heard in any corner of the room, but it did lend a certain importance to the proceedings.

I sat quietly and nodded knowledgeably as Lady Falowell conducted business. There were nearly as many committee reports as there were members. Blessedly, none of them had much to say.

Unable to delay any longer, Gelsey turned to me and made her introduction. She was glad to have me there. We were all grateful for the work I was doing. Yada yada yada. She finished without once cracking a smile. Then she motioned for me to come to the mike.

Nothing was riding on this. Not really. But my hands were sweating anyway. I smiled my best Junie smile and settled myself at the lectern, unobtrusively turning off the sound system since I've never met a microphone that doesn't screech.

"Over the last months it's been such fun," I said, "to go through the church archives. I've really only just begun. The guest bedroom in the parsonage is a warren of some of the boxes and memorabilia I still need to sort. But I'm making headway. I hope to have everything viewed, organized, and labeled by the end of the church year." *Just in time to turn it over to the new minister's family after you fire my husband.*

"You've removed some of our papers from the archives?" Fern Booth, one of Gelsey's supporters at the infamous board meeting, interrupted pleasantly enough. "I didn't know that was allowed."

"The storage room really isn't a good place to keep documents or photographs," I said pleasantly, too, "although I've had to return some of them temporarily to make room at home. There's too wide a variation in temperature and humidity. Once everything is organized the board will need to decide on a better place. We should preserve everything."

"I would hardly have thought a house with rambunctious children was the right place."

The woman was openly declaring war. I let the initial salvo pass over my head and answered as if I didn't understand her point.

"Thank you, Fern, for reminding me about children. We need to share our history with the religious education classes, so they'll realize they're part of a church that's been important to Emerald Springs almost from the beginning of its founding. So I'm planning another presentation, similar to this one, for them."

I flicked on the projector to forestall another burst of fire.

"This is just a taste of what I've uncovered so far. But I know you'll enjoy it. Some of you have lived a piece of this history."

One octogenarian beamed. "I could tell you about some of the parties we used to have."

"I'll take notes," I promised.

Everybody laughed. With two notable exceptions.

I prayed to the PowerPoint gods, asked for the lights to be turned out, and began the presentation. Or tried to.

"This is not a PowerPoint presentation," appeared on my computer screen.

My hands began to drip. "Whoops," I said. "Small problem. Let me fix this."

I had done my homework. I tried one of my backup diskettes. No luck. I tried the other. No dice. Frantically I dragged the file's icon to the PowerPoint icon and dropped it there. Then I tried once more.

The same words came up on the screen.

"Sometimes files get damaged when they're moved from one computer to the other," I said calmly. "Chat just a minute while I fix this."

No one seemed concerned, although I heard a snort from Gelsey's direction. I was thankful for the hour spent memorizing the troubleshooting info in my book. I closed the program, then reopened it and set up a blank folder, then began to insert files into it until I was pretty sure I had reconstructed my original presentation. I saved it under a new name and tried again.

Bingo! My title slide appeared on the screen that had been set up against the opposite wall. A photograph of the church from the early 1900s anchored the left corner, and one of the church in present day anchored the right.

I felt a flood of relief. There it was. Just the way I'd organized it.

Somebody clapped and others took it up. I began my spiel, using notes I'd printed out—or rather that Deena had printed out for me.

When time came for the second slide the transition seemed a little odd. A sepia toned photo of an early congregation posed on the front steps was supposed to dissolve into place. Instead it lurched its way on-screen. I felt vaguely seasick and averted my eyes. I continued my narration, but each slide lurched more drunkenly than the one before.

There had been something in the book about resolution. Frantically I tried to recall what I'd read. I stopped a moment, opened the slide show menu, selected a new resolution, and continued on. The slides flowed seamlessly one after another.

I was really getting good at this. Junie's smile came naturally to my face. I continued the narration. The next portion, showing scenes inside the church over the years, was supposed to be accompanied by sound files of a choir concert in the 1950s. But when I got to it, it wouldn't play. Instead I got another error message.

I continued without sound, but my hands were sweating again. I told myself it didn't matter and changed the narration so there was no reference to the choir.

Then the slides began to skip. Just one at first, then another and another until only every other slide appeared. I scrambled to explain the things my audience hadn't seen, as if the slides weren't there on the computer somewhere. But some of my information no longer made sense.

I came to a chart that illustrated the way the church had grown in the twentieth century. I tried to point out some of the figures and discovered the program's pointer was acting erratically. If I moved the mouse to the right, the pointer went left. I tried thinking like the pointer, but it began moving vertically. Then, as if possessed, it began to spin. I was reminded of Linda Blair's head in *The Exorcist,* a movie that never fails to entertain my dad.

"Forget the pointer," I said with a nervous laugh. I launched into more statistics about the way membership had expanded and declined, tying some of the information to wars and economy, and trying desperately to call up the photos of the Depression era and World War II. No luck there.

The chart illustrating our growth in this century was simply gone. I had hoped to show our sizeable spurt over the months of Ed's ministry, leaving my audience with the indelible impression that things at Tri-C are much better than Gelsey insists. Instead, my final barrage of photos came on the screen. And somehow the multiple images carefully distributed on each slide had piled up like a car wreck. One slide after the other. Distorted beyond redemption, although I could have sworn that in the middle of one was a photograph of my daughters playing in the sprinkler, followed closely by one of me giving birth.

It couldn't be.

I went to what was supposed to be the final slide, the opening service of this church year with Ed at the front of the sanctuary and several adorable little boys dressed up and standing beside him to light our chalice. Instead this slide was a photograph of me in my slinkiest black dress, my hair pushed up in one hand, a shoulder strap slipping down my arm, a come-hither look in my eyes. Ed had snapped it two years before as I got ready for a big night at the Kennedy Center.

I was surprised to find he kept the photo on his computer, and more surprised that as I transferred files, this one had somehow landed in my presentation. Rather than see if the far sexier one taken a few minutes later was in the immediate lineup, too, I flicked off the projector immediately and pulled out the cord for good measure.

"Ummm . . . Modern technology 1, Aggie 0. I'm sorry. This worked like a charm on our home computer. I'll have to get the bugs and the cheesecake photos off the laptop. But I hope you can see where I'm going with this?"

There was applause, and from some quarters enthusiastic applause at that. Gelsey got to her feet, and I steeled myself.

She lifted one brow and smiled thinly. "Well, we seem to have lots of time left for questions. Does anyone have any that our scintillating Mrs. Wilcox might possibly be prepared to answer?"

＋   ＋   ＋

"I'm sure it's not anything you did, Aggie. Gelsey always seems more stressed in the autumn. I've noticed it before.

I suppose it's just getting back into the groove after a restful summer."

I was dejected after my dismal failure and didn't answer. I was only listening halfheartedly to Yvonne, who had volunteered to take Jack's projector back to his office. She was parked in front of the parsonage to leave room in the church lot for the oldest members of the Society.

Yvonne gave a dramatic sigh. "But you didn't imagine it. Gelsey was just plain rude. Maybe she misses New England this time of year. The leaves, the festivals. I know I always miss Santa Fe in the summer, and I'm cranky when I can't get back there."

Chitchat was better than contemplation. "I didn't realize Gelsey's from New England."

"Oh yes. Boston. One of the old Back Bay families."

"Ed's mother grew up just off Newbury Street."

"Well, Gelsey is Mayflower all the way. Her family had a summer cottage in New Hampshire, a ski chalet in Killington. She goes home twice a year to be with her sister and cousins, but I'm sure it's never quite the same."

I was ready to offer the woman one-way first-class airfare to Logan International myself. I helped Yvonne store the projector behind her seat and thanked her for taking it to Jack. Then after I had waved good-bye, I went inside through the front door, just in time to catch the telephone.

"Agate, dear."

"Dear" came out as "deah." Ed's mother Nanette has what Ed calls an "eastern prep school" accent. There are no "R's" after A's or long E's. Of course, with good old Yankee frugality, the R's are never thrown away. They show up in the darndest places.

I fell into the chair beside the entry hall telephone and wondered if my luck could get any worse. "Hello, Nan. How are you?"

"Well, I'm as fine as I always am. I just thought, perhaps, something had happened to you since it's been so long since I've heard anything."

I knew that Ed had called his mother the previous week.

Both of the girls had described their classes in detail. Teddy had recounted my explanation of the body on our front porch in an eerie imitation of my voice. Nan had hung up quickly.

"There's not much to report," I told her now. "Did you have a nice Labor Day weekend?"

"Oh, I lunched with friends, went to a new exhibition at the museum. A quiet day."

We had invited her here for our end to summer celebration, but Nan had pleaded migraines. In advance. In Nan's opinion, Ohio, which was not one of the original thirteen colonies, is wilderness best left to trappers and river boatmen. She came for Ed's installation, and she is still recovering.

I told her about our Labor Day celebration, assured her the girls knew they had to make good grades so they could get into an Ivy League college, promised we would make certain they took part in extracurricular activities to make up for our annoying inability to afford a real school like Exeter or Andover.

"And, I can assume there have been no more . . . incidents on your lawn? You really must be more careful, Agate."

I filed that away. In the future I would murder my victims elsewhere.

I cast around for something else to pass the time and remembered what Yvonne had told me. "Nan, I just discovered one of our members is from an old Back Bay family, too."

Nan perked up immediately. I explained about Gelsey, at least those things which could be said. "Gelsey Falowell." I struggled and failed. "I'm afraid I don't remember her maiden name," I finished.

"Back Bay, you say?"

"That's what I was told. She has a sister, cousins who are still there."

"You say she's a woman about my age?"

"Indeed." Nan brings out my subliminal aristocrat.

"I don't remember any Gelseys. You're certain of her name?"

For some reason the question stopped me. I couldn't remember why. "That's what she goes by," I said. "Might be a nickname, but it's certainly what she's called."

"I know virtually everyone from the important families."

Personally, I thought all families were important. And Nan, if challenged, would certainly agree. But snobbery crept into even her most well-intentioned offerings. She believed in equality, she just believed equality was a sliding scale.

"Perhaps you might find out her maiden name," she said.

I remembered the day Gelsey had showed me a lovely sterling silver monogrammed brooch along with more jewelry she thought me incapable of appreciating. I struggled to picture it. "It might begin with an *R*," I said.

"That hardly narrows it enough, dear."

"Railford!" I was so proud. I remembered now that there had been two coats of arms above Gelsey's fireplace. Falowell and Railford. And I had noted this with a secret smile because a girl named Julia Railford had been the sluttiest coed in my college dorm.

Ed may remember the names of obscure fifteenth-century theologians, but I remember the important stuff.

"Yes, well," Nan said. "That doesn't sound familiar, either. I suppose my son isn't home?"

Nan never seems to understand that Ed works during the day. Despite being a lifelong Unitarian she often calls on Sunday mornings, and is always perplexed when she reaches our answering machine.

I hung up a moment later. Ed is a mystery to me. Either he's a changeling, or else a pediatric nurse with a sense of humor swapped him for Nan's real offspring. Maybe somewhere in the worst slum of Boston there's a man in a bow tie who prefers polo or yacht races to the Red Sox and wonders why.

By the time the girls arrived home I had recovered from my morning and cleaned out our bedroom closet in preparation for painting. When we moved into the parsonage, it was

clear no one had changed anything but the light bulbs in decades. I only agreed to move in if we were given free rein to
paint or paper as we saw fit.

I started my renovation with the girls' rooms and now
Deena's is a pale lavender with a wide stenciled ivy border
that took us a week to finish. Teddy wanted Puritan gray and
compromised on a grayed blue with ruffled white curtains
and one of Junie's quilts, country churches pieced in cheery
reds and golds. Junie's handmade dolls adorn chairs or tables in every corner.

For our room I wanted deep red, but like Teddy, I was
willing to compromise. I did not want anyone from the
Women's Society, on the way to an upstairs bathroom, faint-
ing in horror at my solution to the dingy flocked wallpaper
that had graced the master bedroom walls since the 1970s.
So I was going to settle for a medium sage green with sheer
curtains and botanical prints on the walls instead of the
Kama Sutra batiks Ed brought me from India before we were
married. Those were, regretfully, stored away.

I planned to start painting in the closet to see how well I
liked my color choice. No matter what I decided for the
room itself, the closet interior can remain this shade. No
time wasted.

I had oatmeal cookies, apples, and milk out for the girls
when they walked through the door. Deena took one look at
my expression and shook her head.

"How did you screw it up?"

I poured the milk. "I did not screw up the presentation. It
more or less self-destructed."

"You are so totally lame with anything that plugs in."

I couldn't fault her. It hadn't been said with malice or dis-
respect. "Maybe you can help me see where I went wrong.
Next month when I can face looking at a computer screen
again. How was school?"

"I'm surrounded by lunatics."

The choices were many. "Administration? Teachers?
Custodians?"

"Shannon was supposed to sit with us at lunch. She sat
with Jeff Matthews instead, and his friends."

"I'm surprised you care where Shannon sits. You have a lot of friends to sit with, don't you?"

"For how long? They're all paying more attention to boys than they are to each other. Carlene says she's going out with Sean Hutchinson."

"Going out? Dating?" Even for Crystal O'Grady's daughter, this seemed premature. The girls were eleven.

"No." Deena shook her head as if I were hopeless. "They don't go anywhere. They just go out."

I scrambled to understand. "What do they do when they go out?"

"They don't do anything."

"So going out means they're not doing anything together. And this is somehow different from *not* going out?"

"Tara, Maddie, and I are the only Meanies who still have a brain." Deena took an apple, polished it against the hem of her T-shirt, and carried it upstairs.

Teddy arrived next. This was her first day of walking to and from school with two third graders who live on the next block. Teddy's school is only three blocks away, and there are crossing guards at every intersection. I still felt bottomless relief when the front door opened.

After the mandatory hug, I served cookies and milk at the table and sat for the mandatory blow-by-blow description of her day. Teddy is careful not to leave out any detail, a stickler for accuracy. When we got to recess, the news—good up to that point—soured.

"Some of the kids won't play with me."

I was irate. I managed not to show it. "What bad taste they have."

"They said somebody died in our yard."

I sat back. "I'm not sure I understand what that has to do with playing with you."

She shrugged, apparently less concerned than I was. "Me, either."

"Just some of the kids?"

"Mostly friends of Jimmy Betts. He said I'm scary."

"You're not scary, Teddy."

She frowned. "I know that."

Of course she did. I gave myself a mental slap. "Do you like Jimmy Betts?"

"I don't know. He won't play with me, so I can't find out."

"What did you do instead?"

"I ran around a lot and climbed on the jungle gym with the other girls."

Clearly Jimmy's prejudices had not ruined her day. I hoped they faded.

By the time both girls had gotten a start on homework and Ed had come home from a day of committee meetings and hospital visits, I had put my morning in perspective. By the time the four of us had washed dishes and set the kitchen to rights, I'd almost forgotten my presentation until Deena reminded me.

"Where's the power strip you borrowed from my room this morning?"

I had taken the strip to be sure I had enough outlets for my equipment. Unfortunately, I hadn't remembered to bring it home. I threw myself on her mercy and promised to go over to the parish house and retrieve it so she could work on a book report.

Ed was on the telephone in the study when I went to tell him where I was heading. From his end of the conversation, I knew this was a discussion of the church budget that could last until bedtime. I pointed toward the church and rummaged on the desktop for his keys to the parish house. "Ten minutes," I mouthed. He waved me out.

The sun had already set and a light rain was falling. Autumn wasn't yet official, but the temperature was dipping into the fifties at night. I cut through our yard and the church parking lot. There was only one car, and it didn't look familiar. Sometimes people use the lot when they're shopping or eating in town, even though we have signs asking them not to. But clearly there were no meetings here tonight or Ed would be in attendance. Only a few lights were on inside for security.

I unlocked the backdoor and entered through the kitchen, turning on lights for company as I went. The parish house is meant to be filled with noise and laughter and people. When it's not, it seems bereft, and somehow, accusing. I hummed under my breath, hoping to appease it. I wasn't at all sure that helped.

January, our sexton, had already vacuumed and set the lounge to rights. Of course he had thoughtfully stored the power strip somewhere out of sight, as well. I began a search, humming louder, turning on lights everywhere I went.

There are one million, possibly two million places where someone could hide in the parish house. There was no reason to think of that, of course, except that not long before a body had turned up on my porch. My imagination is vivid, but I'm not given to paranoia. Still, the longer I searched the more aware I became of every creak of the old building, and every darkened nook and cranny.

The power strip turned up in the religious education supply closet on the second floor, between an antiquated 8 mm movie projector and a cardboard box of tempera paints.

"Yowsa!" I snatched it and started downstairs, flicking off lights as I went. By the time I made it to the kitchen, I slowed down and began to breathe normally again. Everything was fine. No cause for alarm. I was out of there.

I locked up behind me and took the steps down to the yard.

Somebody stepped from behind the nearest shrub and grabbed my arm.

The sound I made should have shattered the parish house windows.

"Hey, cut it out!" The voice was menacing. The man was Rico Marina.

I shook loose, although more accurately I shook and he finally let me go. I took two steps backwards, unfortunately out of the direct light cast by the security lamppost at the parking lot's edge.

"What do you think you're doing?" I demanded. "You scared me to death."

The last part didn't seem to bother him. "I've been following you."

"Well, that's reassuring. Now I feel a lot better about this." I looked around. The car that had been parked there was gone, and the lot was completely deserted. Worse, from this angle, all I could see of the parsonage was a row of over-grown lilacs.

I thrust my shoulders back and glared. "My husband knows where I am, and if I don't get home in a minute or two, he's going to come looking for me."

"Well, if you don't answer my questions, he's not going to find you." He snarled the words with finesse, as if he'd been practicing.

I should have been more scared than I was. For all I knew, this man might have murdered his wife and left her for me to find. But Rico seemed more angry than menacing. And un-less he was the oddest kind of serial killer, there seemed very little to gain from murdering me when he was probably a suspect in Jennifer's murder.

"What kind of questions?" My knees were shaking, but I straightened even more and locked them in place. "And why stalk me? Why didn't you simply use the telephone or knock on my door?"

Rico was dressed in black again. I wondered if he'd had his colors done and someone had told him he was a "winter." I wished I could remind him that red or royal blue were good choices, as well, if less intimidating.

My question seemed to perplex him, as if approaching this in such a normal way was completely out of his frame of reference. "You wouldn't talk to me," he said at last.

"I'm talking to you now when I could be screaming for help. What's on your mind?"

"Jenny's body was found on your porch, right?"

"'Fraid so. I was the one who found her."

"Why you?"

"Because I was the first one to go to the door after some-body dropped her there."

"You're saying you don't know anything about it but that?"

"That's what I'm saying."

"You must have an opinion."

"Not yet."

"So why were you nosing around Don't Go There? Keely

says you were asking questions. You showed up at the funeral."

"A dead woman turned up on my porch. Try to put yourself in my position. I'd like to know why. I'd like to be sure nobody else ends up there. I'd like to be sure my family is safe. Is this making sense to you?"

"So what did Jenny tell you?"

For a moment I just stared at him, although I was sure that was not the best of approaches. His scowl deepened as I gazed at him. I shook my head. "I never spoke to your wife. The only time I ever saw Jennifer Marina was when she was already dead."

"I don't believe that. I want to know what she told you."

"She wasn't exactly talking, Rico. She . . . was . . . dead. And you won't find one person anywhere in this town who ever saw me talking to her because I never did."

He stepped closer. I had to steel myself not to step back farther into the shadows. "She told you about her family, didn't she?"

"Dead," I repeated. "She was *dead*. And that's the first time anyone has mentioned her family to me. What family?"

He cocked his head. "I'm not getting the answers I want, lady."

His brows had knit into one angry line. I felt a thrill of alarm. "I'm a really rotten liar. Nobody tells lies worse than I do. I could try lying to you now, if that's what you want, but you'd see right through me."

He took another step and I held up my hand. "One step closer, buster, and I'm going to scream loud enough to bring everybody in the neighborhood running."

"That won't be necessary." A man stepped out from the side of the building. "Get away from her, Marina. Now."

I darted a glance in the newcomer's direction. Detective Sergeant Roussos. Under any circumstances he would be a pleasure to behold. Under these, something of a miracle.

My knees unfolded and began to knock.

"I want to know what happened to my wife," Rico said. The menace in his voice had cranked down to a whine. "I thought maybe, you know, she knows more than she's saying."

"Do you want to swear out a complaint?" Roussos asked me. "Harassment for starters?"

I looked at Rico and felt some distant cousin of compassion. From all accounts, Rico Marina had abused his wife and lost custody of children he didn't want. But I had sensed—call me an optimist—a nugget of concern for Jennifer in his questions. Sure, he was a bully, and not a very smart bully at that, but somewhere deep in this man's psyche was a flicker of love for the woman who had died.

"No," I said. "Of course if he ever comes within ten feet of me again, I'll be at the station in a heartbeat."

Roussos grimaced and shook his head. "Bleeding heart liberals."

"Nope. First sign of blood I'll swear out a warrant."

Roussos fingered the lapel of Rico's jacket. "We're looking at you for the murder, Marina. I'd be careful. I'd be on my best behavior." He released him.

I knew Marina was about to take off. "What family were you talking about?" I asked him.

Now Roussos was scowling at me, but I ignored him. "If you're talking about your kids, Keely told me they're in Pennsylvania." My maternal genes were in an uproar. "If they're here, who's taking care of them?"

Rico looked confused, but he covered. "I don't know what you're talking about."

"You asked me if Jennifer had told me about her family."

Roussos was the one to answer. "He's talking about the Cobras," he said. "They call themselves a family. A real perversion of the word."

"The Cobras?"

Rico rose to the bait. "Yeah, the Cobras. You got a problem with that? Jenny rode with them. And that lowlife Sax Dubinsky, too."

I was trying to imagine how a gang of thugs had ever represented family to Jennifer Marina. Had her life been so sad, so devoid of love, that she had settled for this?

"*Lowlife* is the right word for all of them," Roussos said.

"Yeah? Well, they're everywhere you look. No town in

America they haven't invaded. Hell, I hear your mayor's brother rode with them for a while. Nobody's safe who gets in their way. Look behind you, there's a Cobra standing there. That's where you should be looking for her murderer."

Roussos didn't look impressed. "Tell you what, I'm going to look behind me, and when I turn my head again, you'd better be gone. Got it?"

Rico shrugged and took off around the building.

"The mayor's brother?" I asked, once Rico was well and truly gone.

"Half brother."

I struggled to recall why the mention of Browning Kefauver's half brother rang a bell. Then I remembered. Lucy had told me that Brownie's half brother had rented the house across the street while he was waiting to move to Dallas.

The house where Jennifer had been murdered or at least taken afterwards.

Half bro had been a Cobra. The Cobras were a family, dysfunctional as all get-out, but still with strong ties. Lucy had said half bro had given his key to our uptight mayor to oversee the moving of his furniture, but who was to say that he hadn't made a copy first and passed it on to one of his Cobra buddies? Maybe somebody had needed a place to crash, or hold orgies. Someone like Sax Dubinsky.

"You know," I started, "the mayor's half brother—"

"Lived in the house across the street for a few months. I get it. We've already checked. He claims he never gave out a copy of the key to his motorcycle pals. Said they would have trashed the place. Besides, nothing hinges on a key."

"According to a friend who, umm, knows about these things, locks are the only things the owners have spent any money on. She says the backdoor is like Fort Knox. And the front is in plain view of Church Street. There wasn't any sign of forced entry, was there?"

Roussos ran a hand through his mop of dark curls. "You are thinking too much. With thinking comes action. No more action, okay? Wasn't tonight enough?"

"Hey, I didn't ask Rico to stalk me. I was over here getting a power strip for my daughter's computer." I held it up as evidence.

"And I suppose you were at Don't Go There the other night to convert sinners?"

I bristled. "Can you think of a better place?"

"Mrs. Wilcox, back off. We'll find out who murdered Jennifer Marina. But it will be easier if you stay away and let us do our job. I don't want to worry about protecting you."

"What were you doing here tonight, anyway? I'm fairly sure you're not following *me*, waiting to play guardian angel."

He didn't answer. I answered for him. "You were following Rico, weren't you? You think he's the murderer."

"You're not listening, are you?"

"There are no laws against using my brain, are there?"

I could swear there was the faintest glint of approval in his eyes, although his words belied it. "Stay out of this. I can't say it any more clearly."

I was sure this was good advice. I was equally sure I wasn't going to take it.

8

The first time I saw Emerald Springs I had a moment of recognition, a déjà vu experience, if you will. As a child following Junie coast to coast from craft show to Renaissance Fair, Emerald Springs was the kind of town where I always dreamed we would put down roots.

We weren't on the move every day. There were lengthy sojourns in cities from Maine to California while Junie worked on her inventory. Junie has been married five times, and although I've forgotten some of the names of my stepfathers, I've never forgotten the states where we lived with them. Sid's dad was Georgia. The next stepfather was Iowa—a particularly short-lived relationship since Junie missed hills and mountains. My mother's standards are her own.

Now, of course, I see the benefit of all this travel. Junie is a good mother, although completely unorthodox. The husbands were decent men. Whatever trauma we suffered each time we were uprooted was balanced somewhat by Junie's ability to make a home anywhere, her desire to give us the broadest education possible, her genuine love for each of us.

Still, to offset all those moves and parading stepfathers, I dreamed of a town like the one where I am now—at least temporarily—planted.

In some ways, Emerald Springs is the American Dream. Population: just large enough for decent schools and small enough for individual attention for our children. Climate: too cold for killer bees but warm enough to swim in surrounding lakes in July. Geography: sky, old hardwood trees, and at the outskirts, the beginning of rolling hills that eventually give way to picturesque Amish farms. Location: close enough to both Cleveland and Columbus for culture, shopping, and glimpses of diversity. Special Attractions: warm mineral springs discovered in the early nineteenth century with a sprawling old hotel and spa that attracts small conferences and tourists who trickle in to spend a dime or two in our fair city. Also a small liberal arts college with an excellent reputation. Economy: not so great, but the citizens of Emerald Springs make an attempt to take care of their own. Politics . . .

Well, no town is perfect.

The citizens of Emerald Springs are suspicious of strangers, of new ideas, of progress in almost any form. At the same time they are generous, ardent about the things they believe, and, reluctantly, capable of change. The result is a local government run by officials who must carefully analyze cultural standards and gently, slowly nudge to get things done. The good officials make an art form of nudging. The bad ones only analyze and regurgitate whatever they think the voters want to hear.

Browning Kefauver epitomizes the worst of these. When the stork dropped the infant Brownie into the Kefauver chimney, Baby Brownie probably measured the width, the buildup of soot, and whether the bricks had been recently repointed so he would know, without a doubt, where he had landed and what angle to play. Since that historic moment, Brownie has never stopped trying to figure out what to say to keep everybody happy.

Today, on my first morning at Book Gems, Brownie, a small, balding man with protruding ears, had decided that giving interviews to the media outside the bookstore's front entrance was the best way to go.

I had walked to work, one of the charms of this job. In a move to make Emerald Springs even more attractive and quaint, the city council spent big bucks this summer tearing up our concrete sidewalks and paving them with bricks. New planters, recently sown with chrysanthemums and pansies, dot the curb and sturdy saplings divide each block into thirds. I had enjoyed my stroll right up until the moment I heard chanting around the next corner.

I did not kid myself that the Hare Krishnas had invaded.

I made the turn and saw Brownie waxing profoundly for WQFT, the college radio station. Behind him were half a dozen picketers with signs and half a dozen more marching beside them. Having witnessed any number of protests on Washington's Mall or the steps of the Capitol, I'm a connoisseur of protest signs. These were pathetic. No rhyme, no play on words, no interesting fonts or graphics. Just Ban Pornography and Save Our Children, hand-lettered on poster board and taped hurriedly on yardsticks. I was tempted to organize an adult ed class right there on the spot.

One of the picketers spotted me, and broke ranks to come and greet me. "Mrs. Wilcox. You've come to join us?"

The man holding out his hand to me was the minister of an independent church half a mile from ours. The Reverend Cal Perkins was far more conservative than Ed, but I never would have expected to find him picketing a bookstore.

"Umm . . ." I took his hand. "I work here. It's my first day."

Cal's eyes widened. He has a scrawny build, prominent bulbous nose, and a thick head of hair combed straight back from a widow's peak, televangelist style. I've heard that his sermons last an hour and get steadily louder until his closing words can be heard on the next block.

"You work here?" Cal sounded stunned.

"Well, I will if your good friends let me through the front door."

"Do you kn-ow what kind of lit-er-at-ure you will be selling?"

"Sure." I left it at that.

"Do you understand the evils of pornography?"

I was beginning to get ticked. "Do you understand the evils of suppressing the First Amendment?"

"Surely you don't advocate the kind of filth for sale in there. You have children!"

"And my children won't be allowed in the adult section any more than yours will be. For Pete's sake, the bookstores you shop in offer the same stuff, just not in a separate room. We're not talking hardcore. You've heard of D. H. Lawrence?" When he looked blank I tried again. "Are you planning to ban Harlequin Romances next? How about the Song of Solomon? That's pretty hot stuff. Do you let your children read the Bible?"

"I can see talking to you won't make a difference."

"You're a man of some judgment after all." I moved past him and toward the door. I am not a fan of pornography, but by the standards of almost any community this was not what Bob was selling. Racy, yes. Too explicit for many tastes. Certainly not appropriate for children. But wasn't that the point of separating the sexy stuff from everything else?

I passed Brownie and the young reporter getting the interview. The girl, twenty at most, looked as if she needed a nap. Brownie's signature bow tie was bobbing to the rise and fall of his Adam's apple.

I'm not sure what came over me. I leaned over her shoulder as I passed. "Ask him if he's ever ridden with the Cobras," I whispered in the direction of her ear. Then, smiling my way past the chanting protestors, I made it through the front door.

I had stopped by Book Gems for a tour two days ago. The store was small but impressive. Bob and two other employees had stocked most of the shelves, arranged easy chairs at the ends of rows, designated a children's corner, and set up four round tables in another corner beside a tiny coffee bar. The infamous room in the back was only about eight by eight feet, with narrow shelves hanging from three walls. It was sparsely stocked. There were no Nazis, naked teenagers, or Great Danes haunting magazine covers. I had noticed the newly revised *The Joy of Sex* and had to laugh. I had bought my own copy years ago at a chain bookstore.

Now Bob was behind the cash register with the wooden shades fronting Sparrow Street drawn tight. For once, the smoke wreathing his head was not from a cigarette. He was furious.

"I'll have them arrested."

"Can't," I pointed out. "Free speech, remember?"

"It's restraint of trade. No one can get through the door."

"I just did. They didn't try to stop me."

"Did you see our mayor out there?"

"I didn't vote for him."

"I'm ruined."

"Oh, I don't think so." I looked at my watch. "That's WQFT out there interviewing him for their morning show. Everybody I know listens to it on their way to work or while they're doing car pool or taking their morning jog."

"So?"

"I believe they'll come by to see what the excitement is all about. Free coffee for the opening makes sense to me. What do you think? And I suggest we make some and take it outside to the protestors, too, as a goodwill gesture."

Bob looked as if he was trying to remember why he had hired me. Then slowly, as all the ramifications occurred to him, a smile bloomed. "Let me show you how to use the cappuccino machine."

"Oh, that's not a cappuccino crowd. The cappuccino folks will be here in about . . ." I glanced at my watch again. "Say thirty or forty minutes?"

"Plain old Colombian, then. Watered down. And flip the sign to Open."

+ + +

I won't say the day was a roaring success. But neither was it the unqualified disaster we had feared. At any given time once we opened our doors—but not our blinds—there were as many people inside buying books as there were out-side picketing.

I actually felt almost smug until lunchtime, when I was

preparing to eat a veggie sausage sandwich. Bob had put me in charge of the children's corner, and I had spent most of my time stocking and arranging books for the underage crowd. I'd made a list of more furnishings and props we needed, as well as gift items like stuffed animals and toys to go with the most popular picture books.

At noon, Bob pulled me into the stockroom and pointed to a television set in the corner. A stream of profanity followed. Bob can swear as well as read, I'll give him that.

It took me a moment to figure out what the problem was. Then I realized I was watching State Senator Carlisle in front of the Emerald Springs Hotel and Spa.

"What's he saying?" I leaned forward.

"He's here for some conference. Listen."

The interview was almost over, but I caught the gist of it. The senator was still a handsome man. Silver hair, olive skin, features that hadn't blurred with age, in particular a strong Roman nose. He was waxing enthusiastically against the evils of pornography and the creeping tide of permissiveness in our society. A little sermon on school prayer. A diatribe against gay marriage. An esoteric quote from Revelations. A warning that we must all be vigilant.

"Sodom and Gomorrah started with less," he finished. "We will not have Sodom and Gomorrah here."

Bob strode to the television and flicked it off.

"Sodom and Gomorrah? Give me a break." I couldn't believe what I'd heard.

"You missed the part about murderers in our streets."

Suddenly this was getting personal.

"It's kind of a strange time for an interview," I pointed out. "I wouldn't worry too much."

"He gave it this morning! This is the second time it's been aired. That damned interview will be on every local news program for the rest of the night."

"Not so good." I turned up my hands. "But now everyone who thinks the senator is a pompous, well, you know, will show up and buy books. We'll be okay. You just have to tough it out until the excitement dies down."

"Sodom and Gomorrah." He shook his head. He looked like a man with a dying dream.

There are many fine vegetarian food products. I had not chosen one of them. The sandwich went in the garbage and I made do with a crumbling granola bar from the nether regions of my purse.

Apparently protestors need to eat, as well, because the noise from out front began to falter. Fewer voices yelled "Go back where you came from," and "*Hell* is a four-letter word." That last slogan actually made me smile. At least somebody out there had a sense of humor.

At one the chanting escalated with a vengeance. When Bob tried to show me yet again how to use the register and had to shout, I knew something had changed besides recently ingested carbohydrates.

"Shall I stick my head outside and see what's up?" I asked. "Maybe they're hoping for more coffee."

Bob was so angry his hands were shaking. There's nothing like shared misery to develop a friendship. I was beginning to like the guy, and I definitely felt sorry for him.

"I'll go," he said.

"Not a good idea. You're too upset."

"My store."

"Maybe it will just die down. Why don't we wait and see?"

But Bob was already halfway to the door, leaving me with a register that swore I had grossed half a million dollars on my last sale.

Bob was an adult, and I was fairly sure the chanters were harmless. Nevertheless, I followed unobtrusively. The moment he opened the door we were hit by a wall of sound. I had a flashback. I was walking up Pennsylvania Avenue in the Million Moms march.

I don't know why it hadn't occurred to me that Senator Carlisle would join forces with Brownie and Cal and all the local citizens who were sure that the existence of Book Gems portended a storm of fire and brimstone or maybe even the Rapture. But there he was, flanked by four men in dark suits, chanting with the rest of the crew as a reporter from the *Flow* snapped his photograph.

I wasn't close enough on Bob's heels to stop him. He charged through the crowd and grabbed the senator by the arm before the suits could intervene.

"What in the hell are you hoping to accomplish?" Bob demanded. "You're supposed to be a representative of the law, and there's nothing illegal in my store! You're a damned politician, as corrupt as they come. What gives you the right to pass judgment on me?"

Carlisle's quick response belied his age. He twisted his arm and snapped his elbow into Bob's chest, thereby freeing himself and sending Bob—not the finest of physical specimens—sprawling. I was just close enough to catch my new boss as he stumbled backwards. I was barely able to keep us both from going down.

"Do you want to get arrested?" I demanded as I helped him straighten. "Or beat up by Carlisle's bodyguards? Come on, Bob. Get a grip."

"You think I'm going to close?" Bob turned to include Brownie, who was only a few paces behind and turning pale. "You think you can chase me out of here? Well, you've got another thing coming. I've got friends higher than either of you, and I'll use them. I'll expose you both for what you are. You hear me? Just try and shut me down. I'm staying. And I'll use every last cent I have to end both your political careers! See if I don't!"

Brownie really looked shaken now. "You don't have to close down. I'm an advocate of any upright and decent business opening here. But you are offering—"

"I am offering you a chance to shut up and get out of here so my customers can get in the door. If you don't and quickly, I'll be calling my attorney."

My eyes sought Cal's. He looked as if he were lost in prayer. I hoped he wouldn't find his way back.

"This is a peaceful, legal protest," Frank Carlisle said. "If you make it anything else, you *will* need an attorney, Mr. Knowles."

This was our cue. I took Bob by the arm and guided him toward the front door. To his credit, he let me.

Fifteen minutes later Carlisle and his escorts left, and the bulk of the other protestors began to drift away. By two when I went into the supply room to get my purse so I could leave for the day, we were down to maybe ten. This batch were good Midwesterners, polite enough and subdued.

Ed was waiting for me when I came back out front. This I hadn't expected. Clearly he thought I needed an escort, since I knew he had a full schedule today.

"Hey, boyfriend. Are you here to carry my books?"

"I thought you might like a little company on the way out the door."

I'm almost always glad I married Ed, but sometimes I like being reminded why. "How many of your colleagues are still out there?" I asked.

"Enough to organize a prayer meeting to save our souls."

"Remember when we thought we were moving here for a quieter life?"

"When was that?" He smiled.

Ed has quite a smile. I felt hopeful. I linked my arm through his and squeezed. "Ready to run the gauntlet?"

"Ag, I'd run through fire for you."

I kissed his hairy cheek. "Considering the way things are going around here, I'd be careful what I wished for."

9

The next morning Ed was already at work when our telephone rang. I was barely conscious, having spent my hours in dreamland trying to reason with a crowd burning copies of *Peter Rabbit*. As the flames leaped higher Cal screamed a hell-and-damnation sermon about bad boy bunnies and cabbage theft.

Ed sent the girls off to school without my help.

I took my mug of coffee to the kitchen telephone.

"Agate, you sound as if I got you up."

"Nan . . ." No one else could sound so sweetly accusatory. I took one huge steaming gulp. Nan without coffee was unthinkable. "You just missed Ed. He's at work."

"So early?"

"The birds have been singing for hours. Ed's been gone for one of them."

"I suppose he needs to look busy now and then."

Sip number two. "Now and then," I agreed.

"As a matter of fact, I was calling for you."

This surprised me. I don't think Nan really dislikes me. I just don't think that anybody would have been good enough for her only child, and I was in the bottom 50 percent of the reject pile, at that. She likes me marginally better now that I have twice proved my fertility.

She continued. "I did some checking around for Railfords in Boston. There are some, of course, but none of them important. And all fairly new."

Sip number three. I let the comment about importance sail over my head without grabbing and hanging on. "Interesting," I managed.

"Then I mentioned it to my bridge club. Someone knows a prominent Railford family in Billerica." This emerged as "B'ricka."

"Hmm . . ."

"Well there are no *Gelsey* Railfords from Billerica, either."

I was not sure what I supposed to say to this. I contemplated over sip number four.

"I imagine you heard incorrectly," Nan said, while I remained in contemplation. "You're certainly not from here, so you wouldn't know the nuances, would you?"

I had a slight twinge in the region of my backbone. "It's possible, isn't it, that the bridge club might not know everybody in Massachusetts? Or is this unthinkable?"

"You'll have to take my word for it, dear. My friends are very well-connected."

I was not sure what they were connected to, but I hoped I was never stuck in that web. We chatted a moment about the weather, the safest subject I know, then Nan hung up.

Nan's desire to imprint her values on our daughters is one of the reasons we left New England. She dotes on Deena and Teddy, and her love for them pleases me to no end. But as I finished my coffee I hoped that if our stay in Emerald Springs was fated to be short, we would continue moving west.

✦   ✦   ✦

Ed wasn't in his office when I found my way to the parish house after lunch. Harry Grey, our secretary, was watering the plants when I arrived.

He didn't wait to be asked. "Ed got a call from Tom Jeffrey. Some sort of emergency."

I like Harry. He's sixtyish, a sharp dresser, and financially independent. He took this job years ago to get away from his partner, Greg, an architect who works at home, and because the job gives him lots of free time to travel.

Harry hails from just outside Chicago. Decades ago the Grey family stopped milking cows and turned to milking commuters. The family pastures are now a bustling bedroom community, complete with tract housing, condo developments, and enough strip malls to satisfy even Crystal O'Grady. Although none of the Grey heirs are still pitching hay, Harry invested his portion of the sale in Wal-Mart before the rest of us had heard of Sam Walton.

I rearranged the collection of hand-blown glass paperweights on his desk. "When Ed took this church he expected emergency to mean a plugged toilet. You don't suppose someone in the congregation robbed a bank? Burned down the hotel? Had a torrid affair with Hillary Clinton or Katherine Harris?"

"He looked glum."

"Not good."

"If it's any consolation, Gelsey Falowell is not one of my favorite people."

"Oh?" I wasn't surprised. Ed and I couldn't be the only people in the world who saw Gelsey's dark side.

"She tried to get me fired, too. Said I wasn't a good influence."

"Come on!"

"I stayed. I hope Ed stays, too."

"I'm glad you prevailed." I looked around. We seemed to be alone in the building. "You'll be here awhile?"

"I'm typing up the new address directory. I'll be here the rest of the afternoon."

"I'm going up to the storage room to get more stuff from the archives. My last trip over here didn't end well. If I don't come back in half an hour, call the cops."

My PowerPoint presentation had been so lame I was determined to make things up to the Women's Society. For the most part, these are the kind of older women I hope to be someday. Generous, intelligent, committed. I wanted to make them happy. Clearly the best way was the old-fashioned way. Nothing that plugged in or went "beep."

Last night, waking from one of Cal's sermons against wascally wabbits, I came up with a solution. I would assemble my presentation—and then some—into a scrapbook.

Unlike Junie I'm not crafty by nature, but I am capable of cutting and pasting in real life, if not on a computer screen. This I could do, at least as a stop gap until Deena and I could work out the kinks in PowerPoint. Perhaps if this went well, I could have the pages copied and bound for those who wanted their own. I wasn't expecting to make bestseller lists, but it was an idea with merit.

The storage room is at the back of the building on the third floor. There's not much on this level since it's really just a finished attic, hot in the summer and cold in the winter, home to squirrels, mice, and occasional leaks. It really was exactly the wrong place to keep precious documents and photos, and I was determined that if nothing else, I would find a new place for them.

I unlocked the door and left it wide open while I turned on the light, a pull chain hanging from a bare lightbulb in the center of the room. In defense of my predecessors, most of the archival material had been stored in varmint-proof containers of thick plastic or metal. An old trunk held compilations of sermons, thoughtfully transferred to tape when almost everyone had a reel-to-reel tape recorder to play them on.

I had come for a box of photos from the 1950s that were quickly fading. I was hoping to do a decade by decade collage of church events. I would assemble them and have them copied at the local office supply store. When someone else pushes the start button, things always go better.

I had already done something similar with the few photos left from earlier decades, except Deena and I had scanned those to the computer for my presentation. Once I had worked my way up to the twenty-first century, I would decide what to do with the originals.

I knew exactly where the box was that I planned to take

home with me. A metal shelf system rested against the far wall, the basic gray model most people buy for garages or workrooms. The photos had been haphazardly placed there, with no thought to order, so I had arranged them chronologically.

The box I was seeking wasn't there. I stopped and reconsidered, inspecting the room as I did. The changes were suddenly so obvious to me I was perplexed I hadn't noticed them the moment I walked in. Someone had been in the storage room since my last visit.

This really isn't that surprising. The storage room is a hodgepodge of old tables and chairs, banners too worn for decoration but too beloved to discard, candleholders, boxes of mismatched cutlery and chipped china. The list is long. But the archives take up one wall and a portion of another, and that area is clearly marked. No skull and crossbones, but you get the picture. This is clearly not the correct side of the room to store outdated religious education curriculums or checkbooks and receipts from fiscal years long past.

Our church sexton January Godfrey is a neat freak, and for a moment I assumed he had been here dusting shelves and setting mousetraps. But cobwebs hung engagingly in the corner, and the general storage area clearly hadn't been touched. I also knew from experience that January would put things back where they belonged. He would clean but not rearrange. Even Deena's power strip had been shelved in the most obvious place he could think of.

Fifteen minutes later I was sure that someone had been rummaging through the archives. Seriously rummaging. No sin, really, since there's nothing valuable here, but baffling. I found the box I was looking for behind another. Not as if it had been hidden, but as if it had been shoved there as someone pawed through the materials.

Now I was curious. Exactly why would someone be up here in the first place? And why not take the time to put everything back? I was more than a little exasperated as I straightened and reshelved. I even found a few things from the archives across the room. Fern Booth had accused me of subjecting historical materials to rampaging children, but someone, most probably an adult, had done some genuine rampaging here.

I had finished and started out the door when I realized that something was missing from the shelves. Today I'd had more than enough room on the third one for the boxes I had straightened. But that hadn't always been true. Last month the third shelf had been packed so tightly I had removed a box of slides and placed them elsewhere, just to make a little room. So what was missing now?

I went back, snapped on the light, and sorted through the boxes again. And by the time I got to the end, I remembered. There had been a box of 8 mm movies here. I had kept them at home for months, hidden from childish eyes in the pullout storage drawer under our guest room daybed. I had been sure the temperature extremes in the storage room would seal their doom and had hoped to get a little money from the budget so we could have them put on a DVD. In the end, I had brought them back here to wait for the board's verdict. The drawer was packed to the brim and one day, simply wouldn't close. I just hadn't had room for everything.

Fifteen minutes later I was digging through piles on the other side of the room when Harry came up to check on me.

"You've had your half hour," he said. "I thought I'd check before I call the cops. I'm armed." He held up his letter opener, which is shaped like a shark and no doubt intimidating to tropical fish. If a neon tetra was my culprit, we were in business.

"Harry, has anyone asked you for the key to this room?"

"Nope."

"There's a box missing, and things have been rearranged."

"Any number of people have keys. Religious education teachers, January, the folks who put together the rummage sale."

I sat back on my heels. "It was a box of old home movies. I didn't get to view more than a couple. Somebody's ordination. A couple of potlucks and outdoor events." I shrugged. "Probably more of the same. Why would anybody want them?"

"Maybe somebody decided to have them restored."

"Wouldn't they let me know? Or Ed?"

"You think they're over here?" He squatted beside me.

"Enough stuff was out of order to make me wonder. I found a box of photos there." I pointed to the top of the pile beside us.

Harry helped me search, and in the end he was the one who found the movies. They were buried under a pile of costumes from an old production of *Noah's Ark*.

"Now, that's strange," I said. "I can't imagine how they ended up over here."

We both stood and I took the box. "I had these at the house awhile ago. I guess they all go back to the parsonage for safekeeping. Maybe I'll borrow the projector some time this week and catalog them."

"You'll need caffeine. Intravenously."

We locked up and I headed home with the box of movies. I was trying to decide whether adding beef bouillon cubes to my homemade vegetable soup constituted a violation of principles, when Teddy arrived. We exchanged hugs, I marveled over her crayon drawing of Moonpie eating my houseplants, then I sat her at the kitchen table with a mug of warm cider and a peanut butter cookie.

Deena was next, trailing Carlene. I'll have to admit I gawked. Carlene was wearing a three-layered white skirt that barely covered her bottom, a pink T-shirt that did not cover most of her midriff, shoes that looked to be a cross between hiking boots and strappy sandals, and hair that looked as if it had been styled with a butcher knife.

"Carlene and I are in the same group in history. We're all doing a paper together and Carlene and I are supposed to do the research. Can we do it here on my computer?"

I had suppressed my first comment about Halloween being early this year. "Would you like me to bring cookies and cider upstairs for you?"

Carlene's eyes widened. "I haven't had a peanut butter cookie in years and years."

She had only been alive for eleven, although you wouldn't

know it to look at her today. "They help grow strong bones and teeth," I told her.

"You are so funny!" To my ears, the phrase sounded rehearsed, as if she had been practicing this dulcet uttering with a tape recorder.

We monitor sugar intake in our house, but this child needed to remember what childhood felt and tasted like. At that moment I wanted to drag her mother down to Don't Go There for a little old-fashioned mud wrestling.

"You two run upstairs. I'll be up in a few minutes."

"My mom's not home," Carlene said. "This is her hair day."

I nodded and smiled and bit my lip. The moment the girls clattered up the stairs I got on the telephone. By the end of the afternoon I had organized a gathering here on Saturday afternoon for the mothers of Deena's friends. I hadn't been able to reach Crystal, of course, but I had left her three separate voice mail messages, each more strongly worded than the last. I had stopped short of offering to shop for clothing that was more Carlene's size.

Ed arrived home just as I was ladling vegetable soup into bowls and setting them on the table. He'd left a cryptic message on our answering machine, so I knew he was alive. Since there'd been no ransom demand, I had survived on hope.

I stopped before bowl number four to give him a quick hug and kiss. "You look beat. Where have you been?"

"Roussos wanted to talk to me. Then I had an appointment with Tom."

Neither boded well, particularly since he was home so late. "Were you arrested or fired?"

"You like to get right down to the nitty-gritty, don't you?"

"I believe in getting the worst over fast."

"No to both."

I exhaled gratefully. "Start with Roussos."

"Let's wait until the girls are in bed."

"Basics now, please? It's only vegetable soup, but I'd like to be able to digest it."

"Nothing new. Roussos wanted to know what Jennifer Marina and I discussed. He applied pressure and made threats."

I knew I was talking to a brick wall, but I tried again. "Why are you being so stubborn? She's dead. What's left to protect?"

He ignored me. "Roussos mentioned that the ex-husband's not a suspect anymore. His alibi finally checked out. Now they're looking harder at everybody else."

At least I didn't have to worry about Rico skulking around the church anymore. I bet he'd gotten out of town now that he was no longer a person of interest.

Ed stroked his beard. "Tom says a petition is circulating. He doesn't know who's signed it, or how many. We decided what to do about it."

I swallowed a surge of anger. "What did you decide?"

"Tom's going to get out the word that this is not the way things are done and that he won't accept a petition now or anytime. When and if the board decides to call a congregational meeting, that's what he'll do."

"Tom's a good president."

"He's under the gun." Ed shook his head. "Not the best expression to use, I guess."

I heard the girls at the top of the stairs. We were about to be invaded. "You win the bad day award. You get a back rub after the girls go to bed."

"How about a three-week vacation in Hawaii?"

Didn't I just wish?

10

There were no Weiss–Bitmans at the Weiss–Bitman Funeral Home, but on Friday a Mr. Sawyer called me. This was the same man who had conducted Jennifer's funeral service at a gallop. A few sentences into the call it was clear he hoped to make short work of our conversation, too.

"Let me get this straight," I said, when he paused for a breath. I pictured him gasping for air and a fresh onslaught. "You want *me* to take Jennifer Marina's ashes?"

"That's right."

"No way."

I waited through another torrent of speech, buffing my fingernails on my sweatshirt until he was gasping again.

"Look, I didn't know the woman. I was there to pay my respects, but I never met her in person. Not exactly," I added, to be fair.

"Maybe your husband—"

This time I cut him off. "My husband left town this morning for a wedding in the country, and he won't be back until late. But I can speak for him. Our church doesn't have a memorial garden or any place appropriate to inter them."

I wondered how Ed would like me speaking for him. Not so much, I was afraid.

"I've done everything I know," Mr. Sawyer whined. "Her husband paid for the funeral, but he didn't want them. He said I could give them to anybody, he didn't care what happened to them. Then he gave me a phone number, but it's been disconnected."

I perked up. "Phone number?"

"Somebody in Pennsylvania. Mrs. Foster or something like that. He only told me as he was heading out the door."

"Did you try calling him to see if you got the number right?" Going on what Ed had told me about Rico, I already knew the answer.

"He left town."

Score one for ESP.

"Why don't you give me the number and I'll see what I can do," I told him. "I'm not making any promises, but I have some time today. Maybe I can track this down."

"We can store them here. We would certainly prefer not to."

I could just imagine what storing Jennifer's ashes might do to the sanctity of the Weiss–Bitman home.

It was just as well Ed hadn't been here to intercept this call. He would not approve of what came next. I took Mrs. Foster's number and went to the phone book. The area code Sawyer had given me was for Pittsburgh. Before I did any further sleuthing I tried the number, and also got a recording that said it had been disconnected.

I dialed directory assistance and explained my problem to the operator. I told her I thought the name was Foster and gave her the number. "If there's a new number," I said, "I would appreciate your help."

I hung up a few minutes later, a little wiser. The operator had gone the extra mile for me. The number I had given her had never been registered to a Foster. And searches of Fosters in that area code hadn't turned up any numbers that were remotely similar.

This wasn't going to be as easy as I'd hoped. I decided to

call Lucy, who chases leads for a living. Six months ago when
an old woman passed away in one of the mini-mansions
of Emerald Estates, Lucy found the heir camping in a re-
mote fishing village in Portugal. It took Lucy two days and
three hundred dollars in long distance bills, but her per-
sistence earned a valuable listing and the undying gratitude
of the probate attorney, who was both rich and single.

Of course, he turned out to be a workaholic whose ideal
Friday night date was a trip to Blockbuster and a nap in front
of the television. But you see my point.

I explained my problem as Lucy listened.

"Do you know where Jennifer was living?" she asked.

"With Sax."

"Oh, that's right." Lucy was quiet, but I could hear her
thinking.

"You should tell him the problem," Lucy said at last. "See
if he knows anything, or if he still has the bills for any long
distance calls Jennifer made. Maybe she called this Mrs.
Foster and you can get the number that way."

"Oh sure. Sax strikes me as a man who would help me
out of the goodness of his heart."

"Just call him. You don't have to go back to the bar."

I hung up. In the middle of our conversation I'd had a revelation. Mrs. Foster. *Foster* mother. Rico had probably told
the funeral home to give the ashes to Jennifer's foster mother
or the foster mother caring for her children. And Sawyer,
busy vaulting up the steps of the mortician career ladder,
hadn't bothered to get this little detail correct.

Now I had no name to go on, and I was pretty sure that
child welfare in Pittsburgh wasn't going to give up information easily.

If I had to, I would try to track down the caseworker for
Jennifer's kids, tell her the problem, and turn it over to her.
But first, I decided to try Sax Dubinsky. I called our local directory assistance and got his phone number. For the record,
the man's real name is Saxony, which probably explains a
lot of his pathology.

Since Sax didn't strike me as an early riser, I waited until noon. Then I dialed the number. Just to be on the safe side I blocked my own number first. I didn't want Sax breathing heavily on the other end of my line every time he got lonely.

He answered with a growl. What a cutup.

I explained quickly why I was calling. "So I'm trying to help," I finished. "And since Mr. Marina gave the funeral home the wrong number, we're hoping you have the right one."

He unleashed a stream of noontime profanity. I got the feeling it was more or less a warm-up for the day.

"You oughta stay out of what don't concern you," he said at last.

I'd pretty much had it with good old Saxony. "Listen, buster, I was the one they called because I cared enough to go to her funeral. And I didn't even know her. So don't lecture me. I'm trying to do the right thing here for Jennifer and her kids. You can help or you can hang up. Surprise me."

"I don't have time to go through a bunch of damn bills."

He really *had* surprised me by not slamming down the phone. "I think the phone number belonged to her foster mother, or maybe the foster mother of her kids. Maybe she kept it handy?"

"You think she'd need to look up something like that?"

Bested by the bartender. He was right. If this was such an important number, Jennifer would have memorized it.

"I'll look through the bills if you want," I said. "If there's a similar number I'll know it's the right one." I was sure he'd say no, considering that his calls would be listed there, too. But Sax surprised me again.

"I guess I've got Jenny's cell phone bill somewhere."

"And you'll let me look at it?"

"I'm going into work now. I'll bring it with me." He hung up.

✦   ✦   ✦

Don't Go There seems different in the daytime. The serious drinkers are just getting started. The trash in the parking lot is newer, fresher, almost hopeful. Inside the smell is more homemade chili than backed-up plumbing.

I marched up to the counter where Sax was washing glasses. "Did you find the phone bills?"

He pulled a wad of paper out of his pocket and shoved it at me. "Don't say I never gave you nuthin'."

A poet and a comedian. I thanked him and looked around for Keely, but there was no sign of her. I left while I could.

It didn't take long to locate the number. The one Sawyer had given me was off by two digits. A one where a three should have been and vice versa. I made myself a cup of Earl Grey with a dollop of half-and-half, then I settled on the living room sofa to make the call.

The woman who answered had a lovely, mellow voice. She sounded like she was in her late fifties, maybe older. I told her who I was and why I was calling.

"Yes, I know about Jenny," she said softly. "The social worker informed me. I've told the children."

"Then you're the children's foster mother? I thought that might be the connection."

"I was Jenny's, too. She came here when she was sixteen. She only stayed a year. Then she took off to live on the street. When the state said they were taking her children, she asked me to keep them. I was still licensed, and I've had them ever since. My daughter helps. She and her husband would like to adopt them."

"How are they?"

"Cindy, she's ten, well, she's about the brightest, sweetest little girl in the world. A good student, too. Randy, he's eight. A little rebellious, but I think that's because he's so smart. My son-in-law knows how to keep him busy and out of trouble. They went off camping together a few weeks ago. Before, well, you know."

"I didn't get your name."

"Oh, I'm sorry. Maude Stingle."

I liked Maude Stingle. And I thought Jennifer had showed good judgment in asking this woman to take the children. I told her exactly what Mr. Sawyer had said and explained that Rico wanted her to take the ashes.

"Of course we will. There's a park not far away where Jenny liked to take the children. There's a stream and a pond with ducks and woods. We'll take the children there one evening and scatter her ashes. It will help them say good-bye."

I was liking her better and better. "Why don't I get them from the funeral home, then you can come here and we can talk. When do you think you can come?"

We made arrangements to meet that evening. Jennifer's children were going to spend the weekend with Maude's son and daughter. Maude said she could get here by seven.

I hung up, aware that I'd asked her here because I wanted more information about Jennifer. I was sure Ed wouldn't approve. On the other hand, if I figured out why Jennifer had been in Emerald Springs, then perhaps he and I could discuss it. He would not have violated her trust, and maybe I could help him figure out what to do next.

With Ed gone, the girls and I made pizza just the way they like it, dripping with cheese and nothing else. I was feeling particularly mushy after the conversation with Maude. Jennifer had loved her kids. She had taken them to the park to feed ducks. She found them the best foster placement she could.

I gave Deena and Teddy Ben & Jerry's for dessert, which seriously shot a hole in our food budget for the month.

I was washing dishes and they were finishing homework when the telephone rang. I thought it might be Ed or Maude, telling me she couldn't make it after all. In fact the woman on the other end was unfamiliar, a fact she sought to change over the next ten minutes by talking nonstop.

By the time I hung up, I had something brand-new to consider.

"Who was that?" Deena asked. "You just stood there. Wasn't anybody on the other end?"

"It was somebody from a church in Boston, nobody you know."

"She was calling you?" She sounded incredulous.

"Hard as this is to imagine, I am considered dazzling company by many. My opinion has been sought by kings and Democratic presidents."

"She wanted Dad, didn't she?"

"Of course she did."

Deena went back to studying synonyms. I slid the phone conversation in the "things to discuss with Ed" file and went to help Teddy learn her spelling words.

By the time Maude arrived Deena and Teddy were upstairs watching *Wheel of Fortune* in my bedroom. I hoped Pat and Vanna kept them occupied long enough that Maude and I could have an uninterrupted conversation.

The woman on my doorstep was not my vision of a Maude. This Maude was thin and fit, with brown hair that was only slowly going gray and more fashion sense than I'll ever have. I told her I loved her pistachio sweater, and she told me where to find a clone online. I did not explain why this was a bad idea.

She settled on my sofa and I served coffee. The polite chitchat ended quickly. I told her that Jennifer's body had been placed on our porch. She was horrified and suddenly a little weepy.

I put my hand on hers. "Jennifer's death must have been hard for you. You must have been close to her if she asked you to take her children."

"Jenny wasn't close to anyone but her kids. She was suspicious, wary, hard to love. It's just so sad. She had so much potential, but by the time I got her, the damage was done."

"She obviously felt some affection for you and some trust."

"Not in the last few months."

I sat back and waited. She took a tissue from her purse and wiped her eyes.

"We argued," she said at last. "I feel so badly that the last things we said to each other were in anger."

"It must be hard to be a mother to someone else's children without some disagreements."

"Oh, that wasn't it. She approved of the way I took care of Cindy and Randy. I let her have as much say as I could, and for the most part, she made good choices. No, it was . . ."

I waited without prodding, but it was tough. As if she needed time to compose herself she rummaged through her purse and pulled out her wallet. She unsnapped it to show me a photograph of two adorable children. Both were dark-haired, like Rico. Cindy's hair was a mass of ringlets. Randy's was as straight as a board. They had huge dark eyes and button noses.

Maude put the wallet back. "My daughter already has three children to put through college. As much as she and her husband want to adopt Cindy and Randy, I don't know if they'll be able to afford to."

"I hope you're not beating yourself up for arguing with Jennifer."

"Coming here caused the trouble."

"You wanted her to stay closer to home so she could see more of the children?"

"No, I didn't want her looking for her birth mother."

There it was. The secret I hadn't been privy to. I didn't know what to say.

"I'm not against adopted children looking for their birth parents," Maude continued. "I want you to understand that. I see why it's necessary, and sometimes it even works out. But Jenny wasn't trying to get her medical history or find out why she was given up for adoption. She didn't want a relationship. She wanted money."

"Money?"

"Jenny thought finding her birth mother would be the quickest way to get the children back. I wanted her to do it the right way, the old-fashioned way. I wanted her to get a real job, clean up her life, and make a fresh start for all of them. Maybe it would have taken a year or even more to get a nice apartment and prove she could keep a job, but she had access to the children. It wasn't like she was desperate to see them."

I could see Maude was beating herself up about this. "For what it's worth, everything you've said makes sense to me."

"Jenny never learned how to wait for anything. If she thought she needed something, she took it. She thought she deserved it after the life she'd led. Shoplifting. Petty theft. That's why she ended up in jail this last time. She forged a couple of checks. With absolutely no remorse."

My mind was going a mile a minute. Jennifer Marina had

been in Emerald Springs to find her birth mother. She had talked to my husband. My husband steadfastly refused to say why. It was all coming together now.

I probed. "So, she was here to look for her mother? Why? Was she born here?"

"It's a sad story, really. Jenny was given up almost at birth. A private attorney did the groundwork. She was placed with a wealthy family in Pittsburgh who said they were too busy to go through the regular channels. Unfortunately they were unfit and abusive and never even completed the adoption. By the time she was four and the state rescued her, Jenny was damaged goods. They placed her for adoption twice more and neither placement went through. So from that point on she stayed in foster care, and for the most part the foster placements were disastrous, too. She was finally assigned to a residential treatment facility. Then, when they thought she had improved enough, she came to me. She was a little better, but far from being over the trauma. And then she was simply out on her own with too few coping skills and no support from the state."

The story was too familiar, but horrifying nonetheless. "So she came here to search for the woman who abandoned her," I said.

"Not quite."

I took that pause to pour more coffee. Upstairs I heard the *Jeopardy* theme and no pounding of tennis shoes on the stairs, so I knew we were good for a while longer.

Maude took her mug and cupped her hands around it. "Jenny wasn't starting the search here. She was *finishing* it. She'd been looking for a long time. She felt her mother owed her. She was furious at the woman. Every therapist she visited tried to help her see reason, but she just couldn't. She blamed her mother for her life. She wanted to make her pay."

"So she was here in Emerald Springs to force her mother to give her money."

"She tracked the woman down. See, Jenny found out she was born in Las Vegas."

"How?" Immediately I wished I hadn't asked. It really wasn't important. But inquiring minds . . .

"She slept with somebody who works for the lawyer who did the placement. She threw that up at me the last time we spoke."

"I guess she traded whatever she thought she could."

"The name on the birth certificate was—" Maude stopped and sipped her coffee. "I don't think I should say. I'm going on and on here, and you're really just a stranger."

I tried to explain. "I wish I *felt* like a stranger. But her body was dumped on my front porch. I have her ashes in an urn in my coat closet. My husband counseled Jennifer, and I'm beginning to understand now why he can't tell me what they talked about."

Maude seemed to consider. She stood. "I can trust you not to reveal this in a hurtful way?"

"I'd like to see this murder solved. I'd like to get my husband out of the loop. I'd like to know we're safe. That's all."

"Jenny's mother left Las Vegas not long after she gave Jenny up for adoption. She moved here and married a realtor. I don't know her husband's name, Jenny didn't say. But she did say the woman was, in her words, 'stinking rich.' "

"And that's why she thought she could ask for money." It all made a sad, perverted sort of sense.

Maude stood. "I've got a long drive back."

I knew Maude would give me the name, or she wouldn't. It was not my place to push.

"I'll get the ashes. Thank you for taking them." I put my hand on her shoulder and squeezed. "I'm a mother. I know Jennifer understood how lucky her children were to be with you, Maude. In her own way, she must have loved you, or she wouldn't have asked you to take them."

Maude blinked back tears. She followed me to the closet, and I took down the urn, a simple metal vase that was as perfunctory and cheap as Jennifer's funeral service. I handed it to her. We started toward the door as Maude clutched the cremains to her chest. She turned on my front porch, in much the same place I had found the body.

"I don't know if Jennifer ever contacted her birth mother. She was only here in Emerald Springs a short time before she died. I don't know if you should talk to the woman or not. If she doesn't know Jennifer was her daughter . . ." Her voice trailed off.

I nodded and waited.

"Please, just use your best judgment. Jennifer's mother's name was Wanda Ray Gelsey." Maude turned and walked away.

11

I'm not an expert on these things, but I know there are two kinds of monograms. One uses the first letter of the surname as the middle letter. For instance, *W.G.R.* might read *Wanda Gelsey Ray*—but would really represent *Wanda Ray Gelsey.* The other is more straightforward, using the initials in order. *W.R.G.,* or *Wanda Ray Gelsey.*

After more than an hour of digging into my memory I was almost sure the brooch that Gelsey had showed me so many months before had read *W.G.R.* At the time I assumed the monogram was the straightforward type and that since her maiden name was Railford, like many people, Gelsey had simply chosen to go by her middle name. That bit of trivia had slipped my mind when I talked to my mother-in-law. Perhaps with her blue-blood past Gelsey had been saddled at birth with an unforgivable first name like Winifred. Winifred Gelsey Railford.

Now I suspected "Winifred" had never been the problem and that indeed the heirloom brooch had used the more common monogram for females.

I was still pondering this extraordinary turn of events

when Ed arrived home. For once the girls, tired from their week of school, had gone to bed without a fuss and I'd made popcorn and cocoa for myself. When I heard the car door slam I heated Ed's cocoa in our ancient microwave.

At first glance I knew he was exhausted. The wedding had been held at a farm deep in Amish country, not such a long drive, but the couple had crammed everything into one day, a morning rehearsal, a long celebratory lunch, an outdoor ceremony followed by an old-fashioned barn dance for all their friends. I was sure the dance was still going on.

I greeted him with a kiss, then motioned to the table. "Sit down and relax. How'd it go?"

"I wish you could have come with me."

"That good, huh?"

"To share the pain. The mother of the bride despises the groom and refused to speak to his family. She tried to relay messages through me, and when I wouldn't play go-between she threatened to leave for good."

"Sounds like a plan to me."

"The whole day was more of the same. The good news is the bride and groom were oblivious. They had a wonderful time."

"That's good, at least." Nan flicked through my mind. "Tell me they're moving away."

"Japan, if you can believe it."

"Good for them."

"How did things go here?"

I set his cocoa in front of him and pushed the bowl of popcorn closer. "Well, I figured out that you haven't been protecting Jennifer Marina these past three weeks."

He lifted the cocoa to his lips. "Oh?"

"You've been protecting Gelsey Falowell. She's Jennifer's mother, isn't she?"

He wasn't ready to give up the information yet. He lifted a brow in question. *Tell me what you know Aggie, then I'll tell you if you're right.*

"It all makes sense now," I said. "Jennifer Marina came to you and told you she wanted to contact her mother. You wanted her to tell Gelsey who she was in the kindest possible way. The morning we found the body Teddy told me Jennifer had yelled something at you in the parking lot about not caring who got hurt. I think you were trying to protect Gelsey."

"How did you come to this conclusion?"

I told him about Maude's visit, about the ashes, about Jennifer's background and her children. I finished by exhorting him to suggest a different funeral home if anyone asked for a referral.

He was half finished with the cocoa when he put his cup down. He reached for a handful of popcorn. "You couldn't leave it alone, could you?"

I decided he and Roussos should be friends. "Now that I know, will you talk to me?"

"It's something of a relief."

I had expected him to be angry. I slumped. "Have you been debating what to do about Gelsey all this time?"

"More or less."

"Can you tell me if she knows?"

He shook his head. "Jennifer came into my office on the pretense of needing counseling. She told me right away that Gelsey had given her up for adoption. She said she wanted to get to know her mother, but she didn't know if that was a good idea. She seemed sincere enough, although I was skeptical. It took two sessions before I realized she didn't want counseling, she wanted information. She wanted to know her mother's status in the community, how much she was worth, how much integrity she had."

"Integrity?"

"Simply put? Would Gelsey pay Jennifer to keep quiet about who she was. She said she needed money, and she had a couple of choices. One was to go to Gelsey directly and ask for help. She could have played on her mother's sympathies, even her guilt, and asked Gelsey to help her regain custody of her children. The other was blackmail. Jennifer figured the second was a sure thing and worth a lot more."

"And she went to you because she knew the counseling relationship kept you from revealing her intentions or identity. She could trust you to keep silent while she black-mailed her mother."

"You got it. And even if I was willing to betray her, who would I go to? If Gelsey didn't want to reveal Jennifer's identity, then what would she do if I revealed it? Even to the police."

I grabbed a handful of popcorn, too. "Yikes."

"I tried to talk her out of it. Once in my office, once in the parking lot, once at the bar. She was determined." He pushed the bowl back toward me. "More than that, she was enraged. She wanted to suck her mother dry, wring her out, and throw her away."

"She had a very difficult childhood." I knew it was no excuse, but it was definitely part of the explanation.

"I tried to get her to talk about it. She told me her first memory was struggling to escape from a toolshed in the backyard. At night."

I shuddered. "So what are you going to do now?"

"That's the thing. I don't know. I'm pretty sure Jennifer never told Gelsey who she was. She was getting her ducks in a row, making sure she had the best angle. I think she was savoring everything about it. Imagining what Gelsey would say, figuring out how much to demand, planning what she was going to do with all that money once she had it in her hands."

"We both know how grateful Gelsey will be to hear this news from you."

"That's an issue, but not much of one. It's true I'm the last person she'll want to hear it from, but I am her minister. And right now I'm the only one who can tell her. The question is whether I should or not."

"You'd keep it a secret?"

"What's the point of telling her, Ag? As far as Gelsey knows, the daughter she gave up for adoption is alive and well. Maybe Gelsey fantasizes she's a lawyer or a doctor. Gelsey used a private attorney, Jennifer told me that much. She probably asked for a wealthy family that could take good care of her little girl. Who am I to spoil that and tell her that her daughter was a petty criminal who rode with a motorcycle gang and died violently after she came to Emerald Springs to extort money?"

"That's quite a mouthful." I pondered this, as I had pondered the strangeness of the situation all evening.

"That mouthful was Jennifer's life. Her very sad life."

"I've been thinking about this ever since I made the connection. And here's my conclusion. Do you want to know?" I've found it's always good to ask.

"I do. I could use a fresh viewpoint. Even if you went behind my back to get one."

"You weren't here when the funeral home called." I held up my hands. "Okay, I knew I was treading on your territory. But the body was on *my* front porch, too. I have a stake in this."

He nodded without looking convinced.

"Two things come into play here. One is that Gelsey has grandchildren she doesn't know about. According to Maude, they're bright, wonderful children despite or even because of the way Jennifer raised them. Gelsey has the right to know this and to do something for them as a memorial to the daughter she gave away."

"And what if she doesn't want to?"

I shrugged. "No one's demanding it."

"She's not a young woman. What if knowing the truth ruins the remainder of her life?"

"I can't imagine Gelsey wallowing in guilt. I'm sure she'll be sad for a while, but giving up her baby for adoption was probably the best choice she had at the time. How was she to know it would turn out this way? She'll pick herself up and move on. And if she does something for her grandchildren, then she'll feel she went the extra mile."

"You know her well, don't you?"

"I've had to learn. That rings true?"

He nodded.

"The other thing is this. Jennifer was murdered and dumped on our porch. Who showed up just a bit later? Gelsey. Coincidence? You know what Freud says about that?"

Undoubtedly he had loosened his tie the moment he left

the wedding. Now he stripped it off and unfastened the top two buttons of his shirt. "Go on."

"I think you have to tell her because, for all we know, her life might be in danger, too."

"How do you figure that?"

"I don't. It's just that we know so little. Maybe whoever killed Jennifer will try to extort money from Gelsey, using the same logic Jennifer did. Gelsey has a reputation to uphold, and she doesn't want anybody to know about her sordid past."

"Do we *know* her past is sordid?"

"We know she changed her name. We *know* she had a child she gave up to a terrible future. If you're somebody like Gelsey, that would do it, don't you think?"

"So you're saying the murderer might be someone Jennifer shared her ambitions with? Besides me, that is?"

"Definitely besides you."

"You know I've already gone over and over all this in my mind, don't you?"

"I was pretty sure you had." I reached across the table and squeezed his hand. "One more point. Putting the body in Gelsey's path could have been a warning of sorts."

"Only if she knew Jennifer was her daughter."

"No, I'm apt to agree with you on that. I've tried and tried to remember her reactions that day. And I just can't imagine that she knew that morning. She acted the way you'd expect her to act if Jennifer was a stranger. But who can guess what she knows by now? If someone killed Jennifer so he could blackmail Gelsey himself, then she may know now, or may be about to find out."

"It's good to be able to talk about this." He lifted my fingers to his lips.

"It's nice to see you need help once in a while."

"This doesn't mean you should keep on snooping."

"I am not snooping. Things keep happening that draw me in."

"I suppose that's why you went to Don't Go There with Lucy? You just happened to be going to, what, catch the show?"

"How do you know about that?" I paused. "Roussos! Right?"

"I think he mentioned it while he interrogated me." He smiled. "Have fun?"

"We should go together. I can introduce you to the gang. Keely, Sax, Bud . . ." I put my fingers to my lips. "Oh, I forgot you're a regular, aren't you?"

"If they're closing down any business in town, that one would get my vote." He sobered. "I'm still not sure what to do or how to go about it."

"Just call Gelsey and tell her you need to see her privately. Ask if you can come over. It's what, nine fifteen? It's not too late. Get it off your chest."

"She'll come after me with both guns now. Shooting the messenger and all that."

I sat back. "Maybe it doesn't matter."

"Why?"

"Because you got a call tonight. Third Church in Boston is looking for a minister. Four of the people on their search committee want you to pre-candidate, even though you're not officially looking. They've heard you in other places and know your record. It's early in the year, I know, but she said this could be something of a preemptive strike. If they like you they may not even look at anyone else."

"Third Church?" Ed's eyes lit up. And well they should have. Third Church is one of the plums of our denomination. It's not a large church, but a historic and influential one. Asked to name his dream church, the Ed I married would have named it. But the Ed he had become?

"When? Did she say?" he asked.

"She asked me what weekends you had off. She'll be calling again to see if you want to be considered, so she can arrange to have you preach nearby." That was the way the process worked. One by one ministers the search committee wanted to consider would meet with them. Then the committee would hear them preach somewhere in the vicinity of Boston. Finally they would choose their candidate to present to the congregation. All very hush-hush.

"How's that strike you?" he asked. "You'd be back in the

city. All those opportunities you've missed since we moved here. I'm pretty sure there's a house to go with the job, or at least a large apartment."

Of course the church came with Nan attached, although neither of us voiced this. Nan would be a factor in our everyday life. She might not be interested in visiting the wilds of Ohio, but she would be Johnny-on-the-spot if we lived in Boston.

Nan was just one problem though. There were others. Third Church was formal and a bit stuffy. I would need to pour tea and look gracious, and Ed would be swamped with work. His dream of scholarly research would remain a dream.

Oddly, too, I had to face something that had eluded me until now. I was afraid I might be learning to like this little burg. Midwesterners are warmhearted and standoffish, not such a bad combination when you think about it. They don't pry, but they stand beside you if you've earned their respect and trust. I had made friends here. Despite myself, I was learning to enjoy our Dutch barn of a house. With adolescence knocking at our door, I liked the idea of enduring the onslaught in a place where everyone knew us and would warn us if things were going awry.

"I don't know," I said. That covered a lot.

"One thing at a time." Ed stood, placing his hands against the small of his back and arching. "Right now I have to decide what to do about Gelsey."

"I guess you could wait until tomorrow. You look pretty beat."

"I have some notes in my office about my sessions with Jennifer. I'm going to go over there for a while and see what I come up with. If I don't come back right away, don't worry."

"You'll be at Gelsey's?"

"I will." He kissed me. "Thanks for your help."

I didn't envy him this decision, but I thought I knew what he would choose tonight. Gelsey needed to be warned, and Ed was the only one who could do it, no matter what the personal consequences. I felt good, knowing I had helped him make a difficult choice. In fact, I felt, at least briefly, important.

After he left I cleaned off the table and started the dishwasher. Upstairs I got ready for bed and settled under a light blanket to read the first of a tall stack of library books about parenting teenagers. I was roused somewhat later from a psychologist-induced sleep by the telephone. I squinted at the clock across the room as I fumbled for the receiver. It was almost midnight, and Ed wasn't in bed beside me.

I managed "hello" without difficulty. I was hoping to wing the rest.

Ed was on the other end. By the time I hung up I was fully awake, with no hope of sleep for the rest of the night.

Thanks at least partly to me, Ed had decided to talk to Gelsey. Unfortunately, he arrived at her house too late for conversation. The front door was ajar, and her tiny twin poodles were yapping uncontrollably on the front porch.

Inside, Gelsey was lying on her precious Persian silk rug, as dead as her daughter.

12

Gelsey had been shot. One bullet at close range to the side of her head. Funny how in times of stress you imagine things. When I heard where Gelsey had been found I had a vision of the ghostly dowager shaking her head over the damage to her beloved rug. *"There is not a single dry cleaner in Emerald Springs who can be trusted with this!"*

I was ready for a sleeping pill or a good stiff drink. One is as unavailable in my house as the other.

I settled for opening a bottle of cheap Spanish wine, and I poured Ed a good-sized glass, too. I clinked mine with his, although he was clearly not in the mood for a toast after two hours of interrogation and a stern warning that he was under suspicion for the murder.

"To Gelsey," I said sincerely. "Gadfly, philanthropist, friend to many, enemy to some. But a woman who made a difference and lived life on her own terms."

"It's two A.M.," Ed said. "Why are you still articulate?"

I was unaccountably sad. After weeks of paying close attention to all the havoc Gelsey could wreak, now I remembered all the good things she had done. Charities that were better off, friends she had supported through difficulties, an entire library of books for our religious education program, because she had believed that a well-read child was a child who could change the world.

"I have enough adrenaline in my system to keep me awake until Easter." I sipped the wine, but my throat felt numb.

"I'll sleep for both of us, then."

"You must feel awful."

He tried a sip, made a face, and set down the glass.

"Do you want to tell me how the night played out?" I wasn't quite sure I wanted to know, but I thought he needed to tell someone besides Roussos.

"After we talked I went over to the church. I got out my notes and looked them over. In the end it was something Jennifer said that convinced me I had to tell Gelsey."

"What was that?"

"That she hoped her mother burned in hell, but not before Jennifer got her payback."

"Ouch."

"I'm sure she'd had a number of skilled therapists over the years. I tried to get her to talk about the feelings under all that rage, but that was useless. So I asked her if she intended to injure Gelsey. If she did, of course, that was something I could report."

"And she said?"

"No, but she hoped somebody else would."

I didn't know what to say. A car with a booming bass cruised past our house. I recognized "Time of Your Life," an old Green Day hit about turning points and not being able to avoid them. I suspected a heavenly messenger.

Ed touched his chin to his collarbone, to work out kinks in his neck. "At the time, I thought she was saying that someday, some way, she hoped Gelsey got what was coming to her. But looking at that phrase tonight, I wondered if the words were a threat. Maybe Jennifer knew someone else was after Gelsey. I don't know, but it pushed me over the edge. I decided I had to see her. I debated whether I should call, but decided it would be better to drop by. I knew Gelsey always stayed up past midnight. She's an insomniac. I wouldn't be welcome at any time of day, but late was no worse than any other."

"Did you go straight over?"

He twisted his head from one side to the other. "No. And that's the problem. I knew I was going to tell her. But I wasn't sure how to go about it. So I took a drive. Maybe a half hour of aimless wandering out in the country. Then, after I'd decided how best to approach her, I turned back to Emerald Estates and parked in front of her house."

I wasn't sure I wanted the rest of the details, but I thought he might need to repeat them. He told the story without prompting, but I'm sure he spared me the worst.

"Her poodles were on the front porch. I know she never lets them out without supervision, so this was a warning sign. And the door was ajar. I hoped she had just put the dogs outside for a moment and would be close by when I knocked. But I knocked and rang the bell, and nobody answered. That was odd enough. Then I heard a strange noise and I realized that somewhere inside a CD was stuck. You know the sound I mean? One syllable, over and over, like a jackhammer. Nobody lets that go on."

"So you went inside?"

He looked away and spoke a little faster. "I called her name, pushed the door a little, and walked in. I kept calling as I walked through the entryway. Then I saw her on the rug."

"What did you do?"

"Ran over to her, knelt, and put my fingers against her throat to see if she had a pulse. One of the dogs nipped my arm. Still protecting her, I guess, even though there was nothing to protect anymore. I fended him off, but he scratched my arm with his teeth." He turned back and held it up to show me.

This is not a man who wants to be babied, but my maternal instincts gushed. "Ed, we've got to get something on that."

"I washed it at the station. They had some ointment. I'll

go in for a tetanus booster tomorrow. Of course it didn't help my case to have the dog attack me. Or to have Gelsey's blood on my pants and shirt when the police arrived."

"*You* called them?"

"I didn't have a chance. The moment I shook off the dog and got up to find the phone, one of her neighbors appeared. She'd heard the dogs and gotten worried. She made the call, but we both knew it was too late for Gelsey."

"How long do you think she had been dead?"

He looked away again. "One of the cops guessed about an hour."

"And the gun?"

"Nowhere in sight. I'm sure they'll tear the house apart."

"What do they think? That you shot her, hid the gun, left the door open and the poodles yapping the whole time, then went back to kneel beside the body?"

"I don't know everything they think. But they think it's odd I was there so late."

"Did anybody see you at church? January? Esther?" Sometimes Esther likes to practice the organ at night when nobody's around, so she can pull out all the stops. Very *Phantom of the Opera*. If the windows are open we can hear her over here.

"No one was there. And since I knew I'd probably go see Gelsey, I drove to the church, so the car wasn't parked where you could see it."

"Maybe somebody saw it in the church lot."

"Or out in the country while I was driving around. But it's a gray sedan. Who's going to notice?"

"They'll find somebody who saw you to establish you weren't in the house at the time of death. And why would the police suspect you anyway? Even if you were kneeling beside the body when the neighbor arrived." I winced at that image.

He frowned and turned back to me, as if he needed proof it was really me asking such a stupid question. "Jennifer's body was found on our porch, Ag. This is body number two I'm connected with. And they've already dug up a motive."

"What, the problems at church? The fact that Gelsey

doesn't—didn't—like you? If every minister killed every parishioner who disagreed with them, Christians would need some modern-day equivalent of the catacombs for protection. For heaven's sake!"

"It's more than that. She made an appointment to have her will changed. She was writing the church out of it. Since the Grim Reaper appeared before her lawyer came back from vacation, we stand to inherit more than a quarter of a million dollars for our endowment."

I was stunned. A quarter of a million dollars? "How on earth did they find that out so quickly?"

"News travels fast in Emerald Springs. Just about the only thing that does. Her lawyer was notified, and he called the station while I was there."

"I can't believe Roussos thinks you killed her because the church was about to lose some money."

He raised a brow. "Some?"

"Okay, a lot of money. So what?"

"So he's scrambling for a motive and a suspect. I was there, scratched up and bloody. It was late at night. Not the usual time for a pastoral call. And I wouldn't tell him why."

"What?" I couldn't believe this. "Jennifer's dead, Gelsey's dead, what is wrong with you? Who are you protecting?"

He rubbed his beard, as if that would help him stay conscious. "I just wanted some time to figure out what to say and how to say it. She was a major force in the community. I don't want the good things she's done diminished by vicious gossip. If he'll promise to keep the information as private as possible, I'll probably tell him the nuts and bolts tomorrow. But tonight I was just too heartsick to trust myself."

I stared at the man who had been belittled and threatened by Gelsey Falowell and wondered if somewhere she was finally aware of the mistake she had made.

"I've got to get to bed." He stood, rolling his head in a circle to ease the tension again.

"I'll clean up. Go. I'll be up when I think I can sleep."

"Some ministers only have to worry about sermon topics and end of the year reports."

"Think how bored you would be."
He didn't even smile.

✦   ✦   ✦

When Deena's alarm went off I dragged myself out of bed
and made breakfast for the girls, who were spending the day
in Cleveland at the Rock and Roll Hall of Fame with their
religious education classes. I wasn't sure what this field trip
had to do with religion, but I was sure someone would work
it in along the way.

Since I knew they would hear the news, I told them about
Gelsey. To Deena's credit, she did not sing a chorus of
"Ding-Dong, the Witch Is Dead." She seemed genuinely
sorry, although she didn't try to dig up any good memories
of Gelsey, since there were none to be had. I'm afraid
Gelsey only liked children in theory.

Ed came down about nine thirty. By then I had fielded half
a dozen telephone calls. The membership of the Women's
Society was stunned. I pictured worker bees without their
queen and understood what Gelsey's death meant to them.

Ed decided to spend the day in his office since he'd been
out of town all day yesterday and still needed to finish tomorrow's sermon. He had only been at the church an hour
when Sally Berrigan arrived.

Sally is a tall woman, square, masculine shoulders, a trim
build, no-nonsense silver hair. I think of New York skyscrap-
ers when Sally walks into the room. Inside the imposing fa-
cade a lot of wheeling and dealing is under way. At
sixty-four Sally hasn't even begun to slow down. Had she
been elected as mayor instead of Brownie Kefauver, Emerald Springs would not be in an economic slump, and no one
would be picketing Book Gems. She would simply not have
allowed it.

Sally didn't waste time sharing stories about the departed, although it looked as if she had shed tears that morning. "Ed's in a meeting," she told me. "So I thought I'd see
what you think about this."

I learned upon arriving in Emerald Springs that I was to
become the unpaid assistant minister. Also the carrier of

messages, the substitute sexton, the extra pair of hands in the church kitchen, and the woman most likely to plunk out hymns on the piano when Esther has the flu. As a bone-deep feminist every part of me knows I should be outraged, but secretly, I enjoy this. It's just that kind of church and town.

Without asking I set a cup of coffee in front of her. This is the major food group at the bottom of Sally's nutritional pyramid. "Think about what?"

"I was able to get Gelsey's address book from the police. After they copied it, of course. I told them I would call her next of kin to let them know what had happened."

Sally was the most likely person to make the calls. She and Gelsey had been close, and to my knowledge, there was no family in the area.

"I'm sure everyone is upset." I sounded sincere, but all my systems were on alert. Had Gelsey's family referred to her as Wanda Ray, or was that only a false name she had used on Jennifer's birth certificate? How deep did the deception go?

"There is no 'everyone,' Aggie. Every single phone number was a sham. I got a deli, a library, and a nursing home. Two others were disconnected. Information has no listings for any of the names in the book. I checked addresses on the Internet. Some of the streets don't even exist. Those that do have different numbering systems. The only address I could find that actually exists is a doggie day care center. That was supposed to be her sister's house."

Even knowing what I did, I was surprised. "Did you check names of residents at the nursing home? Did you check for staff at the other places?"

"By the time I got off the phone I knew the names of everybody who had ever walked through the doors."

My mind was whirling. "What do you make of it?"

"I have no idea. She went to Boston regularly to see family. She came back with stories."

"Photos?"

"No one our age takes photos of contemporaries. Why do we want more evidence we're falling apart?"

I let the editorial pass. I found it interesting there was no physical evidence from Gelsey's "family" visits. "Did any of these relatives visit her?"

"She always said she preferred to see them at home. That way she could visit her beloved Boston."

"I wonder why she never moved back after her husband died."

"I believe there was something in his will that made that difficult. But I always thought it mostly had to do with her place in the community here. Boston is so large, and even with her family connections it seems unlikely she would have had the status or influence she had here. We all looked up to her." Her voice broke.

I went for the tissues, but of course, Sally had her own and had finished wiping her eyes by the time I returned.

"Leave this with me awhile," I told her, patting her hand. "I'm going to check around a little. Ed has family in Boston." I didn't add that those last two statements had nothing to do with each other. In her own way my mother-in-law had done her share of checking in Beantown. Now I was going to do some on my own.

Sally straightened her shoulders. "I want to do something. I don't want to feel helpless."

"I think you should help Ed plan Gelsey's memorial service. Why don't you talk to a few of her closest friends and see if she ever told them what she wanted? Who knew her better?"

Of course that was the real question. Who *had* known Gelsey better? The real Gelsey, that is. I was scrambling to figure out the answer as I showed Sally to the door.

I spent the rest of the morning cleaning house and making a list of what I knew for sure about Gelsey Falowell. The former was particularly necessary, because today was the Meanie moms powwow in our living room. I still wasn't sure Crystal O'Grady had gotten my messages, but everyone else would be here.

The Gelsey list was not as long as I wanted it to be. I knew Gelsey had lived here more than thirty years, that she was a force in the community. I knew she claimed to be from

Boston's Back Bay. I knew she claimed her maiden name was Railford, although Nan was dubious. I knew she'd had a daughter out of wedlock in Las Vegas, that Wanda Ray Gelsey was the name on the birth certificate, that she and the daughter were now dead. I knew a lawyer had facilitated the adoption and that I could sleep with one of his associates for more information.

That last part was no help at all, for obvious reasons.

I mopped and waxed the kitchen floor since no one had thought to install a new one since no-wax floors hit the market. I added: "Gelsey played tennis, loved expensive, tasteful jewelry, and took an instant dislike to me," to my list. I cleaned the bathrooms and added: "Gelsey wanted to fire Ed and seemed to be searching for a reason to do so. She was a woman of strong opinions." I dusted, and in between the coffee table and the fireplace mantel I added: "Gelsey kept false information in her address book, which is carrying deception to the ultimate limit."

By the time the house was clean enough to suit me, I still had very little to go on.

Wanda Ray was not a name I would associate with the Northeast. It's a Southern name, an Appalachian or Ozark name, perhaps. Of course if she pulled these syllables out of thin air, this didn't matter. But somehow, that didn't ring true. After all, there's an accent that goes with this name, just as there is with Gelsey Railford Falowell. Why would she choose a name that didn't seem to fit?

Or perhaps it did fit at the time.

Perhaps she didn't choose it. Perhaps it was chosen for her at birth.

Taking my life in my hands, I turned on Ed's computer and thanks to lessons from yet another Dummies book I ran "Wanda Gelsey" through the Internet. When nothing turned up I searched for "Gelsey," subtracting "Kirkland" after I realized I was getting numerous references to the dancer. When I still wasn't getting anywhere I added "genealogy," then "family tree."

Since the computer was still working, despite freezing twice for old time's sake, I went to Cyndi's List, one of the most popular genealogy sites on the Web. I found my way to Social Security records and made a list of the states where "Gelseys" had died. Not surprisingly, Florida came up repeatedly. I envisioned an entire sun-drenched village of snowbirds with the same last name. The only other state that seemed to have a surplus of Gelsey graves was Kentucky, and those seemed to center in a town called Hollins Creek.

A few minutes later I was on the telephone to Frankfort to the Kentucky Office of Vital Statistics, but of course, they weren't open on a Saturday. Since it had been a long shot they would help without birthplace and date, I hung up and considered other avenues.

The phone rang and Lucy screeched in my ear about Gelsey, Ed, and the rumors in town. I waited for the atonal overture to subside.

"I should have called you," I agreed. "I'm playing amateur detective here."

She agreed to put on her Sherlock Holmes deerstalker and deposit herself on my doorstep—breathing, of course—in a jiffy.

I had two hours before the Meanie moms arrived, so I made a large pan of gingerbread and checked to be sure we had enough apple cider.

My breathless pal was dressed in pumpkin-colored silk and black velveteen jeans when she arrived. I won't say she looked excited about Gelsey's death. She's not unfeeling. But she did look ready for action.

"Tell me," she panted, sliding into her usual seat at the table.

I did, scratching up every detail except, of course, the truth about Jennifer's parentage and all that went with it.

I had considered whether to tell her about the false addresses in Gelsey's book, but in the end I swore her to secrecy and related what Sally had told me that morning. Lucy can keep secrets. She won't tell me the selling price of a house until the records become public. And even if I torture her, I don't think she'll give details about the night her broker celebrated the sale of a prime corner property by swimming naked with two unnamed females in Emerald Springs. What little I know came from the *Flow* and the reporter who found him a towel and a pair of pants.

"So Gelsey was living a lie?" Lucy gnawed at her lip. I was sorry the gingerbread was still baking.

I debated some more and companionably chewed my own. "Looks that way."

Lucy knows me well. "What?" she demanded.

"Well, I think she has another name. And I can't tell you everything I know or why. Can you handle that?"

"You bet." Lucy had made an attempt to tame her hair with a tortoiseshell barrette. It hadn't worked. Curls whipped both cheeks as she nodded. "What is it?"

"Wanda Ray Gelsey." I explained what I'd found on the Internet.

"Did you look up the Hollins Creek white pages? You know white pages are on the Net, don't you?"

At my sheepish expression, she shook her head. "Let's go."

Ten minutes later Lucy was on the telephone with Amy Howard, one of the two realtors listed for Hollins Creek, a virtual hotbed of Gelseys. We had learned Hollins Creek was in Kentucky's mountainous eastern coal field, nothing more than a dot on the map, mines and two blocks of small businesses.

Lucy introduced herself. She claimed she had a client who was interested in purchasing a second home in Kentucky, Hollins Creek to be specific. She needed more information. Lucy listened awhile, then she made a circle with her thumb and forefinger and winked at me.

"Yes," she said. "It is rather a ways to go, isn't it? But her family's from that area. She's sentimental."

She listened. "Gelseys, I think," Lucy answered a question I could only imagine. "Oh, I'm not sure of first names. I think she mentioned a Wanda Ray?"

She hung up eventually and rubbed her ear. "Wanda and Ray Gelsey had a daughter, Wanda Ray. She left town a long time ago when she was still a teenager and never returned.

Amy says Wanda Ray always thought she was worth more than anybody in Hollins Creek, or at least that's what she's heard."

"Gelsey was seventyish? Is this woman you spoke to a hundred?"

"Even better. She's *related*. If Wanda Ray and our Gelsey are one and the same, Amy Howard is a distant cousin. Ray Gelsey was Amy's mother's uncle."

"What, is this Amy a walking Hollins Creek genealogy?"

"Just because your mother macramed her way across America and you never put down roots, don't assume everyone else chopped down the family tree."

"Junie's macrame was brilliant. She wanted to macrame my wedding dress but my nipples kept poking out between square knots." I tapped my lip. "It might be the same Gelsey. Or it's possible Gelsey made up the name *Wanda Ray* for some other reason."

"Amy said Wanda and Ray were devastated when their daughter abandoned them, and it's probably prudent for my client not to tell anybody if she's related to Wanda Ray. They'll hold it against her. Oh, and there are a lot of houses for sale in Hollins Creek." Lucy glanced at her Cartier knockoff and frowned. "I'm showing a condo in ten minutes. Gotta go."

I took the gingerbread out of the oven and set it on a rack to cool. So there really had been a Wanda Ray Gelsey, and it wasn't such a common name that I'd expect to find a hundred more. But what did this tell me?

The Las Vegas connection had been gnawing at me. It was possible Gelsey had simply gone there to give birth. It was an anonymous sort of place, large enough where she could sink into the shadows, the kind of town where nobody would notice a pregnant woman or care about her situation. Flights and hotels were cheap, surely medical care was excellent.

But wasn't Las Vegas also a lure? The kind of place a young woman might yearn to live after a childhood in a Kentucky coal patch? Bright lights, city life. I've never seen photographs of a younger Gelsey, but I imagine she was lovely.

Ed has a colleague in Las Vegas, and it was time to ask for help. I had an hour and a half before the moms descended, and I left a message.

George returned my call an hour later. George Bentsen went to seminary with Ed. He visits us whenever he's in our neighborhood, so we probably won't see much of him while we're in Emerald Springs.

George is something of a high roller. He figured out quickly that life in a normal parish held little appeal, and he turned his sights to other things. About five years ago he wandered west and founded the Las Vegas Chapel of Bliss, three acres with a view of the mountains, a gazebo that holds fifty guests, and a full-time wedding coordinator who insists on at minimum a fifteen-minute consultation. His niche is tasteful weddings without Elvis impersonators, *Star Trek* captains, vampires, costumed cupids, or the bright lights of the Strip. His wife does the floral arrangements. They make out okay.

I was lucky it was a slow day and George could call me back between weddings. I told him quickly what I needed and why. He was outraged that anyone would suspect Ed of murder, and promised to see what he could find out. Not surprisingly, George knows a fleet of private investigators. Checking credentials is a booming business in Vegas.

By the time I hung up, the moms were knocking.

May Frankel arrived and immediately set to work cutting gingerbread and putting it on plates. Tara's mom, Rachel, came into the kitchen and ladled the cider I had heated into mugs and mismatched china cups. Both of them knew the reason for the meeting. We had held a mini-conference about it in the middle school parking lot.

I am surrounded by women who dress in hand-decorated seasonal sweatshirts. Today Rachel's was forest green with appliquéd apples, a harbinger of fall. Shannon's mother, Grace, was still clinging to summer, and hers was sea green with a peach collar and cuffs and embroidered sand dollars.

With local fashion in mind I wore one of Junie's creations, a short-sleeved sweater knit from ribbon yarn and something that may well be hemp. I hope not to get arrested if I stray too close to a bonfire.

The others streamed in until there were ten of us. I wasn't sure how interested they were in the topic, or if they had turned out to get away from their families. Just as I was about to give up on Crystal and abandon the kitchen she arrived with her customary flurry, white blond hair billowing around her shoulders.

"I hope you didn't start without me?" She said it playfully and wagged a finger.

I held out the last plate of gingerbread. "We saved you one."

"Oh Aggie, you are the perfect mother, aren't you? The closest I get to baking is the tanning bed at my salon." She followed with a peal of laughter and set the plate on the counter. "I won't have any cider, I don't think. But thanks."

"Everyone's in the living room."

"Goodness, is there room for us?"

"There's a spot on the rug just for you, Crystal."

She looked down at white linen pants, and I left her to wrestle with what was probably the most serious problem she had encountered that day.

She joined us, but she stood and leaned against the wall, the mistress of compromise.

Everyone was chatting about the beginning of the school year, what their brilliant and talented daughters had already accomplished, and whether the fifth graders should be allowed to try out for junior varsity cheerleading. I took Crystal's spot on the rug, a worn oriental heirloom from one of Ed's cousins, and leaned against the sofa between May and Rachel, who were discussing the relative merits of two English teachers. I heard Gelsey's name mentioned across the room and tried not to react.

The moment there was a lull, I cleared my throat. "I'm so glad everybody could come."

Unfailingly polite on the surface, they all made the appropriate noises.

"The girls are such good friends," I continued. "And it occurred to me that their friendships give us a little clout. They're going to be making a lot of changes in the next years, and maybe if we make some decisions as we go along and stick together, we can make sure they don't grow up too fast."

May jumped in. "I'm already concerned. Seems to me there's just too much pressure out there for them to turn into adults. Television, the music they listen to. Maddie has a good head on her shoulders now, but I worry."

Grace leaned forward. I don't know Grace Forester well, but I remembered that Deena had said her daughter Shannon was sitting with a table of boys at lunch this year. I was expecting no help from this quarter.

"Let me tell you," she said. "These girls are just one step from having sex between classes! Mark my words."

No one said a word. I cleared my throat. "Umm . . ." It was the best I could do.

"Well, I'm not quite *that* worried," May said smoothly. "But I do think we need to protect them a little. From themselves as much as from the world. We need to help them send the right messages, don't you think?"

I recovered. "I agree with May. I think we need to make sure they don't have to compete with older girls, just because they're at the middle school. They should be dressing like children, having sleepovers and pillow fights. They should still be viewing boys as the enemy. At that age I was playing dolls with my sisters."

Crystal pushed away from the wall. "I'll just have to disagree. Children grow at different speeds. Now some of your girls haven't developed yet. But my Carlene certainly has. And she's not interested in dolls. She's interested in boys."

"Your Carlene is as flat as a pancake and she dresses like a slut," Grace said. "You'd better watch out, Crystal, or you'll be the youngest grandmother in Emerald Springs history."

I considered throwing myself between them, but apparently the two women had known each other forever. Crystal just giggled. "Grandmother? Me?"

"She looks like she's having sex or wants it badly, Crystal. Either that or she's trying to get a gig on MTV. Where have you been, woman?"

One of the other moms interrupted. The poor woman's eyes were popping, as if she'd developed an iodine deficiency from her last sip of cider. "What were you thinking of doing, Aggie? Any suggestions?"

"I'd like to see us come up with some rules, a dress code, maybe, before the school gets around to it. For better or worse, a lot of the other girls look up to the Meanies. They're role models."

"Dress code?" Crystal sounded appalled. "You want me to tell Carlene what she can wear? You want me to police her?"

"Didn't you get your badge the day you gave birth, Crystal?" Grace glared. "The rest of us did. They misplace yours or something?"

I broke in, glad there was as yet no fistfight and determined it would stay that way. "It's so much easier to stick to rules if everybody else does, don't you think? There shouldn't be too much work to do. We just tell the girls we've agreed that this is the way things are going to be. We come up with reasonable standards. Nothing too strict . . ."

The kitchen door slammed, and I heard the scuffing of feet and Teddy's voice. Before I could warn them, my girls plowed into the living room. Teddy in denim and cotton knit looked just as she had that morning. But Deena, my level-headed Deena, was wearing a hot pink tank top with thin lace straps and a tight knit skirt that stopped midthigh. My jaw dropped.

She saw my expression. "What?" she demanded. "Jill Mollincroft and I traded clothes in the girls' bathroom. So?"

I looked at the other mothers, all of whom were staring at me.

"We'll start with chastity belts," I said. "Any objections?"

13

Deena had switched clothing with Jill Mollincroft, three years her senior, because Jill had been too cold in the Hall of Fame's moderate air-conditioning and Deena had been too warm. They had locked themselves in adjacent bathroom stalls and tossed clothes over the top, the logical solution. Deena couldn't understand my reaction. She didn't know that I had glimpsed the knockout teenager in training and aged a decade knowing what awaited me.

Life goes on, even post-murder. In the next two weeks the police took their time combing Gelsey's house and life for clues; Ed went about the business of the church, although it was clear more members seemed uncomfortable with him, and I went to work and sidestepped the diminishing number of protestors in front of Book Gems.

Bob was doing enough business to stay open, but barely. Those upstanding citizens who were no longer carrying signs were still not coming inside to buy books. After all the furor, Bob's little room in the back had never found an audience. Readers who looked like regulars at Don't Go There came once and left quickly, since the material was too tame for their taste. Readers who might have been interested were too traumatized by the publicity to set foot inside. Bob confided that once the protests died down completely, he was going to scrap the idea, redecorate the nook, and move all our magazines and gift items there. But he would be damned if anyone thought he was doing it because of pressure from the right wing.

I was at loose ends. Ed was even quieter than usual, the girls were involved with school activities, and with business so slow, Bob only needed me one day a week. In an effort to stay busy I dove into the church records, working on the scrapbook I planned to present to the Women's Society.

On the last Friday of September I went up to the spare bedroom to rummage for more photos. Somehow I had slogged my way through to the fifties. If this sounds deadly boring, don't blame me. The project kept me busy, and I knew some of our older members would love it. This was my one shot at a legacy.

I perched on the edge of the daybed we'd installed for family visits, and rifled through one of a series of old boxes. When I tried to hold one photo closer to the light another fell to the floor and floated under the vintage chenille bedspread.

I retrieved it, but as I did I spotted the box of 8 mm movies I'd taken from the storage room, wedged under the daybed drawer. I pulled them out, as well, and decided to change my plans. It was raining outside, the skies were gray, and I could use the movies as an excuse to make popcorn. My kind of day, even if Johnny Depp wasn't making an appearance.

Half an hour later it was just me, Orville Redenbacher, the old projector from the religious education closet, and the box of home movies. I had finished the popcorn and three reels before I took a break from making notes. I'd seen an ordination, an anniversary dinner thirty years ago in the parish house, and a nativity pageant. The anniversary dinner was the most interesting since people were laughing too heartily not to suspect a wee hint of the grape. I thought one of the women looked like the oldest member of our Women's Society, and set the reel aside to show at the first opportunity.

Perhaps we could attach some names to the anonymous faces before it was too late.

I stretched and resumed, making notes. Some of the film was ruined. Some had even begun to smell like vinegar as it decomposed. I put the best aside, dusting boxes and canisters and making sure the film wasn't wound too tightly, with the hope that we could transfer it to DVD soon. Considering the storage conditions, more of the film than I had hoped was still good. By now I was beginning to suspect that at one time somebody had cared about the archives and stored things more appropriately. Perhaps the storage room on the third floor was a fairly recent development.

By the time I had finished all the reels it was almost time for an invasion of girls. I cleaned up and put the projector back in the case. I was boxing up the salvageable film when I realized that one of the movies was missing.

When I had agreed to take on the job of historian I had viewed a sampling, just to see what we had. I remembered now that I had watched a picnic, from maybe twenty years ago. The film itself had been well-preserved and recent enough that I had recognized faces. I'd gotten a kick out of the padded shoulders of the women's dresses and the big hair, sort of an Emerald Springs rerun of *Dallas*.

The picnic reel was not here.

For good measure I shuffled through the movies I'd seen today, now clearly and carefully labeled and annotated. No picnic.

I knew better than to hope the movie was still somewhere in the storage room. Two weeks ago when I had noticed the movies were missing, Harry and I had searched thoroughly. When we had found the box mixed in with junk in the opposite corner, we had sorted the rest of the pile carefully to be certain we'd retrieved everything. The movie was gone.

Someone had searched through the archives. I had discovered that weeks ago. Now I had a pretty good idea what they had found and removed. I wondered if photographs were missing, too.

I had just enough time before the girls arrived to search the photographs from that decade. I was grateful I'd organized them enough to make this possible, but there were no photos of the picnic.

Who had taken the movie and why? Nostalgia? Something to hide?

Gelsey had certainly hidden a secret, but what could have been on that movie to make her steal it from the archives? It was a long shot, at best.

The girls arrived home, Teddy first, then Deena, who was thankfully still in the clothes she had left home in that morning. I wasn't sure what was going on in the other Meanie homes, but in ours we were sticking to the guidelines the moms and I had drawn up: no bare midriffs or shoulders, skirts at least midthigh when seated, jeans loose enough for oxygen intake, no T-shirts with provocative slogans. So far there were no problems, since Deena didn't even own the forbidden clothing items.

The telephone rang while I was helping Teddy find magazine photos to illustrate a story she was writing about a cat who dies and comes back to haunt its owners—I think we've progressed from funeral services to what comes afterwards.

George Bentsen was on the other end.

I had heard from George last week. He'd turned my information about Gelsey over to a private investigator friend named Leo who planned to trade his services for an upgrade to one of George's super deluxe weddings. Super deluxe means half a dozen extra white roses in the bride's bouquet, a bottle of premium champagne, and two tickets to a Friday night performance of Cirque du Soleil. The PI is something of a connoisseur, since George has already married him twice. Apparently PI-ing is tough on a marriage.

At that time there hadn't been anything to report, but today George sounded enthusiastic.

"We traced Wanda Ray Gelsey to the old Grandstand Hotel and Casino. *Wanda Ray* was the name on her official documents, but she went by the name of *Gorgeous Gelsey.*"

"Gorgeous Gelsey?"

"Showgirl. He found a photo I'm sending you. Legs you wouldn't believe. She was what they called 'a real dame' in those days. Feathers, sequins, black stockings. She worked at the Grandstand for two years, '51 through '53. Then she drops from view until 1964, when Wanda Ray Gelsey gave birth to an unnamed baby girl at North Vista Hospital. She was discharged with the baby in arms, and there's no record of the baby from that point on, not even a birth certificate."

"Maybe they sealed it when the adoption took place, or at least when it was initiated. I don't think it was ever completed."

"That's all we've got so far."

I was pondering Lady Falowell in ostrich feathers and spangled blue eyeshadow. Could this really be the same woman?

"Does Leo have any theories about what might have happened to her in those missing ten or so years? Does he think she left town?"

"Left town, cozied up to some sugar daddy, and lived off him so she didn't have an income to tax, or maybe took up something illegal and dropped out of sight. Showgirls burn out fast. They all hope they're going straight to the top, and instead they're stuck with the same boring, sweaty dance routines under twenty-five-pound headdresses. And at a dump like the old Grandstand, making nice to the same boring guys in her spare time, too. Being a showgirl's not glamorous, it's plain hard work."

"Three possibilities there. Does he have any guesses which it might be?"

"Leo's got a hunch she moved on to something illegal. She just disappears too fast. Now you see 'em, now you don't. I told him to look a little harder. I'm throwing in a video of the wedding and matchbooks with names and the date for their friends."

"We owe you, George."

"If you and Ed ever move somewhere I want to visit, I'll come and stay awhile."

"How about Boston?"

"How about Paris?"

We hung up.

"Why did you say Gelsey is gorgeous?" Teddy asked. "Is she going to be gorgeous at her funeral? Can I come and see?"

I thought of the urn I'd turned over to Maude with Jennifer's ashes. "Mrs. Falowell asked to be cremated. So that happened early last week. But there'll be a memorial service for her in our church tomorrow morning. You can come, but you'll have to be quiet and sit still the whole time."

Teddy pushed her glasses farther up her nose. Moonpie, perhaps to see if he agreed with the theology lessons in Teddy's story, jumped up on the table. "Not if the body's not there," Teddy said at last. "Someday I want to see someone who's dead, just so I'll understand."

I brushed her hair back from her face. "Understand what, sweetie?"

"Why people die."

"Oh." I searched for answers, or at least something to offer her. "I've been to a number of funerals, and I still don't know the answer to that. People live and they die, and it's all part of an amazing mystery."

"Doesn't that *bother* you?"

I felt chastised. "No. It's good to ask questions, but we have to accept we may never have all the answers we want."

"I think I'm going to hear that a lot."

I thought she was too smart for her own good.

✦   ✦   ✦

The girls had a sleepover at the Frankels' that evening and left before dinner. At six a distracted Ed ate couscous with chickpeas and eggplant and managed all the right responses to my inquiries about his day. But the real Ed Wilcox was clearly not there. The imposter disappeared into Ed's study after dinner to work on Gelsey's memorial service. We expected a large crowd. After all, how many memorial services are conducted by the very minister who is under suspicion for the departed's murder?

I was tired of having nothing to do. The television schedule held no surprises, the movies playing in town were rated IQ13, and there were no cultural events at Emerald College unless I counted a lecture by the chairman of the computer department on the running times of algorithms. By the time the phone rang I was aching for a stimulating conversation on the merits of switching my long distance service. Even better, it was Lucy.

"You won't believe this . . ."

I was breathless with anticipation. "Don't fail me now . . ."

"Well, you just *won't* believe it. In fact, I have to see your face. I'm coming over."

"We can make fudge and do each other's nails. I can tell you what Johnny Vincuzzo said to me in American History a million years ago."

"Better yet, get that quilt thing out of your closet and put it on. We're going out."

I hung up and went to tell Ed I was leaving him. Ed-imposter was still in residence. He nodded like something out of a body snatchers movie.

Out front Lucy honked, and I grabbed my quilted jacket and took off down the front steps. The night was clear and cool, and there were a million stars over Emerald Springs. Other people had noticed and the roads were filled with people going anywhere they could. I was thrilled to be included.

"You and Ed having problems?" Lucy asked first thing.

"No. Just a tough time. He withdraws when he's under stress. There are zombies in Haiti with more charisma."

"We need to find the murderer so he'll get his energy back."

I snorted. "On a list of reasons, that's somewhere at the bottom." I noticed we were driving out of town toward the burbs—if Emerald Springs is large enough for such a thing. More exactly, we were driving in the general direction of Emerald Estates.

I touched Lucy's shoulder. "Turn around quick. At the least I was expecting another go 'round at Don't Go There. They've got an all-female band on stage tonight, the Hot Mama Express, with a surprise guest appearance. I'm thinking maybe Sax is dressing up like Janis Joplin to sing a couple of choruses of "Bobby McGee." I'm primed."

"You'll like this better."

"That good, huh?"

"Hang on." In a daring move, Lucy sped up to forty in the thirty-five mph zone. It was that kind of night.

When we pulled in front of Gelsey's house and parked, I didn't know what to say.

"Here we are." She gestured.

"Don't tell me there's a lockbox on that door, Luce. Even if there is, I don't want to be caught snooping inside."

Lucy turned. "No lockbox yet. There's going to be an estate sale in a couple of weeks, then the house goes on the market. And guess who's been hired to sell it?" She dangled a house key in front of me. "My listing, and you're here to help with the appraisal. You can tell me what we need to do to get the best price."

"You have the listing!" I paused. "Who gave it to you?"

"Gelsey's heir. Or I should say her husband's heir."

"Explain."

Lucy was clearly thrilled to do so. "When Herb Falowell died, he left everything to his only living relative. Gelsey was given use of the house and everything they owned until her death, as well as a generous annual allowance. She had some money she'd brought into the marriage, and that's probably what's going to your church. But she couldn't sell any of Herb's assets. It was some sort of paper she signed before they were married. Did they call them prenups that far back?"

I remembered Sally Berrigan telling me that Gelsey had been forced to stay in Emerald Springs because of some technicality in her husband's will. Hel–lo technicality.

Of course Gelsey hadn't really wanted to move to Boston, anyway, since as far as I could tell, she'd never known a soul there.

"You're missing something important here," Lucy told me.

"The reason you were given the listing?"

"Not exactly. Who gave it to me!"

"The relative." I narrowed my eyes. "Who? It's some-body I know, isn't it?"

"Not only know, work for. Bob Knowles is Gelsey's hus-band's nephew. Bob's mother was Herb Falowell's sister."

"Go on!" I sat back. "How come nobody ever told me?"

"I'm not sure how many people know. Bob never lived in Emerald Springs until he moved here to open Book Gems, and Herb's been dead a long time. I doubt Gelsey introduced Bob to friends as her beloved nephew. And why would Bob want people to know he was in town counting the heartbeats until Gelsey flatlined?"

"You think that's why he moved here?"

"I imagine he could taste that money, don't you? And Gelsey wasn't getting any younger. I think he was just waiting to pounce."

I remembered my conversation with Joan Barstow. "Did Herb own salt mines in Cleveland?"

"Herb was Mr. Salt Mine himself. And that was family stuff, stuff he inherited. On top of that, he made a fortune here in town. Herb was the guy who designed and developed Emerald Estates." She gestured to Gelsey's fake Tudor. "This is one of the very first houses. He knew exactly what people wanted and gave it to them. Houses that look more substantial than they are. Traditional exteriors with luxury touches inside. Space, views, a bit of grandeur. Houses where people can feel a little superior, even in a nowhere place like this one. Have you been inside Gelsey's?"

"When we first arrived and once afterwards. The first time, Gelsey gave me a tour, but I was in a daze. I couldn't believe Ed and I were moving away from the land of lobbyists and orange alerts."

"I bet you're sorry you did."

I considered that. "Really? No. If we leave—and these days it's more like when we leave—I'm going to miss Emerald Springs. And you, of course."

"Ah, Aggie . . . Maybe you won't have to go."

"Maybe we wouldn't if I hadn't talked my husband into coming over here to see Gelsey the night she was murdered."

"I still don't understand what was so important that visit couldn't wait until morning."

"You and most of the town."

"Well, come inside with me. We're going to check out

everything." Lucy wiggled her brows. "I do mean everything. And if you just happen to open a few drawers and paw through a few papers, who will know?"

Lucy was giving me the opportunity to search Gelsey's house to see if there was anything that might help Ed. Of course, the police had been here first. But what did they know?

I reached for the door handle, and my hand froze. "Good grief, Luce. Bob Knowles is the *heir*. Bob Knowles told me he was having serious financial problems."

"Not any–more . . ." She sang the words with glee.

Without a doubt, Bob Knowles had possessed the best possible reason to want his aunt dead. Since he had never mentioned Gelsey, and she had never mentioned him, I was pretty certain they had not spent Christmases and birthdays together. More likely he had been half a mile away hoping she choked on a turkey bone or cake crumbs.

By why would Bob want Jennifer dead? Unless he had somehow discovered her real identity and knew if she told Gelsey who she was, Gelsey might find a way to override Herb's prenup and leave some of his estate to her daughter.

"Oh, brother . . ."

Lucy opened her door. "You're already thinking and you haven't even gone inside. It's showtime."

I followed Lucy up the walkway. As fake Tudors go, this one's not bad. Although the crossbeams have never held anything heavier than a nail, the stucco is well done, the windows effectively multipaned, and the steep roof has an attractive side gable. I remembered now that the architecture had helped generate the "Lady Falowell" nickname.

The walkway was vintage brick, bordered on both sides by what must have been truly lovely gardens in the spring and summer. Now they looked sad, as if the weeks since Gelsey's death had taken the heart out of them. No one had told the gardener to replace the spent snapdragons with pansies, the ageratum with chrysanthemums, or to cut back the lifeless black-eyed Susans.

"I'd tell Bob to spend a few bucks getting the borders in shape," I told Lucy. "Nobody wants to be reminded of the work that goes into a garden. They just want to bask in the glory."

"Any other impressions?"

"A new doormat, maybe, and the door needs cleaning . . ." I stepped closer. "No, it needs a fresh coat of paint, maybe something other than black? I'd have to see the house in daylight, but maybe spruce green or burgundy? The front should look welcoming. The windows are an asset. I'd have them cleaned so they sparkle like diamonds."

"Wow, poetry."

"You did ask, right?"

"I'm making notes." She wasn't, at least not literally. In fact the only thing in Lucy's hand was the key. She opened the door.

The house had been closed up too long, and under the stale odor of uncirculated air was Eau de French poodle. I hadn't thought about the dogs since the night one had chewed on my husband. "By any chance do you know what happened to Trixie and Dixie?"

"Please! Jean Pierre and Genevieve. I think a woman at the end of the street took them."

I was sorry the dogs couldn't talk. For that matter, I was sorry at least one of them hadn't been smart enough to tell the difference between a murderer and a friend.

I wrinkled my nose. "Tell Bob he needs to have the house cleaned top to bottom, especially the rugs, and all the windows opened for at least twenty-four hours before he puts the house on the market."

"I already have. He argued, but I told him my commission depends on the selling price, and that shut him up."

I was glad to help, but I was less interested in whether the house sold for two hundred thousand or two twenty-five than in what I might discover about Gelsey. I was also wondering if I was going to happen on a certain 8 mm movie. This was one flick I wanted to see.

The rooms were filled with antiques. I wandered the first floor, fingering everything, and stopped at a cranberry opalescent epergne with three lilies and a central trumpet on a drop leaf mahogany table by the window. "This will bring

Bob enough money to stock a couple of shelves with children's books."

In the glass case beside it I noted a particularly fine collection of Staffordshire figures depicting stories from the Old Testament and stopped to admire them. "There's too much stuff everywhere for today's tastes. I suppose the estate sale will take care of that?"

"I think I've talked Bob into getting rid of the collectibles and just about half the furniture. The house will show better if it's still furnished. I think once the house is sold, a good auction house will take the rest on consignment."

I found this sad. Gelsey had been so proud of her house and all the contents. Now it was just so much cargo to disperse.

We discussed what to keep while the house was on the market and what to sell, whether to paint rooms and what neutral shades were best. As we strolled through the cherry-paneled study I opened side table drawers, lifted a few books from shelves and thumbed through them for hidden documents, searched through cabinets, checked under the few photos in gilded frames. I even checked behind paintings for a hidden safe. I've learned everything I know from A&E's reruns of *Murder She Wrote*.

The kitchen needed to be updated. We pondered the possibilities and decided the most effective and least expensive solution was to have the small patches of striped wallpaper removed and the walls painted a peachy white to neutralize the celery green laminate countertops. I suggested Lucy clear everything from the counters except the Majolica canisters. The drawers were a bonanza of kitchen utensils that looked as if they had never been used. There was nothing else of interest.

"The police left the house in pretty good shape, considering," I said as we started upstairs. We had both carefully stepped around the spot where I assumed my husband had found Gelsey. The Persian carpet was missing now, a "dead" giveaway.

"I'm not sure how hard they searched, but I called Detective Sergeant Roussos myself and told him once they were finished, this house had better not look like Genghis Khan and his hordes were visiting."

I was sorry I hadn't been a bird on that telephone wire.

Lucy was seriously taking notes now, and we progressed from room to room. I searched, she asked for advice on what to do about wood floors and outdated bathroom tile. Turquoise and salmon may yet come back in style. Gelsey was prepared.

Our last stop was the master bedroom. I paused in the doorway and had a prolonged attack of guilt. I felt like an intruder. I could smell the faintest hint of Chanel.

"What do you think?" If Lucy knew what I was feeling, she didn't let on.

"Not as large as they build now, but not too bad. The carpet looks newish." The carpet was white plush, the walls were white, the heavy brocade bedspread was white. The antiques ranged from dark oak to rosewood. Not my taste, but effective.

"I thought we'd clear away this and this." Lucy walked around the room pointing to a bookshelf, a writing desk from the nineteenth century, a table holding a small carved oak chest. "We'll leave the bed, one dresser, maybe the nightstand. What do you think?"

I thought the chest was exquisite. It was maybe sixteen inches high, about the same width and perhaps twice as long. It was intricately carved in what looked like Renaissance style, with angels glaring from each side. The middle panel was set with lovely, detailed marquetry. As I had expected, it was unlocked. If the chest had been locked at Gelsey's death the police had made certain it no longer was. Inside, I sifted through a collection of delicate lady's handkerchiefs from another age, all with *R* embroidered in different colors and scripts.

"Look, she made a collection of old handkerchiefs. More ersatz heirlooms?" I wondered if the young Wanda Ray had haunted flea markets and antique malls.

Lucy stood beside me and shook her head. "A Railford to the end, huh? Do you suppose she pulled them out at appropriate moments to prove her lineage?"

I put the top down gently. Something was niggling at me. As a teenager I had seen a chest like this one at a booth at one of Junie's fairs. There were often antique dealers at these events, and through the years I had learned a lot from them, as an antidote to boredom. Junie had been selling floral headdresses that year, and my sisters and I had been forced to wear them and walk through the crowds to advertise, ribbons streaming behind us.

One of the antique dealers had called me over to get a better look, and we had struck up a conversation. He had shown me his stock and told me a little history, sensing my interest. There had been a chest like this.

"Whoa . . . Watch this, Luce."

She had wandered off. Now she came back to stand beside me. "Watch what?"

"If I'm right . . ." I grasped the panel on the side and began to inch it upwards.

"Aggie, you're not going to destroy a valuable antique here, are you?"

"Not if I'm right. If I'm wrong, Bob can dock my pay for the next decade."

The panel slid up and off. And under it, at the bottom of the chest, was a drawer. "Voila!"

"How'd you know?"

"I've seen another one. Chests like these were made to protect old documents."

"It's locked."

"Right." I deflated immediately. "Right . . ."

"If it's locked, that means there's something inside worth locking away."

"Where would you keep the key?"

Ten minutes later we found the key under the moss in a pot of white silk orchids beside Gelsey's bed. It was pretty clear she hadn't been too worried about anyone sneaking in and opening the hidden drawer. I was relieved we wouldn't have to jimmy the lock, although Lucy assured me that she was up to the task.

The drawer slid open to reveal a stack of papers and photographs. "Be still my heart." I took the drawer to the bed with me and perched on the edge. Lucy joined me. If I'd had any lingering doubts that Gelsey Railford Falowell was really Wanda Ray Gelsey, they were laid to rest immediately.

"Gorgeous Gelsey." I held up the top photo, autographed by the former resident of this room, and Lucy snapped on the bedside lamp so we could see better. "My God, she *was* gorgeous, wasn't she?"

The woman who stared back at us had heavy black hair in waves to her shoulders, a pout, and a figure that predated silicone implants. The photo showed large God-given breasts covered in sequins and rhinestones, a wasp waist covered in nothing at all, and rounded hips barely disguised by chiffon harem pants with glittery adornments in strategic places. On her head she wore a massive creation of ostrich feathers, beaded flowers, and cascading sprays of rhinestones; on her arms, elbow-length satin gloves.

I saw the Gelsey I knew. Not clearly, of course, since the photo was probably fifty years old, but she was definitely there.

"What a babe," Lucy said.

I turned it over and saw *Gorgeous Gelsey* stamped in faded red ink, along with the name of an agency of some sort and a telephone number.

"I don't suppose they're still in business, do you?" I asked. "Maybe a booking agency?"

"I doubt they've been around for decades."

I set the photo down and quickly went through three more photos of Gelsey in different costumes, one as extravagant as the next. All had the same stamp on the back.

"I wonder if she worked in more casinos than George knows about?" I wondered this out loud.

"George?"

Lucy only had pieces of this puzzle, and what help was that? Besides, I was tired of being the only one besides Ed and the police who knew the whole story. I made a snap decision and filled her in on everything I'd discovered from beginning to end. I trusted her not to tell the world about Gelsey's peccadillos.

"It's too bad there's no date on the photos," she said when

I was done and she had properly oohed and aahed about the connection to Jennifer.

I set the photos aside and pulled out a manila envelope that was next in the pile. I opened it and carefully dumped out more casino photos, snapshots this time, of showgirls on the stage. I suspected she was among them. There was a neon sign visible in one: Welcome to the Grandstand.

"Okay, still the Grandstand days." I put the photos back and went to the next item in the pile. It looked like an address book or a journal, an old one with a leather cover and gilt-edged pages. The leather was powdery with age. I opened it, expecting to see names and addresses, four-digit phone numbers with two-letter prefix codes. I have my grandmother's address book from the forties, and treasure it.

Instead, each page had an odd name like Hazelnut, Tomboy, and Tarzan, followed by a page of letters divided into groups of five with the occasional number mixed in. None of it made any sense to me. "Codes? What do you think? She was running a numbers racket? She worked for a bookie?"

"Beats me."

We set that aside and I struck paydirt. A business card that read: "Gorgeous Girls. Why ask for any other?" And a phone number.

"Gorgeous Girls?" I handed the card to Lucy, who was trying to read over my shoulder. "You think she started her own talent booking agency? Gorgeous showgirls? Courtesy of Gorgeous Gelsey?"

"Ag, what experience did Wanda Ray have booking talent? She had a face, she had a body, and she had no problems showing the world. That's all we know."

But I was already rifling through the rest of the contents of the drawer. Another photograph, not of showgirls at work, but of three Lana Turner look-alikes in furs and low-cut dresses in what looked like an upscale cocktail lounge. Another of a man and a woman, taken at a distance and blurry. I was just as glad I couldn't see too clearly what was going on. Another woman, an exotic redhead this time, puckering up for the camera. Yet another of a couple undressing each other too close to a window. Both appeared to be men.

"Gorgeous Girls," I said. "Gorgeous Gelsey's Girls . . . and Guys? Gelsey was running a brothel?"

"Prostitution isn't legal in Las Vegas."

I didn't ask Lucy how she knew. "An escort service then?"

"Either she was running one, or she was participating," she agreed.

I looked down at the address book and back up at her. Lucy nodded. "Running," I said. "And I just bet if we play around with those numbers and letters long enough, we'll probably know the likes and dislikes of every john who walked through her door."

14

By the time Lucy and I had finished our Friday night treasure hunt, we had learned a lot about Gelsey Falowell a.k.a. "Wanda Ray Gelsey" a.k.a. "Gorgeous Gelsey" a.k.a. "Madam Gelsey" of Gorgeous Girls fame.

That last title hadn't really turned up anywhere, of course, but we had seen plenty of evidence that Gelsey had gone from strutting on stage to sending gorgeous girls strutting in strange hotel rooms. The coded book plus an old bankbook in Gelsey's name with substantial deposits and withdrawals strongly suggested she had been in charge, and the name of the service made us think she had been the founder, as well.

We had turned up letters, too, at least one that seemed to indicate Gelsey hadn't been above a little old-fashioned blackmail. The snapshots of couples embracing had suddenly taken on new meaning. When the circumstances were right, Gelsey caught her customers in compromising positions and documented those Hallmark moments.

But even at that, the most difficult items to view had been at the bottom of the drawer. A birth certificate for Baby Girl Gelsey on March 14, 1964, and below that, a snapshot of the baby in the hospital nursery. Jennifer Marina's defenseless little face scrunched up in sleep, her head covered in a pink knit hat, her fragile body wrapped tightly in a pink plaid blanket.

Even Lucy had blinked back a few tears.

We discovered a history, but the 8 mm movie had not turned up. Nor had any obvious reason for someone to murder either woman. I suspected that Gelsey's days as a blackmailer were long over. Many of her former clients were probably dead. Those still alive might actually cherish a reminder of their youthful "vitality." Surely that cash cow had turned into pot roast at least a decade ago.

I was thinking of all this the next morning at eleven as I filed in with two hundred other Emerald Springs citizens for Gelsey's memorial service. The Women's Society had prepared a lunch reception and decorated a table at the back of the sanctuary with framed photographs of Gelsey, an old letter from Brownie Kefauver thanking her for her work in the community, several others from charities she had assisted, and a guest book for mourners.

I wondered who would receive the book after the service. Bob Knowles, who was absent today and clearly would not mourn her passing? The owner of the doggie day care center in Boston where her mythical sister was supposed to reside? It seemed unbearably sad, somehow, that Gelsey's life had been built on so many lies that at the end, it had simply collapsed.

After giving the service a lot of thought, Ed had opted to say little. He had asked Sally, Yvonne, and Fern Booth to speak about Gelsey's life. Sally was careful not to mention facts that were now in question, but Yvonne and Fern, oblivious to the charade, repeated stories Gelsey had told of her childhood in Massachusetts. Other church members stood one by one to give readings or came forward to speak a few words. At the end, after our little choir sang "Turn, Turn, Turn"—a performance and choice Gelsey would have hated—Ed gave a benediction, and we filed out to the parish house for the reception.

I had no duties in the kitchen today. The Women's Society

has been organizing receptions for so long that a new pair of hands just confuses them. Instead, I moved from group to group, chatting and listening to stories about Gelsey and earlier years in the church. Several people questioned why no one from Gelsey's family had come. Apparently, I am surrounded by detectives in training.

After ten minutes I was cornered by Fern and Samuel Booth. Rotund Samuel had a plate heaped with some of everything from the serving table. He seemed especially fond of cheese. Fern, a square-faced woman with a graying Prince Valiant haircut, had no plate at all. Fern strikes me as someone with little time to eat. I have never encountered her when she isn't too busy passing judgment on somebody to take time for herself. Even her scowl is permanent, as if she hopes this might save time in her race to condemn.

"We'd like to know your husband's plans," Fern said, getting straight to the point.

"Well, this afternoon we're going to the dedication of the new service center. Then I think Ed's planning a nap."

"Fern means long range," Samuel said, as if I really needed clarification.

"Ed would like to retire to Maine. I'm more inclined toward someplace in the Caribbean. It depends on where the girls are living."

"Are you purposely trying to misunderstand?" Fern demanded.

I took a deep breath. "Are you purposely trying to communicate with my husband through me?"

They both looked aghast.

I decided to be even more direct. "Because the best way to find out what Ed is planning is to ask Ed."

I started to leave, but Samuel took my arm. "We're just worried about the church."

"Gelsey was worried, too," Fern said. "God rest her soul, she disliked your husband from the first moment he appeared."

I couldn't answer. I was too busy swallowing every additional word that tried to force its way between my lips. But Sam was shaking his head. "You know, Fern, that's not true.

Gelsey voted to bring Ed Wilcox here, and at first she was as enthusiastic as I've ever seen her. She thought he was a man of intellect and wisdom. She said it was a miracle he would agree to come to a little church like this one."

I opened my mouth and luckily only a question emerged. "Why did she change her mind?"

Fern was glaring at her husband, but Samuel shrugged. "I don't know. She seemed to change from one day to the next. But don't make the mistake of believing she had it in for him from the beginning. Gelsey wasn't like that. She was fair. He must have done something."

"When did she change her mind? Do you know? After the first sermon? The first board meeting? When she realized he wouldn't do everything she wanted?"

He shook his head. "A month, maybe two after you arrived."

I tried to think back. That meant last year about this time. We had arrived just at the end of summer. So what had gone wrong?

"I don't see why any of that matters," Fern said. "The point is that this church has not been the same since your husband arrived."

"I'll second that," I agreed. "It's been more interesting, more dynamic, and better attended. Of course you might not know that, since you so seldom come yourselves."

Yvonne McAllister seemed to sense the brewing storm. She wound her way through the guests, grabbed my arm, gave a huge smile to the Booths, and steered me to a corner. "I don't care what the Booths said to you, Aggie. It's not true, and it doesn't matter."

I let out one long breath through flared nostrils. "Fern has hoisted herself into Gelsey's place as Ed's biggest detractor."

"She won't stay long. Gelsey's shoes will be hard to fill."

"Do you have any idea what set Gelsey off? Samuel said she was one of Ed's biggest fans until we'd been here a month or two."

Yvonne shook her head. She kept shaking it until I had to look away to avoid getting dizzy. "I just don't know. But they're right. That's about the time she changed. At first she didn't have enough good things to say. I remember being so surprised when she started complaining. He'd give a wonderful sermon and she'd pick it apart. He would make great suggestions at committee meetings and she would do whatever she could to see they weren't implemented. It was like she had a vendetta against the poor man."

"Yes, well . . ."

"The first time I noticed was after one of the Women's Society meetings," Yvonne continued. "It was the oddest thing. Gelsey went into the meeting as a supporter and out a detractor. And poor Ed was hardly even there. It was the first meeting of the season. He opened with a prayer, did a little talk about a sermon series he was planning, made a suggestion or two about what he'd like to see us do for the church, but not until he was asked, of course."

I remembered the meeting now. I had attended so the women could get to know me better. The staff had been present for this welcome, and we were all treated to lunch afterwards. I'd even given a short presentation about my interest in the archives. I laughed about some of their parties and picnics and said when everything was put to rights we'd have a film fest and charge admission.

By now Yvonne had finally stopped shaking her head. "Maybe it was Ed's suggestion that we use some of the proceeds from our bazaar to start a Friday night soup kitchen. Gelsey was old-fashioned in that way, you know. She believed people should pull themselves up by their bootstraps."

Gelsey certainly had given her own a good yank, although I doubted that *her* way was one we ought to recommend to any woman needing help in our little burg.

I wished, once again, I could remember details from the missing movie. "Yvonne, is there any chance I was the one Gelsey disliked, not my husband? Did I do something so despicable that she wanted both of us out of here?"

Yvonne looked dismayed. "Oh, dear, I just—"

"I'm not going to be hurt."

"Well, she didn't have good things to say, I'm afraid. But her complaints were odd, like she was manufacturing them out of nothing. It was rather unlike her, actually. Gelsey was more than able to find real reasons to dislike anyone."

"Did anything in particular bother her?"

"Your frankness, I believe. You do have a way of going straight to the heart of every matter. An admirable trait, I think, but she claimed it was inappropriate for a minister's wife."

I had seen Jack earlier at the service; now he came over to join his mom and me. He looked like a successful young lawyer on casual Friday. Jacket, no tie, khakis with the requisite crease. He took my hand and kissed my cheek.

"I hear you've had a little excitement in your life," he said.

"A murder here, a murder there."

"I was thinking about the protests at Book Gems."

"Those? I think the good citizens of Ohio are just trying to make me feel at home."

"Bob is incensed. I've had to remind him this is a death penalty state."

"You must know him pretty well to make any kind of suggestion."

"We do his legal work."

Yvonne was clearly proud of her son. "Jack's being modest. Bob asked for him specifically."

"I bet he's high maintenance," I said.

Jack looked like he had stories to tell, but couldn't. We chatted a few minutes until he was called away.

"Bob *is* a nuisance, although of course Jack would never say so," Yvonne said. "But I know he's in Jack's office making one demand or another a couple of times a week."

I wasn't surprised. My boss had a lot to protect, or so it seemed. Now he had a whole lot more.

Protecting assets reminded me of something I'd been meaning to ask Yvonne. "You know, I heard that you have a key to the house across from ours."

Yvonne made a face. "Had a key. I gave it back to the owners after I found out Jennifer Marina might have been murdered there."

"You were checking on the house?"

"The Gilligans travel a lot, and it was no trouble for me to pop in when I was over at the church. If I couldn't do it, Jack did it for me."

"Jack, huh?"

"I had an extra key made so he could go directly from work if need be. We were called a couple of times to check out plumbing repairs that had been done while they were out of town."

I remembered Lucy saying that the owners were neighbors of Yvonne's brother and only acquaintances of hers. Even for Yvonne this was extraordinarily conscientious. "That seems like a lot of work for you both."

"Oh, since I live so close I didn't mind. And when my brother was ill last year, both Gilligans were over there every day with homemade soup or books from the library. We take care of each other in Emerald Springs. That's why it's so terrible to have murderers in our midst." She sniffed and searched her purse for a tissue. "Poor Gelsey."

I gave her a moment to pull herself together and patted her shoulder.

"I'm sorry," she said, once she was under control again.

"You and Jack are good, generous people. I hope the Gilligans understood when you had to give back the keys."

"Key. Just one. Jack lost his somewhere along the way. We never got around to replacing it."

"Oh . . ." I tried to sound nonchalant. "I bet Jack dropped it somewhere. I'm always losing keys." It wasn't exactly a lie. Surely I had lost a couple in my thirty-five years?

"No, he kept the key in a tray by his telephone at the office. He's sure it got mixed in with his junk mail one morning and tossed."

"Well, a key's just a key. Who would know what door it opened, even if they found it in the garbage?"

"It had a tag. But who would steal a key off Jack's desk?"

This was a question I hoped to answer very soon.

✦   ✦   ✦

The girls had spent the morning in Stephanie's care. I arrived home to find them on the living room rug at the tail end of a Monopoly game. Deena had the most monopolies, but

Teddy had hotels on Park Place and Boardwalk. Stephanie was a few bills short of bankrupt.

"Six-year-olds aren't supposed to be this good!" Stephanie stood and shook life back into her extremities. "Send her to tutor Donald Trump."

"Here's some of the real stuff. Invest it. Teddy will give you tips." I paid her and sent her away to nurse her wounds.

I turned back to my daughters. "Did you eat lunch?"

The girls were too immersed in skinning each other to do more than nod.

Ed arrived ten minutes later, looking tired and pale. I sat him at the table and made hot tea with lots of milk and sugar. "A tough one," I said. "But you got through it."

"I've decided to pre-candidate at Third Church next weekend. One of the local ministers has appendicitis, so there's an opening for a speaker, and I have that weekend off. The search committee wants to take advantage of it. Unless you have some strong objections."

I sat across from him. Truth was, I would follow him to the middle of the Mojave if I had to, but I was never going to tell him.

I tempered my response. "I like Boston. We'll find a community there. We still have friends in the area."

"But you don't want to leave Emerald Springs, do you?"

What could I say? That after all my jibes and complaints I was actually beginning to feel at home here? That I thought this might be a good place to raise our daughters? That eventually, when the storm passed us by, this might be a very good life?

Instead, I told a different piece of the truth. "I don't want to stay if you're under fire here."

"At a certain point it becomes counterproductive for everybody."

I covered his hand. "We could skip the dedication this afternoon."

"I'm doing the opening prayer. But you don't have to come."

"The girls want to play on the new playground. Hopefully it will be short?"

"Senator Carlisle is speaking."

I groaned. "Call down God's wrath on his head when you have the chance."

"I hope you're kidding."

"Marginally."

By two, Teddy had taken everything Deena had worked so hard for on the Monopoly board and Deena had vowed revenge. I was glad they hadn't yet learned to play Risk. World dominance was more than their relationship could stand.

We drove to the new service center in my van. The city had owned this twelve-acre plot at its outskirts for at least ten years, but there had never been enough money to develop it. Then two consecutive years of crippling winter storms and the absence of well-maintained equipment to deal with them had changed the minds of voters. A levy had passed, and ground had been broken. Now we had an expansive garage to house and service our snowplows, pickups, and leaf blowers, and our very own storage dome.

The Emerald Springs powers-that-be had taken the levy as a mandate and expanded the facility so it would also house the jail and police department. One acre had been set aside for a playground and jogging track with exercise stations, to be joined by a swimming pool and small recreation center, if the voters ponied up again in the future.

The expansion, of course, had come with a price, and apparently this was where Frank Carlisle had come into the picture. My theory was that someone, perhaps our esteemed mayor, had convinced the senator that his help procuring state money for the project would be looked on favorably by local voters. Since Carlisle only won his last election by a nose and was not the favored candidate in Emerald Springs, I suspect the promise of support was too good to refuse.

I told myself leaving Frank Carlisle and Brownie Kefauver behind was one good reason to move. If we didn't move, I predicted many dedicated hours of struggling to get one or both men voted out of office.

I considered staying at the playground so I would miss the entertainment, but in the end, it was clear the girls would stage a rebellion if I stood on the sidelines. I put Deena in charge of her capitalist sister and found a place on the bottom row of metal bleachers that had been installed for the occasion.

Ed's prayer was masterful. He asked that the acres be used for the good of all citizens and that all who served those citizens be strong, courageous, compassionate, and honest in their dealings. Unless there was a sudden change of heart, that left out some of the town council, the mayor, and senator. I hope they noticed.

The rest of the afternoon was not so much fun. I had hoped for quick. I got an hour of speeches. At one point, I slipped out to check on the girls, and when I returned Frank Carlisle was still regaling his slumbering captives with stories of his glory days in the legislature. I suspected a filibuster.

The ceremony ended at last. Carlisle was whisked to the sidelines by his bodyguards, Brownie cut the first slice of a Lake Erie-sized cake, and I spotted Roussos at the edge of the crowd.

Since Ed was tied up talking to several council members, I made a beeline for the detective. I was stopped in my tracks by Harry Grey.

Our church secretary looked particularly dapper today in Calvin Klein country wear. "Ed did a good job on that prayer," he told me.

"What on earth are you doing here?"

"Greg's the architect. Didn't you know? He made me come. Besides, know thine enemy." He nodded toward Carlisle, who actually appeared to be autographing programs.

"I can't believe you submitted to this torture willingly."

"Among other things, he's the biggest homophobe in our Senate."

That did not surprise me. "Maybe we can get rid of him next time around." I almost winced at my own "we."

"The Democrats are scouring the district for a candidate for his seat. And there's already money for a good campaign." His eyes flicked back to Carlisle.

"I guess people feel passionately for or against."

"You know Gelsey Falowell contributed generously to the party?"

"Really? I heard she was big on making people work for every single penny."

"Well, maybe. But she was also big on the environment, on civil rights, on education. She gave every penny she legally could during the last election. She even went door-to-door."

The woman was a mystery to me in every way. Just when I thought I knew how I should feel about her, I was given more evidence to consider.

When I left, Harry was heading for Carlisle to get his program signed, and maybe to engage in a little unfriendly debate.

I caught up with Roussos just as he said good-bye to a small group of cops in uniform and started away from the gathering. He did not look pleased to see me.

I had been debating exactly how much of what I had learned last night to share with him. I knew that Ed had finally divulged the connection between Jennifer and Gelsey. Roussos had not told my husband he was off the suspect list, but Ed felt the information had made a difference.

"Mrs. Wilcox."

"Detective. Just the man I need to see." My breath always seems to clench somewhere between my diaphragm and throat when I talk to Roussos. I've known a lot of charismatic men, but this one's particular combination of, well, everything, sparks a hormonal overload. Having a husband I'm crazy about doesn't seem to shut down the flow, although it helps enough to keep me from babbling uncontrollably.

"Don't tell me. You're on the trail of the murderer, and you need my help." It wasn't said with complete disregard for my feelings. There was a small smile that went with it.

"Well, I have some information you'll be interested in, but maybe I'll pass it on to somebody with better manners. How do I make an appointment with your captain?"

"You try it and we'll put your picture up at the station."

"You try that and I'll come after you for harassment."

His smile broadened a millimeter. I had the oddest feeling he actually approved of me.

I seized the moment. "I know Ed told you Jennifer was Gelsey's daughter."

He didn't respond.

"And that the night he found her body he was there to tell Gelsey who Jennifer was."

"That's what he says."

"Well, it's true. He and I discussed it that evening before he went over to the church. He wasn't sure what to do. He didn't want to tell her the truth if it was going to destroy her life. But in the end, there were two factors. First, that someone had killed Jennifer and left her body where Gelsey would see it that morning. And second, that Gelsey had grandchildren she might want to help in some way."

"Your husband told me this already."

"He had no reason to kill her. The bequest wasn't for Ed, for Pete's sake. It was for the church. What does it matter if she left the money to the endowment fund or she didn't? There's no way Ed could get his hands on it."

"Do you know that one of your members came forward and confided that not long before she died, Mrs. Falowell said she was afraid of Ed?"

I stared at him. This just got worse and worse.

He shrugged.

"That's plain preposterous," I said at last. "If she was afraid of him, it was just because Ed wouldn't do what she wanted. She couldn't control him, and that probably scared her to death, considering what we now know about her."

"Maybe . . ."

"This is a man who thinks swatting flies is a moral dilemma. And he doesn't own a gun and never has. Nobody is afraid of Ed. And where is this weapon he supposedly used? What did he do, rent one and return it by midnight so he'd get his deposit back?"

"Just so you know, I really don't think your husband murdered anybody."

"Oh?"

"I just have to cover all my bases."

I took a moment to calm down. When I spoke it was in a lower voice. "Then I have one more for you to cover."

"That would be?"

"The fact that Bob Knowles is going to inherit the entire estate except for the amount Gelsey left to the church."

"That's one of the first things we checked."

"Do you also know that Bob's in financial turmoil? He told me the market played havoc with his investments and for a variety of reasons the store is costing more than he'd expected. He needed an infusion of cash and fast. Gelsey's death equals infusion."

This seemed to interest him a little. "He told you that?"

"I work at his store."

"Remind *me* not to hire you." His eyes flicked to the crowd in dismissal. "We'll look into that."

"Do you know anything about Gelsey's background?"

"I know the family in Massachusetts is a fake. Lots of people invent better identities for themselves."

I didn't think he was as nonchalant as he was pretending. Lots of people didn't get murdered.

I sweetened the pot. "I could tell you who she was and what she did for a living before she moved here. But maybe you'd rather just figure this out by yourself."

"When that dimple starts twitching, Mrs. Wilcox, I know you're trying to get my goat."

So okay, I have a poor excuse for a dimple in one cheek, and it tends to give away a lot. Now I was afraid it was doing the shimmy.

I subdued it and narrowed my eyes. "Listen, I am not Nancy Drew. I'm tired of going to bed at night wondering exactly who's going to end up dead tomorrow and where. So if you'll let me tell you what I know, I'll be on my way. Maybe it will help me sleep a little better."

"Never let it be said I added to your insomnia."

"She was a madam in Las Vegas." I watched his expression change. I definitely had his attention. In a minute's time I filled him in on what Lucy and I had uncovered and promised to bring him the documents.

That was just about long enough for Ed to find us. I lowered my voice when I saw him striding toward me. "I haven't told anybody, not even Ed," I said. "You'll keep it as confidential as you can?"

His expression warmed. For a moment he looked more the man, less the Greek God. "Keep your head down and stop snooping, okay? Somebody's killing women in Emerald Springs. I'd like that dimple to keep twitching."

15

Fall in Ohio seems to be a well-kept secret. Last year I discovered that the change of seasons is a lot like those I remember in New England, and gawker accidents a lot less common. Emerald Springs is proud of its fine old trees, and by the weekend after Gelsey's memorial service, they were beginning to show their colors in earnest. We would view an unfolding pageant for the rest of October and perhaps a week or two beyond.

Early Friday morning Ed left for Boston. Thursday night I realized he did not seem enthusiastic about the trip. I donned a teddy and boxers that even Crystal would blacklist and did everything I could to raise his spirits.

Clearly I had to tell the children something about their dad's absence. By the time Deena came down for breakfast, I was ready.

"Daddy said to tell you good-bye. He's spending the weekend in Boston. There's a church that wants to hear him preach."

Deena was no fool. She was old enough the last time we moved to see how the process worked. "Is he going to change churches again?"

I was casual, friendly, and, unfortunately, transparent. "Nobody's made any decisions. He's gathering information, and this is not something you should tell anyone else."

"I'm not going."

I set whole-grain pancakes in front of her and envisioned myself turning at the edge of town and waving good-bye to my daughter at the year's end. "Oh?"

"I'm tired of you making decisions for me. You do it all the time."

"It's called being a mom."

"Well, I like it here, and I'm going to stay. I have friends. Miss Barstow lets me ride whenever I want. Somebody will take me in."

I put maple syrup on the table with a slight thunk. "I'd advise against that tone when you ask."

"And while we're at it, I think this dress code you and the other moms came up with is really stupid."

"It took more negotiation than a Mideast peace agreement."

"You shouldn't be deciding what we can wear. That's up to us."

"Deena, there's nothing in your closet on that list. Your clothes are fine."

"It's the principle! You're telling us what to do. Clothing is personal. It makes a statement."

This sounded rehearsed. I wondered how many Meanie moms and daughters were having identical discussions over breakfast. Crystal would need more highlights, a manicure, and an hour in a sensory deprivation tank to recover. Of course she'd probably have to drive to California to find a tank.

Internally I chanted my mantra. "Sometimes making a statement isn't a good thing. The other moms and I want to make sure nobody misunderstands what you're saying. When you and your friends are older, you'll be able to face the consequences a little better."

"Gosh mom . . ." She rolled her eyes. "Just think, if we move to Boston you'll have to make a new set of friends and a new set of rules. What a waste of time."

The mantra faded into white noise. I plopped into the seat across from her. "You and I have a lot of arguments ahead. So let's get the rules straight right now. We will respect each other, and we won't use sarcasm. We'll keep our voices down. We'll remember we're on the same side, even though it may not always seem like it."

"What side is that?"

"The side that wants you to grow up to be happy, well-adjusted, and able to make all your decisions without me one day."

"One day? What day?"

"That depends on you." I got up to make another pot of coffee. Clearly, I was going to need it.

"I know one rule I want."

"Uh huh?"

"I want you to listen to me."

"I plan to listen. I expect to learn a lot from you."

"You're just so reasonable."

I didn't remind her of the rule against sarcasm. I'd fight that battle with more energy another day. I would fortify myself. I was going to take up weight lifting. Surely Emerald Springs has a gym.

Deena was gone by the time Teddy stood at the front door buttoning a bright red sweater Junie had crocheted for her. "Jimmy still won't play with me."

I had wondered how the saga of Jimmy Betts, boy bigot, was unfolding, but I hadn't wanted to give it undue attention.

"Won't he?" I unbuttoned the cat-shaped button at the top, which was in the wrong hole, and lined it up correctly. Junie had used Moonpie as a model and sculpted the buttons herself.

Teddy took over, brushing my hands away. "Nobody listens to him anymore. I showed them how to balance on the top of the jungle gym without holding on, and now everybody wants to be my friend."

I wasn't sure which was worse, ostracism or broken bones. "Be careful on the jungle gym, sweetie. That's a long, hard fall."

"I feel sorry for Jimmy. He looks sad."

I gave her a big hug. "It's nice of you to worry about him."

"I worry about everybody."

I hugged her again, then forced myself to watch her go. I'm afraid my Teddy is a minister in training. I wonder if it's too early for an intervention.

With the girls gone I got ready for work. Last Friday the only protestor at the bookstore had barely lasted an hour. At the end of her shift she had consumed the coffee I took to her, cheerfully discussed whether the Emerald High Wizards would win their homecoming game, and left for home.

Today when I arrived, there was no one on the sidewalk. Inside, Bob was alone, but whistling. He looked more relaxed and a lot happier than I had ever seen him. I suspect inheriting a fortune does that to a person.

"I ordered every book on your wish list," he said without introduction. "Our shelves are going to be packed solid. I'm going to start staying open late on Friday and Saturday nights and scheduling entertainment. I'll be expanding the menu to include muffins and scones, and bringing in well-known authors for book signings."

I could live without this job so I blundered ahead. "Finances improved, huh?"

"You could say that."

"I heard you're the Falowell heir. News travels fast."

He didn't look surprised. "I waited a long time for that money."

Maybe not long enough.

He must have noted my expression, because his smile faltered. "It was a tough way to come into it," he said.

"Certainly tough for Gelsey."

"She was an awful woman. I'd like to tell you I'm sorry, but I'm not. She could have loosened up the purse strings and let me have enough from the estate to get things going month ago, but she refused. Said if I was starving she wouldn't feed me the crumbs from her plate."

Unfortunately I could almost hear Gelsey saying it. And where had a similar sentiment gotten Marie Antoinette?

"She hated me," he said.

"All that hostility because it wasn't her money free and clear?"

"You seem to know a lot."

"I seem to need to."

Bob felt in his pocket for his cigarettes, pulled one out, but didn't light it. There was a no smoking policy in the store. He spent a lot of time in the alley.

"I've never been sure why dear Aunt Gelsey had such a big problem with me. I was grown by the time she joined the family. She was a lot younger than my uncle, and I think he wanted kids, but she never produced. Considering her warm, generous nature, it's a good thing she never had kids of her own."

Just as well for Bob, since he was now the heir. I debated, then plowed ahead, watching him closely for a reaction. "Maybe she did."

"Don't you think I'd know?" He tapped the cigarette against his palm, hard, like he was stubbing it out.

"I don't mean with your uncle," I said. "I mean before."

"She wasn't married until she met Uncle Herb."

"So?"

"What are you trying to tell me, Aggie?"

"There's a rumor that before she married your uncle she had a child she gave up for adoption."

Either he was a terrific actor, or he was clearly blown away. "How come I never heard it, then? Me, of all people?"

"It's just coming to light."

"So where's this kid?" He paused. "I guess not much of a kid by now, huh?"

"She's dead."

"Double whammy?" He shook his head. "Maybe that explains something, but I don't know what. Except that my uncle married a woman with secrets, and one who didn't have a maternal bone in her body."

"If the daughter was still living she could have caused you some problems."

He seemed perplexed. "Like what?"

"Sharing the inheritance?"

He gave a humorless laugh. "No problem there. The will

is ironclad. That's what made me so angry. There was no way anybody could touch that money except me, but my aunt still wouldn't let me have a penny before she died. She couldn't spend it, but she didn't want me to. Not even for a bookstore the town really needs."

I could see why he had disliked Gelsey so much, but I wondered what he *wasn't* saying. Maybe she had refused to help him, just to keep the upper hand. But maybe she had refused for darker reasons.

Bob was watching me, and I guess my thoughts were more or less clear.

"Hey, I was with friends in Wooster the night my aunt was killed." Bob was scowling now. "Don't start thinking I killed her for the money. My hands are clean. I sure didn't like the woman, but I never hoped she'd die that way."

I wondered. Jack had kept his key to the infamous "murder" house on the desk at his office. Bob was *at* that same office, sitting across the same desk where the key was kept, several times a week. The key mysteriously disappeared. Figure the probabilities.

I went off to shelve books. I hope Bob's ideas to improve the store work and soon, because another day passed with only a few customers. By the time I left, I had resorted to pulling books from the shelves and dusting behind them, just for something to pass the time.

Since Ed was out of town, the girls had gone home from school with the Frankels for a sleepover. At six I was expected to join the crowd for May's superior homemade pizza, but I was so tired from doing nothing that I needed an energy boost before I faced them. I decided to walk home the long way.

Downtown Emerald Springs quietly puts itself to bed about five. Shop bells stop tinkling and Open signs are flipped. The coffee pot at Lana's Lunch is emptied and washed; the post office parking lot is blocked off with fluorescent orange sawhorses. Tellers at First Agricultural and Buckeye State Savings take off for less orderly worlds. Ahmed Bahram—who's taught Ed more about Islam than three courses at Harvard Divinity—sweeps and locks his tiny corner deli with its excellent gyros and falafel and mandatory kielbasa.

Maybe Baskin-Robbins and Joe's Spaghetti House are just beginning to yawn and stretch for the weekend on-slaught, but they're the exception here. Most of our booming restaurants are on the outskirts of town, along with our chain stores and motels.

Tonight I didn't feel like watching Emerald Springs fold up for the night. The setting sun cast a rosy glow, and the air was pleasantly tinged with wood smoke. I followed my nose to the residential area just south of the parsonage and took my time weaving in and out of streets, admiring the late fall gardens that would soon make way for the first snow of the season.

Once this was the nicest part of town, where the old Emer-ald Springs families passed down substantial homes on ex-pansive lots. Many of the houses are still beautiful and well cared for; some have been divided into apartments, and the lawns are strewn with tricycles and basketballs. Every fifth house or so has been demolished and two have been squeezed onto the lot, but it's still a pretty neighborhood, worth enjoy-ing for the architectural furbelows of another day.

Actually, I had chosen this particular scenic walk for an-other reason. Brownie Kefauver lived here, in a house that has graced this street for well over a century. Brownie and his wife Hazel have no children, but the house, a brick Colo-nial with paired end chimneys and arched dormer windows, could easily hold half a dozen. Regal and gracious, it stands at the end of a long drive bordered by gigantic poplars.

Today bronze-colored spider mums and flowering kale accented beautifully trimmed evergreens along the front of the house. I stopped to enjoy the effect and figure out whether I had the courage to follow the herringbone brick path to the front door. I wanted to ask Brownie how he had lost his key to the house across from mine. Asking Yvonne had been easy enough, but I wasn't sure Brownie could even pick me out of a lineup. Why would he tell me when I was nearly a stranger?

I was trying to figure out logistics when something caught

my eye. At the far corner of the house, in a grove of river birch trees, stood a birdhouse mounted on a solitary post. Even from a distance I could see that the tiny house strongly resembled Brownie's historic Colonial.

"Keely." I walked a little farther to get a better view from the other side of the grove. "Keely, I'll be darned." I wondered how Keely had gotten this commission.

The front door opened and Brownie stepped outside. He was dressed in a green jogging suit with racing stripes up the sleeves and legs, and shoes so white I was certain this was their inaugural jog. He put a foot against the brick wall beside his door and unsuccessfully tried to touch his head to his knee.

The opportunity was too good. I walked up the drive, my hand raised in greeting. "Mayor Kefauver . . ."

He looked up. For a moment I was afraid his foot was permanently attached to the brick, because he couldn't seem to bring it back to the ground. He solved the problem by taking the leg in his hands and shaking it loose.

"Aggie Sloan-Wilcox," I said, putting out my hand. "Ed Wilcox's wife."

"Yes, I know," he said, pumping my hand. "I'm just setting off for a jog. Stress, you know. Too much of it in my job. I have to cope some way."

I've heard that Hazel Kefauver is the real cause of her husband's stress. Jack Spratt and his wife have nothing on the Kefauvers. Hazel is twice her husband's size, a wide, muscular woman who could give Sax Dubinsky a hernia on Mudwrestling Mondays. She has a booming voice and as much hair on her forearms as her head. From gossip I know the house has been in Hazel's family for four generations. I also know it was Hazel's idea that her husband run for mayor when it became clear he couldn't do anything else successfully.

I decided to slide tactfully into my questions about the key. "I love the birdhouse," I said, nodding in that direction. "I thought I'd see if you could tell me where you bought it?"

Brownie turned bright red. Now, I've heard this phrase before and thought I knew what it meant. But I have never,

never seen anything quite like this. The poor guy's complexion went from milk toast to chili pepper in the space of seconds.

"Yes, well . . ." He swallowed.

Fascinated, I simply waited and smiled expectantly.

"Yes, well," he said again.

"Is that the name of a shop?"

"No, I . . ." He swallowed once more. "No, I . . ."

I knew better than to pretend "No-I" was his second choice. "It's just so cute," I said, hoping he'd recover as I babbled. "We live in a parsonage, but it would be nice to have one made, wouldn't it? So we could take a little piece of our history with us when we leave?"

Not that I thought there'd really be enough time to buy a birdhouse and pack it before we did.

"I . . . I got it from a young lady in town who makes them herself."

"How on earth did you find her? Such a clever idea."

He unzipped his jacket as if he needed air. Underneath I glimpsed an undershirt fresh from a Fruit of the Loom package.

He wiped his brow with the back of his hand. "She more or less found me. She showed me a sample, and I, well, I thought about it and decided it would be a perfect birthday present for my wife. The details were so lovely and delicate, I knew they would appeal to Hazel."

Hazel is as delicate as Godzilla. Brownie was trying to pull a wooly mammoth over my eyes. From the color of his cheeks and the panic in his eyes, I suspected that Brownie hadn't been thinking about *Hazel* at all. And his interest in Keely, who just happened to have worked side by side with Jennifer, intrigued me.

"I don't suppose she has an address, or phone number?"

"She . . . she lives in Weezeltown. Her name's Kelly or Keely. I'm afraid that's all I can remember."

I didn't ask more since I knew exactly where I could find Keely tonight. I nodded my thanks. "By the way," I said, "I heard the strangest thing. You know the house on Church Street where they think Jennifer Marina was killed?"

He was milk toast again in a second. It was like watching some exotic variety of chameleon. And he wasn't finished. He was growing paler. "I've heard that story," he said. "There's no proof, is there?"

"Not really. But I'm trying to help a realtor friend of mine track down all the keys. And for some reason she thinks *you* had one. Is that just a silly rumor?"

"Why doesn't she simply change the locks?"

I'd been ready for this. "That's the plan. But it's a bit complicated. Old door, state-of-the-art hardware. The locksmith has ordered new parts." The parts about the door's condition and hardware were true enough, so the lie didn't nag too loudly.

"I had a key," he admitted. "I lost it somewhere. I'm sure it had nothing to do with that poor girl's murder."

I hadn't suggested it might, but of course I wasn't surprised he had made the connection. "Do you remember when you lost it?"

"I can't see how that would help you."

"Well, you're probably right. I'm sure you've told the police about this, right? They know the details."

"It's time for my run now, Mrs. Wilcox."

"Oh, just call me Aggie. Even Detective Roussos calls me Aggie. Every single time we discuss the case."

He was now vanilla ice cream. "I lost the key sometime in July, after my brother moved out. I am sure it fell out of my pocket, or it's in my house somewhere in an old pair of pants. Now I really must get going."

Judging from today's ensemble and his usual sartorial splendor, I doubted Hazel allowed such a thing as an old pair of pants in this house. But I smiled.

"Thanks for chatting with me." I started down the path, expecting Brownie to jog past me. But I was halfway down the block before I saw him leave his property.

In the other direction.

+   +   +

Lucy was out of town for the weekend, and May had the girls at her house. So after pizza, I left for Don't Go There by myself. I had agonized over what to wear. Not my Green Meanie mom duds, not my minister's partner duds—which weren't all that different—nothing even faintly provocative. I settled on dark pants, which wouldn't show blood, vomit, or spilled alcohol, and a gray turtleneck sweater I could toss in the washer if necessary. I was ready to roll.

I was beginning to feel at home in the bar's parking lot, the scariest thought of any day. I parked between a pickup and a Ford Expedition so I wasn't particularly visible. Mine may be the only minivan ever to grace the lot.

No one had fixed the sign and the usual "Dons" were hanging out where the Harleys held sway. Since I was now something of a regular, they hooted at me as I walked past. I nodded regally and swept inside.

The entertainment hadn't started, for which I was profoundly grateful. A female vocalist was belting out "Take Me as I Am" on the jukebox. I thought a plea for better understanding of the fair sex might be lost on this crowd.

The exhaust fans were working overtime, but the room was already smoky. Through the haze I noted no familiar faces. Sax wasn't at the bar, and if Keely was in attendance, she'd gone outside to breathe between rounds.

The new guy tending bar was short, completely bald with an unfortunate pointed head. He had gold hoops in both earlobes and a stud in each nostril. As I watched, one of his customers, a big guy in a blue work shirt, apparently said something he didn't like. Before I could blink, the bartender leaned over, grabbed the guy by the front of his shirt, and yanked him halfway across the bar. The room went silent. Even the song ended. I backed toward the door.

"Sorry, man," Work Shirt said.

The bartender deposited him back on his chair and went to fill another order.

The buzz began again, and Willie Nelson, singing about mamas and cowboys, filled in all the cracks.

I had to stop coming here.

I waited until the bartender had filled his order, then went to the bar. "Hi," I said brightly. "I'm looking for Keely. Is she here tonight?"

"Quit. What do you want?"

To humor him I ordered a beer I wouldn't drink and waited until he brought it to me. "I really need to find her. I'm interested in one of her birdhouses. I know she lives around here . . ."

He sized me up, and I guess he decided I looked more Junior League than serial killer. "End of Mill Street. Blue house on the right. Her apartment's on the top floor. But she's leaving town."

He was so much nicer than Sax, almost cuddly. I paid him, tipped him generously so he wouldn't grab me by my sweater, and left the beer on the counter. Work Shirt was drinking it when I left.

I pulled out of the lot without incident and started down Mill. Weezeltown is nobody's inner city, but I wondered if Keely was leaving our fair village because living on this end had creeped her out. Streetlights in Weezeltown are few and far between. The button factory, a substantial brick building, is boarded shut, and a layer of razor wire has been added to the tall chain-link fence that surrounds it. Tonight mongrel dogs wandered the sidewalks, and only a few citizens had braved their front porches to enjoy the evening air.

I cruised Mill for four blocks before the street whimpered and died. Trash strewn, treeless acres rose up before me. There hadn't been any warning, as if everyone but moi knew Mill ended here. I spotted a blue house on the right, not the last but the next to the last, and figured it had to be the one.

There were two scrawny border collies sleeping under the old Chevy hoisted on concrete blocks in the front yard. Luckily they were conserving their strength, and neither seemed to notice as I parked and went around the side where a wooden fire escape led to the apartment upstairs. The mailbox just to the right of it read "K. Henley." Of course Keely has a last name. She isn't Cher or Madonna. I've just never thought about it.

I took the fire escape rather than see if there was a more traditional entrance. I wasn't sure how long the dogs would play dead, and I wasn't anxious for them to start earning their keep.

I rapped on the glass window at the top of the door. My view was obscured by ruffled curtains, but there was a light inside. I was hopeful.

"Keely? It's Aggie Sloan-Wilcox. We talked at Jennifer's funeral?"

The door opened so quickly I stumbled against it. Before I could right myself someone jerked me inside.

Keely, in a tight scoop neck T-shirt and sprayed-on jeans, slammed the door behind us and bolted it shut.

"I thought it was him!" She squeezed her eyes closed. "Nobody ever comes up here."

"Him?"

She was struggling to pull herself together. I was fascinated—and just a teeny bit concerned. She opened her eyes. "Why'd you come here? How'd you know where to find me?"

"The bald guy at Don't Go There."

"Ferret."

"Tell me his mother was kinder than that."

"His real name's Ferris, or something. Farrell. I dunno. We call him Ferret."

"I think I scared you." I touched her arm. "Keely, are you okay?"

"I . . . I'm moving, that's all. Getting out of here. I just . . . didn't expect nobody at the door, you know?"

"Do you have any tea? Let me make you a hot cup of tea."

She looked confused.

"It'll help," I said. "You go sit down. Where will I find it?"

"There might be some in the cupboard."

The apartment was small, a living room with cracked linoleum covered by a rust-colored area rug, which in turn was covered with cat hair. There was a bedroom just beyond and a kitchen nook to the left of the door. Keely had no kettle, but I warmed water in a saucepan and found an ancient box of Tetley in the cupboard to the right of the stove. I opened it and took out bags for both of us. She couldn't evict me if we were having tea together.

Keely was calmer by the time the tea steeped. She took hers sweet. I didn't trust the milk in her fridge, so I took mine plain.

I let her sip for a while before I started in. "So . . . You're leaving? Someplace special?"

She shook her head. One firm shake.

"Then why go? Don't you like it here?"

"Not anymore."

A huge white cat strolled out of her bedroom. The cat hair was no longer a mystery. The cat jumped up on her lap, and Keely rubbed her face against its fur. As if she needed comfort.

"Something must have happened," I said matter-of-factly. "Would you like to talk about it?"

One more firm shake of her head. Her face was still buried, and cat hair flew.

"Well, your name came up in a conversation today."

She looked up. "Why?"

"I saw one of your birdhouses. At the mayor's house."

She stared blankly at me.

"Browning Kefauver? Brownie?"

"Brownie? Brownie's the mayor?"

I wondered if Weezeltown existed in an alternate dimension. Was I slipping through some sort of time–space continuum every time I made the trip?

"I don't believe it," she said, as I pondered the universe.

"Well, it's true. He is definitely our mayor. He never told you?"

"We didn't talk a lot. At first he wanted a birdhouse. Then he wanted more, or leastwise, I suspicioned he did. He's a shy little dude. At first I had a lot of trouble telling what he was after, you know?"

I could only guess.

"Anyway, he got his birdhouse. Do you want one? 'Cause I don't think I'm going to have time now."

"How long ago was this? I mean, when you and Brownie were . . . negotiating?"

"I don't know. Maybe a month before Jenny was killed. Something like that. I think like that now. Before Jenny. After Jenny. I wish I could think some other way."

So Keely and the mayor had engaged in whatever version of a tête-a-tête they'd decided on *before* Jennifer was killed.

Birdhouses or kinky sex or love nests on Lake Erie. None of that really mattered—except for the tantalizing vision of Brownie in his Fruit of the Looms with Keely in the blue satin robe I'd first seen her in. That was going to be hard to erase.

"Here's the thing," I said, shaking off that picture so I could get to the point. "Brownie had one of the few keys to the house where Jennifer was probably murdered. And afterwards he claimed he lost it. Now I know this is a long shot, and I don't want to insult you, but I wonder if you know anything about that key, Keely? Because if we know what happened to the key, maybe we can figure out what happened to Jennifer."

"She got murdered."

I blinked. "Ummm . . . yes. I mean we can figure out who *did* it."

She began to cry. The tears were so sudden that for a moment, I just stared. Then I got up and found a box of tissues in her bedroom and brought them to her.

She took awhile blowing her nose, but by the time she'd gone through half a dozen tissues, she seemed to make up her mind.

"If I tell you something, you gotta promise you won't tell nobody."

"I don't know if I can do that." I bit my lip. "How about if I promise not to tell unless we come to an agreement?"

"I guess."

I sat forward. She looked like she needed a friend. I took her hand.

Her lips trembled. "Brownie was here one night, umm . . . paying for his birdhouse."

"I'm sure he thought it was perfect."

"Well, then he, like, took out his wallet and a key fell on the rug over there. And he didn't notice it, but I did. I didn't say nothing. I was kinda busy at the time, you know?"

I was afraid I did.

"Anyway, after he left I noticed it again. And when I picked it up I saw it had a tag on it, with this address. At first

I thought it was his address, then I realized it couldn't be 'cause I'd seen his house so I could make the birdhouse. So anyway, I went by the address a couple of nights later, looking to see if maybe he had another woman stashed over there or something."

The picture of Brownie Kefauver "stashing" anyone was incongruous. "Uh huh." I nodded sagely.

"When I got there I saw it was just an empty house with a For Sale sign."

Sage redux. I nodded once more.

"So then, I like, well, I—" She gulped and started to sob again.

I held out more tissues. We went through the nose blowing again.

"Better?" I asked.

She began to speak quickly, as if she was afraid once she stopped she wouldn't be allowed to continue.

"Sax was looking for a place to hide some stuff, or leastwise that's what he told me. He wanted to use my apartment. I didn't ask what he was hiding, but I guess it wasn't nothing good. Most likely drugs or maybe guns. I needed money. Root canal." She pointed at a bottom molar. "I didn't have any other way to get enough. Brownie couldn't help. I guess his wife has all the money. So, I—I told Sax he couldn't use my place but I could get him the key to a house that was for sale, but he'd have to pay me for my trouble."

"Why would he want to hide anything in a house that was being shown by realtors?"

"He said that didn't matter, that he'd find a good place in the house where nobody would bother looking."

"So you sold him the key?"

She nodded, looking miserable. "Not for much. And I didn't know he'd use it to, you know . . ."

"Kill Jennifer?"

She nodded again. "I didn't know that's where it happened. The murder, I mean. Not until yesterday. Then I heard one of our customers talking. And I made a big mistake."

"What did you do?"

"I was so mad when I heard. That's the only reason I can think of to act so stupid."

I wasn't going to quibble about her IQ. "How stupid?"

"I told Sax I'd heard where Jenny died. And I told him it wouldn't look good for him if I went to the police and told 'em what I knew."

I sat back. "You were blackmailing him?"

She shook her head wildly. "No! I didn't mean it like that. I was just so angry! He killed Jenny in that house. I know he did. They used to fight, and Jenny told me that once she came into that money, she was going to dump him. Maybe he found out, I dunno. But I wanted him to know he wasn't going to get away with killing her. And maybe I was just hoping he'd tell me he *didn't* kill her and he'd say it in a way that would make me believe it was true, so I wouldn't feel so guilty."

"Oh, Keely." I was suddenly very sorry I was sitting in Keely's house, in a neighborhood where nobody would ever think to look for me. And I was just as sorry for the woman across from me.

"This morning he was out front in a car. I saw him out my window. I've been afraid to go outside ever since. I called the police and told 'em there was a guy parked out there watching my apartment, and they came by and chased him off. But I know he'll be back. I thought you was him."

"Why didn't you just tell the police what you knew?"

She wrung her hands. "Will they believe me? I'm nobody, Aggie. I serve drinks in the worst bar in town. I called Brownie and told him I was in trouble, and he told me never to call him again. And I'm the one that sold Sax the key! How's that going to look? What can I do?"

I got to my feet and peered out the window. There was a new car on the street, just behind my van. I was sure it hadn't been there when I parked. "What kind of car does he drive? Does he have a car?"

"A beat-up Mustang."

I was very afraid I was now parked in front of a beat-up

Mustang. And I was very afraid the driver's door had just swung open. "Where's your phone?"

"Are you going to call somebody? You said you wouldn't!"

I turned back to her. "Do you want to end up like Jennifer Marina?"

Her huge eyes widened. "No. No, I don't."

"Then where's your phone?"

She pointed toward her bedroom.

"Wedge a chair under the doorknob and turn out all the lights. Is there another entrance into the apartment?"

"Used to be, but somebody walled it off before I moved in."

I was grateful to that unknown carpenter who had blithely broken city codes. Thanks to him we had a chance.

"Stay away from the windows. Stay down low, and hit those lights right now. Then get in the bedroom and help me barricade that door, too."

"Who are you going to call?"

"The man who wants Sax Dubinsky for murder as badly as Sax Dubinsky wants you."

16

By the time Roussos and friends arrived Sax had broken into the apartment and was nearly finished kicking in the bedroom door. I was armed with a can of hair spray and Keely was hoping he wouldn't peek under the bed.

By the time it was over I swore I was done playing amateur detective. I don't think it's an exaggeration to say sleuthing nearly got me killed.

On the other hand, I'm sure urging Roussos to pull out all the stops and get a patrol car to the scene saved Keely's life as well as mine. I don't know what she would have done if I hadn't been there to call him. Maybe she would have been smart enough to call 911 when Sax started kicking in her front door. But I think telling Roussos that Jennifer Marina's murderer was working on his next two victims brought help a lot quicker.

I do know that from now on Brownie's going to have to get his "birdhouses" somewhere else. Keely swears she's a changed woman. When we parted after giving our statements, she was heading to confession for the first time in decades. If the priest wasn't available, she was going to confess on the front steps of Saint Mary's to anybody who would listen. I was planning to drive home by a different route.

Our police station sits at the edge of downtown, a two-story frame rectangle sided with gray asphalt shingles. Never an architectural masterpiece, these days the building is an eyesore. Emerald Springs citizens will be delighted when the move is finally made to the service center so that the station can be torn down to make way for public parking.

Inside is much like outside. Paint is peeling; threadbare carpet is patched with duct tape. A uniformed officer took my statement at a rusting metal desk that was old when Eisenhower was president.

As I was heading home to my sadly empty house, Roussos stopped me in the parking lot. I hadn't seen much of him, since he had been busy with Sax.

The temperature had dropped while our little life-altering drama played out. I shivered now, and Roussos tugged off a black leather jacket and draped it around my shoulders. I was enveloped in the scent of anise and pine needles, or that was my best guess. The jacket smelled and felt so good I didn't want to give it back.

"You really couldn't leave it alone, could you?" he said.

I was too exhausted to smile. "Apparently not."

"With what Miss Henley told us, we'll probably have enough to charge Dubinsky for the Marina murder. He's been our best suspect from the start. At least once we knew Rico Marina had an airtight alibi."

"You've got more on him?"

"Dubinsky and a couple of his Cobra buddies have been trading guns for drugs in East Cleveland for about six months now. The cops there know all about it, but they haven't made any arrests. While they're at it, they want to get the guys at the top. When we searched the house across from yours, we found crack stashed in the crawl space under the family room. You get to that from the basement, so you need to get into the house. We were pretty sure we knew who put it there. We've been watching the house to catch him in the act, but he hasn't been back."

"I guess he never expected anybody to make the connection between Jennifer's murder and the house. Or even Sax would have been smart enough to move his hidden treasure elsewhere."

"Now that we know he had a key, that's one more piece of the puzzle. And that SUV you saw at the house the morning you found the body? We're pretty sure it belongs to a friend of his. With what we know we can probably get a warrant and go over it. We can search Dubinsky's apartment, too."

"A confession would be easier."

"Yeah, but we've got a couple of people who heard him fighting with Miss Marina. And he doesn't have an alibi for the night she was murdered. If we find blood in the SUV, the owner will probably turn state's evidence. I don't think you'll have to worry about Dubinsky again."

"You think he killed her because she was going to dump him once Gelsey paid her off? That's Keely's theory."

"He probably wanted *something* from her she wasn't going to give him. Love, money, Coors instead of Bud Light."

"He'd be better off with Bud Light. You could suggest it."

He didn't quite smile. "Maybe they had a fight, and he killed her because it was easier than counting to ten, or she knew about the drugs and guns and was threatening to blackmail him, too. We'll probably never know for sure. But between what we do know and what we'll find out in the next few days, he's going down."

I wasn't ready to give up the jacket. Maybe I'm a vegetarian, but apparently my scruples don't extend to leather.

"What about Gelsey?" I asked, pulling it forward to snuggle deeper.

"What about her?"

"Sax killed her, too?"

"We're working on that."

"Can you tell me what you know?"

One corner of his mouth actually turned up. His gaze warmed. "You tell me."

I'd thought about this while I waited to give my statement. "Maybe Sax knew who Jenny was going to blackmail and why. After all, they were living together. Even if she didn't tell him, chances are he figured it out one way or the other. So after he killed Jenny, he decided to blackmail Gelsey himself."

"Interesting. You think?"

I glared at him. "Yes, and maybe he even killed Jenny so he could go after Gelsey without sharing the payoff. I don't know. Only whatever the sequence, something went wrong. Gelsey refused to believe him, or she threatened to call the police. I can see her doing that, especially if she suspected Sax killed her daughter. She wasn't mom-of-the-year, but she wasn't a moral wreck, either. Jenny was hers, whatever that meant to her. And I don't think she would let her daughter's murderer go free."

"All tied up in a neat little package."

"You have a bigger, fancier one?"

"One murder at a time." His smile widened a little. "But it's possible."

I was astonished. "Wow, that is high praise from you."

"You'll never hear it again. Stay away from my cases, okay?"

Reluctantly, I removed the jacket and handed it back to him. "Keep dead bodies off my porch, okay?"

"It will be my pleasure."

✦   ✦   ✦

Somehow when Ed called the next morning, I forgot to mention the incident with Sax and Keely. I was lying in bed missing everybody despite the fact that when they're here, I frequently yearn for solitude—or at least for an uninterrupted cup of coffee.

"Hey." I sat up and raked my fingers through my hair, as if he could see me. "How's it going?"

"They love me."

"How can you tell? You're in Boston, right?"

"Not everybody in America feels a need to regurgitate an entire life history when they're introduced, including a blow-by-blow of past lives."

"You still don't believe Junie was Cleopatra, do you?"

"It's crossed my mind to be skeptical."

I missed him more. I thought about wrapping myself in his bathrobe, except that he never wears it himself so it just smells like Tide. "So somebody loosened a tie and you think that means you're a shoo-in?"

"I'm afraid I'm a shoo-in, Aggie. This is more or less a pre-empt. If I want the job, I think it's mine."

"Gosh, I'm married to a rising star."

He was quiet, and I waited him out.

"Thing is," he said at last, "I was looking for a quiet life, remember?"

"I do. I wasn't in favor of it."

"And now?"

"I don't know what to tell you. It hasn't exactly been quiet here, has it?"

"Tell me what you want."

"I can't make it simple. Just don't expect me to misplace my *R's* and polish the Revere sterling after social hour."

"I wish you were here."

I slumped against the pillows and thought about last night. "You have no idea how much I wish I was, too."

"I'll be home late Sunday evening."

"Good luck tomorrow morning at the service."

We made smoochy noises and hung up.

The house was quiet enough that I could hear every car pass on Church Street. After I showered and dressed I went downstairs and made toast and coffee from Arabica beans my sister Vel roasts and sends me monthly.

I was reading the comics when I got the first of three phone calls. The girls wanted to spend the day at the Frankels', where they were raking the yard and building a fort out of bags of leaves. I'd expected them to be too smart to fall for this Tom Sawyer trick and gave May a mental salute. I told them I would bring everybody picnic lunches as a treat.

In the second call Bob said he needed me to fill in for someone else, and I said yes to this, too, building on yes number one. I promised to come in after I dropped off the lunches.

Third call, Esther, our organist, had something to give me. Would I be home for a while?

Esther has multiple talents besides music. She can make sick plants bloom again. She can knit a wool muffler in the time it takes me to cast on a row of stitches. She bakes a chocolate chip applesauce cake that is so luscious just a hint she's bringing one to a potluck guarantees a large attendance and fights in the food line. Esther is seventy-six, spry as a college sprinter, rosy cheeked, and silver haired. She is also a treasure hunter.

I wasn't surprised she was bringing me something. Esther can go for a walk and return with stones shaped like sail-boats or seed pods for the perfect dried arrangement. She goes to yard sales and comes home with Spode china and Depression glass, discovered in the two-for-a-quarter box under the picnic table.

From the moment we arrived, Esther, who suspects my eccentricities, has brought me things. A bouquet of brightly colored asters from her yard, a filmy lace curtain that's the oddly perfect choice for our bathroom, the chenille bed-spread with pink and blue tufted roses in our guest room. I have a Porky Pig candy dish I wouldn't trade for a gold mine, courtesy of Esther's last trip to California.

I had tea steeping when she arrived in a Barbie pink jog-ging suit.

We hugged and I sat her at the table. We chatted and sipped, going through the usual pleasantries about the weather and autumn colors. She was carrying a canvas bag.

"I'm on my way to practice my prelude," she said.

Tomorrow's speaker was an Emerald College professor who would regale the congregation with his doctoral disser-tation on Sartre. If anything would make our members ap-preciate my husband, this would do it. I asked Esther what she was going to play, and she said something suitably French, and that if he was as boring as he sounded, she might play it while he lectured, as well.

We sat there smiling at each other.

"Ed's not here?" she asked.

"Out of town for the weekend."

"And the girls?"

"At May and Simon's, building forts."

"Then I have the perfect project for you." Esther pulled an old-fashioned scrapbook out of the bag and set it on the table next to her cup. "A find. A real find."

"What is it?"

"I was visiting Dolly Purcell, and she told me she'd been cleaning out her spare room and found this. She was going to bring it herself, but she's down with a cold."

Dolly is a longtime member, now in her eighties. She and Esther are good friends.

"Church photos?"

Esther slid it across the table to me. "Photos, and they're all documented. Names, dates, a little write-up for every event. Dolly was the historian a long time ago. This is just like her. She puts all her energy into learning a job, masters it, then she's bored. But at least for two years she set things to rights."

I flipped pages while she finished her tea. The scrapbook was the old-fashioned variety, a long rectangle with a green plastic cover trimmed in gold. The forty or so pages were black and the photos were held in place with triangular corners. Dolly had carefully typed information to go with each photo. It really was a treasure trove.

"Great. This will help a lot. Now I'll be able to identify some of the stuff that's not cataloged." I looked up and smiled. "Thanks for bringing it to me."

She stood and stretched. "There's a rumor going around that they caught the guy who killed that poor girl."

I set the scrapbook on a counter and walked her to the front door. "I think they have."

"That's a relief. Nobody with a brain in his head believed Ed was involved, of course. But at least the subject won't come up now."

I wondered. Even if Sax was charged for Jennifer's murder, there was no guarantee the police would find enough evidence to charge him for Gelsey's. And Ed *had* been standing over her body when the police arrived.

"I still can't figure out why this no-good dropped the body on your porch," Esther said, standing much too close to the very spot.

"Maybe he panicked and wanted to get rid of it as fast as possible. Or maybe he wanted to point suspicion in the wrong direction." But I knew that was a stretch. There were better places than a public porch in daylight. Sax had taken an awful chance.

"Who would ever have thought we'd be having this discussion." Esther shook her head and started down the steps to the church.

I planned what to take to the girls for lunch and pulled frozen cookie dough out of the refrigerator to go with the pimento cheese sandwiches. As I set the slices on my cookie sheets I flipped through the scrapbook, making sure not to leave grease spots on the pages. Dolly had done a wonderful job. I viewed weddings and child dedications, religious education award ceremonies, even some early shots of my kitchen when the tile floor was being laid. Judging from the volunteer's clothing, I'm guessing the floor went in before the Depression. I need to mention this to our successors to give them ammunition for the next skirmish in the Congoleum wars.

As the cookies baked I made sandwiches and gathered a medley of fruits to put in the picnic basket. I added frozen boxed juices and a plastic bag of trail mix.

As I walked by I flipped to the next scrapbook page and glimpsed another picnic and another time.

The picnic?

At the kitchen table I bent over the scrapbook, brow appropriately wrinkled. I recognized the scene, a public park near the new service center with a sycamore-lined brook and tables covered with gaily printed fabric. If I remembered correctly, the missing movie had been filmed in this same place.

Dolly had carefully typed "End of the Year Picnic at Shadyside," and the date, "1982." Of course it was possible the church had staged annual picnics at this same spot for some years, even though now we celebrate at Emerald Park, which has covered pavilions just yards from the springs it-self.

I tried to remember details. Who had I noticed in the missing movie that might be in these photos? I examined them closely, and grew more certain this was the same event. There was something familiar about this scene, the way the tables were set up, maybe the way the participants were dressed. Preppy, moderately big hair.

I searched my memory. The day had been sunny, like this one. The number of people in this range. And I remembered something else that had caught my eye as I rushed through reels, a group of teens in stonewashed jeans and yes, Michael Jackson-style parachute pants, playing Hacky Sack just beyond the picnic table. My sisters and I had been champion Hacky Sackers in junior high school. We'd found it was a great way to attract guys. So I had noticed these kids, of course, and stored that away.

And here they were again.

Now that I was nearly certain this was the same picnic I took my time going through each photo and carefully read-ing Dolly's commentary. I knew a couple of the people caught on camera. I recognized Fern Booth before I read that caption. Although her hair was longer and darker, she had the same disapproving glare.

Samuel wasn't in the photo, but I recognized Harry in the corner of the next one. He was dapper now and he'd been dapper in his forties, something of a hunk, as a matter of fact. He had his arm around a young woman who was gazing adoringly up at him. I suspected Harry had not yet told the world he was gay.

I continued on, staring at photos, reading captions. I gave my unconscious strict instructions to stop me if anything seemed out of order. I turned the page.

I nearly passed right by the third photo. None of the peo-ple were familiar to me, and the names in the caption meant nothing. This photo had been taken at the outskirts of the ac-tion, where fewer people scurried by with plates of food or children in hand. But as my eyes flicked to photo number four, my unconscious shrieked a warning. I went back and looked more carefully, and there in the shadows, I saw two people.

One of them was Gelsey Falowell.

Maybe I wouldn't have recognized her so readily if I hadn't recently seen photos of the much younger Gelsey. But now, looking at the Gelsey who had lived in time between Gorgeous Gelsey and Grouchy Gelsey, I knew her instantly. Regal, sexy even in middle age and eighties shoulder pads, and as always, commanding.

But who was the man?

There were no captions, of course. Dolly had documented the people in the foreground, but not the two under the tree some distance behind them. I left to find a magnifying glass and located one in Teddy's room. Back at the table I used it with no luck. The man looked the tiniest bit familiar. But not familiar enough that I could add twenty years and place him. The picnic was too recent for this to be Herb Falowell, who, according to my information, had died in the midseventies.

The rest of the photos, only four more, provided no further clues. Whomever Gelsey had been talking to remained a mystery.

And so what?

I closed the scrapbook and stared at my kitchen sink, which, like the floor, has not benefitted from recent technology.

Did any of this matter? Although I was fairly sure the movie had been removed from the storage closet, I couldn't swear to it. Maybe someone had detected an advanced rate of decomposition and tossed that reel. Maybe someone had borrowed it to show friends. It was entirely possible this was the most innocent picnic of all time, and Gelsey was simply busy in the shadows writing a check to fund a guinea pig wing at the local animal shelter.

Or maybe, just maybe, the man beside her had something to do with Jennifer Marina.

The thought would never have occurred to me, of course, if the movie hadn't disappeared after I viewed it and belatedly returned it to the closet. Or if the storage room hadn't been ransacked. Or if Gelsey's dislike of Ed hadn't begun the same day I announced to the Women's Society that I had taken the job of historian and viewed some of their old films.

And hadn't I mentioned that I'd seen a picnic? Had that been the moment when Gelsey realized I might see something on the film, perhaps a film she hadn't known was still in existence? Because, until now, no still photos of that picnic had turned up anywhere.

Almost as if someone had made sure to remove each and every one of them.

The morning had slipped by and it was nearly time to head to the Frankels' to deliver lunch. First I made a quick phone call to Jack, then I looked for a good place to hide the scrapbook, paranoia a new and worthy addition to my repertoire. I stored the book between cookie sheets in the drawer under my stove and went to find my purse.

+ + +

Book Gems was humming when I arrived. Work is so much more fun when you're not making it up. I helped three different customers choose books for gifts, discussed the merits of Julia Child and Marcella Hazan with another, and provided an impromptu story hour complete with a Curious George puppet so a harassed young mother could select a novel. We rang up more sales than I'd seen any other day.

On the fly Bob told me that since the protests seemed to be over, he was going to clear out the little back room and ready it for the painters. The experiment had been a failure. He didn't ask for help, and I didn't offer. I had a feeling Bob might want to fondle the books one last time before he packed them back to their publishers.

By five the crowd had thinned to almost nothing. Bob joined me behind the front counter and watched me ring up my final sale. When the young man left, Bob turned the sign and locked the door.

"Things are looking up." He sounded delighted.

I was feeling more charitable toward Bob than I had yesterday. Gelsey's murder was still a mystery, but at least now I was sure Bob hadn't had any reason to murder Jennifer. My phone call to Jack had affirmed what Bob had told me yesterday. Jennifer could never have touched a penny of Herb Falowell's money, no matter how hard she or her mother tried. The will was ironclad. Bob was the only heir. And Sax was in custody.

Suspicion about one murder is an improvement over two. I decided to enlighten him about Jennifer.

"You know they've arrested somebody for the murder of Jennifer Marina, don't you?"

He looked surprised. "You're kidding. And it wasn't in the papers?"

"They put the *Flow* to bed *way* before midnight. You need to find a better source of gossip." It was time to enlighten him even more. "Remember me telling you yesterday that Gelsey had a child before she married your uncle?"

"Yeah?"

"Jennifer Marina was that child."

He stared at me, as if he couldn't quite make this leap. "The dead woman on your porch?"

"That would be the one."

"Come on. You're kidding."

"Not funny. True. And something you probably don't want to tell the world."

"I'll be damned."

Really, he was a first-class actor or a completely honest man. I decided to go for broke. "Jennifer had two children, a boy and a girl. Gelsey had grandchildren."

He shook his head. "Did she know?"

"I don't think so. Jennifer came to town to tell her, but she probably never got the chance."

He cashed out in silence, making notes and tallying the day's receipts. I left him to it and went through the store straightening and reshelving books, setting chairs back in place. I went for the vacuum cleaner and was plugging it in when he came to stand beside me.

"Where are the kids?"

I didn't trust him *that* much. "In foster care." I didn't say where.

"And their dad?"

"A bum."

"This has to be so hard on them." He looked genuinely sorry.

"Has to be," I agreed. "I hear they're great. The foster parents want to adopt them, but they have three older kids they have to put through college. I don't know if they'll be able to afford to put two more through after that."

"Tough break." He pulled out his favorite prop and tapped the butt against his palm. "I haven't been through Gelsey's stuff. What do I know about women's jewelry and geegaws?"

"Geegaws?"

He gave a humorless laugh. "I doubt she kept anything that mattered to Uncle Herb, but she might have. I need to go over there and see for myself."

"I'm sure you'll want to, before all the stuff goes up for sale."

"How do you know about that?"

I told him about Lucy and our visit to Gelsey's to appraise the house, but not about the documents in the secret drawer. I couldn't see any reason Bob should know the seediest part of Gelsey's history.

"You know about stuff?" he asked. "What it's worth and all?"

"Actually, I was just in the house to help Lucy figure out what needs to be fixed up so you can make more money when you sell. But yes, I know a little about collectibles and antiques."

"Would you know what might be good to pass down? That kind of stuff?"

"Heirlooms?"

"Maybe Gelsey's grandkids would like something that belonged to her. Maybe it would help them feel like *they* belonged somewhere, you know?"

I was so surprised that for a moment, I didn't know what to say.

"I could find somebody else," he said. "To help me. If you don't want to go back to the house."

"No, no I'd like to." Actually I also wanted one more shot

at looking for the 8 mm movie, and Lucy wasn't coming home until midweek. In the excitement of finding the secret drawer, we had forgotten to search the garage. I felt pretty sure if I found the film, I would understand a lot I didn't understand now.

Maybe even the identity of Jennifer's father.

Because wouldn't that be an awfully good reason for Gelsey to fear being seen in a photo with this man? Wouldn't that be enough of a reason to steal the movie that would make him easier to identify? What other secret competed with this one? What else did she need to hide?

"I could go Monday evening," Bob said. "I'm busy all day tomorrow. But Monday I could go after we close. We don't have to stay long."

Bob was giving me enough time to run an announcement in the *Flow* warning the world I was going to be alone with him in Gelsey Falowell's house—or at least to tell Ed. This hardly seemed like a death threat.

"Sounds good," I said. "And I'll think about it between now and then and figure out what might be good to pass down."

"Gelsey with a kid. And that woman on your porch the one." He frowned. "I don't know if you've thought about this, but maybe it wasn't a coincidence."

Now why didn't I think of that?

17

On Monday morning I discovered how Deena had spent her hours in the fort with Maddie Frankel. She came down for school dressed in an old skirt of mine that dipped to her ankles, a dress shirt of her father's which extended to her fingertips and a stocking cap that covered every inch of her hair. I was sure that across town Maddie was dressed the same way.

"I gather you're making a statement?" I said as I dished up scrambled eggs.

"We've decided you're right. Not an inch of our skin should show."

"No Amish mother could be prouder." I added toast to her plate and set it in front of her.

"We're all dressing the same way."

"All being the Meanies? Crystal won't let Carlene out of the house."

"We stick together."

Since I suspected the outer layers covered her usual clothes and would come off behind some hedge on the way to school, I nodded. "You might want to make a will, just in case you die of heatstroke. Teddy will treasure your American Girl dolls."

"You are so funny."

"I'm counting on my sense of humor in the years ahead."

Deena was easier to deal with than Ed. He had gotten home late last night, and right before he turned over to go to sleep, I'd casually mentioned my near-death experience. When he came downstairs this morning he was still angry.

"Aggie, what possesses you to do these things?"

"We're carrying over from last night's conversation?"

He poured himself a cup of coffee and held out the pot in question. I shook my head. I noticed he was dressed as if he was going to church, gray pants, green sweater over a subtly striped shirt.

"If you suspected this Keely woman knew something, why didn't you just tell the police?" he demanded.

"I didn't suspect. I wondered. Besides, what was I going to tell Roussos? That Brownie bought a birdhouse from a woman who also works at Don't Go There? Anyway, I knew Keely wouldn't tell Roussos a thing." I held out the frying pan. "Do you want scrambled eggs with your argument?"

"I've got a clergy breakfast this morning, then I have work to do since I was away the whole weekend."

"Ed, don't be mad. It turned out okay."

"Maybe you need a job you can really sink your teeth into."

It's amazing how fast the human species can go from zero to furious. I set a record. I slammed the pan on the nearest burner.

"Why, so I won't have enough time to sleep, eat, and meddle?"

He sighed and set down his cup. He put his arms around my resisting body. "Listen, you scared me to death. What would we do if something happened to you?"

Back to zero, or someplace nicer.

After Ed left I considered his solution. Actually, I wouldn't mind a job with challenges and financial security. The girls are in school full-time, I have a good education.

It's just that I'd like to set my own hours, so I can do all the extras that come up. Field trips, Christmas parties, Brownies. Maybe I'll be able to find an important part-time job in Boston, or maybe I'll just be forced to do laps on the super-mom track. Neither sounded very good.

I was elbow deep in dishwater when the telephone rang. I toweled dry and answered on the fourth ring.

"Hi Aggie, just following up."

I recognized George Bentsen. I had called last week to let him know what Lucy and I had found at Gelsey's house. He'd promised he would tell his PI pal Leo. Now we chatted a moment before he got to the point.

"I don't have much for you, but Leo did find a little more. Seems Gorgeous Girls started life with a backer. It was a classy operation from the get-go. Nothing low rent about these girls. And you were right, it wasn't just girls. A warm body for every taste."

"What kind of backer?"

"Most likely mob related. Leo caught a strong whiff, but that's about all. It came and went too long ago to dig any deeper without putting in a lot of hours."

"Wouldn't Gelsey have a real problem going out of business and moving to Ohio if the mob was involved? I mean, I watch *The Sopranos*. I saw what happened to poor Big Pussy."

"Maybe somebody had a soft spot for her. Or the folks in charge were sure she would never breathe a word of any of it."

And of course Gelsey had invented a reputation to protect and a life in Emerald Springs society. I supposed it made sense.

But something *had* happened to her in the end.

I told George about Jennifer and Sax, and my feeling Gelsey's murder was part of this.

After I hung up the doorbell rang. I have entire weeks that are less intense than this morning.

Roussos was at the door wearing "my" leather jacket. I invited him in, hoping he would take it off so I could misplace it, but he only got as far as the threshold. He handed me a padded envelope. "I think you should be the one who decides what to do with this stuff."

I peeked inside and saw all the secrets I'd liberated from Gelsey's chest. "You don't need this? It's not in the record now or something?"

"It's old news. I didn't see anything that would help our investigation."

"You don't want this on file, do you? You're trying to protect her."

"A lot of people have access to our files and leaks happen. I don't see a good reason to share this chapter of the woman's life with the general public. Of course, if you hold on to that envelope for a while and put it away somewhere safe, that might be good."

"That's nice of you."

"If I thought any of it was relevant, I wouldn't be nice."

I folded the envelope to my chest. "Any news yet?"

"We picked up the SUV early this morning. The tests could take weeks. Dubinsky spent a restless night and ate raisin bran for breakfast."

"You don't need another detective on the ESPD, do you? Ed thinks I need a job I can sink my teeth into."

He was still shaking his head when he left.

I had already decided to take lunch over to the church as a peace offering.

Rain was threatening and there was a definite chill in the air. I cleaned out the vegetable bin and chopped everything, throwing it in a pot with water and canned tomatoes to make vegetable soup. Now I had hours to either clean a nearly clean house, find a hobby or job other than detecting, or play with the codes in Gelsey's book. The decision was easy.

I took hot chocolate into the living room and made myself at home on the sofa. I have a knack for cryptograms. My sisters and I still sign letters and e-mails with code names we invented for each other. Last year Sid's Christmas card message was written in the alphabet we devised as young teens to hide our exploits from our mother.

I thought it might be interesting to see if I could figure out any of the names of Gelsey's clients, if indeed their real names were part of the code. Taking into account Gelsey's lack of education, I doubted any unusual languages were involved. But I also doubted the codes were the simplest variety, *"A"* for *"Z"* etc. She had gone to some trouble to hide this information.

Unfortunately this wasn't a newspaper puzzle and none of the usual clues were here. There were no single-letter words for clues or repetitious three-letter words like *"the"* or *"and."* The letters following the nicknames were in groups of five. Gelsey might simply have made up a code at random, substituting one letter for another with no rhyme or reason, then hidden the key somewhere else. But somehow I doubted this. With this approach, losing the key can result in disaster. My guess was that she had used a phrase or name to base the letters on, the way Sid and I had based ours on "we hate Junie."

I tried "Wanda Ray Gelsey," which, when identical letters were removed, became "wandrygels." Using this system *"W"* became A, etc. Then everything after *"S"* followed the normal alphabet, omitting letters that had already been assigned a substitute. With this rationale I made a new alphabet and tried to break the code of the first entry, after code name "Hazelnut."

Three lines into it, I gave up. No pattern had emerged, and I had used up half an hour.

The idea seemed sound enough, although just a shade short of a shot in the dark. I checked the clock and the soup and came back to try some more. Using the same system I tried "Gorgeous Girls," "Gorgeous Gelsey," and plain old "Gorgeous." Again, no pattern.

I tried "Las Vegas," then "Las Vegas Nevada." The soup was beginning to smell delicious. The code was unbroken.

Back in the kitchen I was finishing almond butter sandwiches to go with the soup when another idea occurred to me. I had just enough time for one more shot at the code before I took lunch to the church.

Back on the sofa I printed "Grandstand Hotel and Casino," then decided to try the code with just the first two words. If this didn't work I'd try the whole thing later.

I removed identical letters and was left with "grandsthoel." I created my new alphabet, then began the substitutions, and slowly a man named Hazelnut began to emerge. Knute Green, who hailed from the Dayton's Bluff neighborhood of St. Paul, Minnesota, liked blondes, expected an entire night of pleasure, and paid accordingly. He was a big tipper, with fairly ordinary tastes and a wife with money and no sex appeal.

Or at least that was the condensed version. I stopped translating halfway into it. Clearly Knute Green had told his sympathetic "escorts" enough to make blackmail a cinch. I bet somewhere along the way, the big tips became big payoffs.

I couldn't believe I had found the key words. I was darned good at this. Maybe the CIA would offer me a job I could "sink my teeth into."

"Tomboy" turned out to be a businessman named Elton Tompkins, from Murray Hill, New Jersey. I felt no need to translate anything else about Elton. "Tarzan" was some poor guy named Horace. Maybe Johnny Weissmuller had been a favorite at Gelsey's movie theater in Hollins Creek. Or maybe "Tarzan" liked to pound his chest or swing on vines in the bedroom or call all his escorts Jane. I hoped it didn't have anything to do with chimps.

I didn't have time to translate another word because I had wasted minutes patting myself on the back. I probably wouldn't find anything important here, but at least I had proven that all those years of communicating secretly with my sisters hadn't been a waste.

I carried the envelope upstairs, leafing through the photos again as I climbed. In my bedroom I stopped at the window and examined them closer. One of the women in the group of three blondes looked vaguely familiar, but probably only because she was trying so hard to look like any number of silver screen bombshells of the period. By the same token, one of the men in the photo at the window looked vaguely familiar, too, but probably because he reminded me of publicity photos of the young Brad Pitt. This one had been snapped with a telephoto lens and was, at best, blurry.

I buried the envelope under my mattress and went back downstairs to pack up lunch.

At the last minute I decided to take Dolly's scrapbook

with me and show the picnic photos to Harry. He had been at the picnic, and it was possible he might remember seeing Gelsey with a mysterious man. The only other person I'd recognized from those photos was Fern Booth, and I preferred to avoid her.

Ed's office door was closed, and Harry, in a Coogi sweater and black twill trousers, told me Ed was on a marathon phone call. I set the picnic basket on his desk and pulled out the scrapbook, delighted with my luck. I really didn't want my husband to catch me snooping so soon after our argument.

"Trivia quiz," I told him. "The year was 1982. The scene, Shadyside Park." I flipped open the scrapbook and put it on his desk next to the basket. "And here you are. Weren't you a hunk?"

He raised a brow. "Look at that tan. I must have spent some part of spring in Florida that year."

"Do you remember the picnic?"

"I remember her." He put his finger on the woman staring up at him. "She was the daughter of the minister. And she decided I had never married because I just hadn't found the right woman."

"It wasn't a good time to be yourself, I guess. Or a good place."

"I got tired of the charade and came out of the closet a few weeks later."

"That was one way to stop her, huh?"

He smiled a little.

"There's another photo I thought you could help me with." I flipped the pages. "There's no caption for the people in the background. Can you identify them?"

Harry leaned over and squinted at the photo of Gelsey and the mysterious man. "That's Gelsey, isn't it?"

"I thought it was. I just wondered. I can't place the man."

Harry leaned closer. He shook his head slowly. "I'm sorry, Aggie, but it was more than twenty years ago. He doesn't even look familiar."

"Darn."

"You need to go easier on yourself. It's a good idea to

update the archives, but nobody expects this level of commitment."

I let him think that was the only reason I cared.

Ed finished his call, and I set up our picnic on his desk. Two committees were meeting in the parish house, and we were interrupted three times. Our religious education director needed to be sure that Ed and I liked the design for new robes for the children's choir. I did, but I was pretty sure my girls wouldn't.

Sally came in to tell us she was going to serve out Gelsey's term as chairman of the Women's Society board. We told her sincerely she would do a terrific job.

As I tried for the third time to tell Ed where I was going that night and why, Harry came in.

He looked distraught. "The spring social committee is frothing at the mouth."

I brushed bread crumbs off my palms. "In October? Isn't it a little early for a meltdown?"

"Gelsey took the crystal punch bowl and cups to her house for safekeeping. Now they're afraid the whole shebang will be sold with the contents of her house."

I remembered the punch set from the social last May. Huge, beautifully faceted lead crystal. The committee raised money to buy it several years ago and considered it a treasure. And now that Harry mentioned it, I remembered seeing the bowl and cups in a cupboard in Gelsey's dining room. For once, sticking my nose where it didn't belong had been a good thing.

"It's there," I told him. "And I'm going over tonight with Bob Knowles to look at some of Gelsey's things."

"You're doing what?" Ed said.

"There's no reason to worry. He's giving me plenty of time to tell the world where I'll be and with whom. So don't tie yourself in knots, okay?"

"Can you ask Mr. Knowles about the punch bowl?" Harry said. "I could give you a photo of last year's social to prove it's ours."

"I bet he'll be decent about it. I'll take some newspaper and boxes and pack it up while I'm there," I promised.

Harry looked relieved. "I'm the one who fields all the phone calls from the spring social committee, you know. I'm the whipping boy. I don't know how many more calls I can handle."

"The church couldn't stand without you."

Harry shut the door, and I told Ed the real reason for the trip to Gelsey's. I hadn't wanted to mention Jennifer's kids to Harry. Ed was calmer by the end of my explanation.

"So I couldn't say no," I finished. "He's trying to be generous."

"Do you have any reason to think Bob killed Gelsey, besides wanting to spend the Falowell fortune?"

"Well, he couldn't stand her. But I don't really think it was Bob. He had an alibi. And hiring somebody else is just plain tricky."

"How would you know?"

"I watch A&E."

"I could go with you."

"Don't you have a meeting tonight? And besides, it would be pretty insulting to my boss to arrive with an escort. Can you have the meeting at our house so I don't have to get a sitter?"

He shrugged a yes.

"There's nothing to worry about," I promised him. "Sax is in jail and he probably killed them both."

"These days I walk around worried, Ag. Let's see if we can change that to mild concern, okay?"

I gathered up the soup bowls and kissed him on top of the head. "Everything's going to be fine. The police will charge Sax, you'll be offered a church where nobody suspects you of murder, and I'll be home tonight before your meeting ends, punch bowl in arms."

"If you're predicting the future, I'm making plans for Sunday. How many people will come to hear a sermon on Unitarianism in the fifteenth century?"

"Sometimes it's better not to know."

18

Bob was waiting at Gelsey's house when I arrived. The storm had finally blown in, and I had driven through pouring rain to get here. On the porch I shook myself like a Labrador retriever and put my rain jacket by the door. Inside I debated whether to remove my shoes, but they were thick-soled ankle boots, not that simple to slip on and off. I didn't think I was tracking anything with me, and Gelsey wouldn't even know.

I found Bob in the living room, his expression pained. "Years ago Uncle Herb used to have this great collection of hunting prints in the den. Now it's flowers and Audubon lithographs."

"Afraid I haven't noticed hunting prints anywhere."

"I'm sure she sold them and anything else I might want."

I was sympathetic. "She could be spiteful."

"I suppose there's no point in speaking ill of the dead."

"The best revenge? Be nice to her grandchildren. Even if she couldn't be nice to you."

"I like kids. That's why I'm doing it."

Just as I was about to apologize he relaxed visibly. "But knowing I'm taking the high road sweetens it a little, doesn't it?"

We shared a laugh. Whatever tension I'd felt getting out of my car was disappearing. "Where do you want to start?"

Slowly we toured the house and I showed Bob interesting things I'd discovered in the living room. When we got to the dining room I opened the cabinet and pointed out the punch set.

I explained the problem. "I brought a photo and the receipt," I finished. Harry the worrywart had found both and brought them over to the house that afternoon to be sure I had all the proof I needed.

Bob waved away the evidence. "Take it back to the church tonight if you want."

"Good, I came prepared to pack. Thanks."

We proceeded through the rooms, and I told him what I thought might be valuable. By the time we started upstairs, Bob hadn't found a thing he wanted to keep for himself, but he was interested in a delicate Bavarian china tea set with crimson roses for Gelsey's granddaughter.

I'd expected to introduce Bob to the house and its contents, but he was the one who found the lamented hunting prints. They were stored in a space just under the rafters, reached through a ceiling panel in the guest room closet. The panel wasn't hidden, but the closet was packed with Gelsey's summer clothes, and I hadn't thought to crane my neck. Bob remembered the storage area from a long ago visit.

Bob brought a stepladder from the garage and by the time he reached the second floor, he was huffing and puffing. The prints were his reward, along with two mounted fish, a Remington bronze, and four bowling trophies. When Herb died Gelsey had removed every trace of him, but apparently she hadn't had the heart to throw his things away.

Bob was in a much better mood after he handed everything down to me and descended the ladder. Old Bob has a sentimental side. Inheriting the family salt mines probably pales in comparison to the bowling trophies. Or maybe not.

"That's a good evening's work." He polished one of the trophies against his shirt.

"Anything else up there?"

"Just a box of odds and ends."

I wondered if one of the "odds" was a certain 8 mm movie. I knew I'd arouse his suspicion if I shoved him out of the way to check.

"Why don't you just leave the ladder, and I'll tell Lucy to have a workman remove it." I hoped I would be able to climb it later.

He looked grateful. "Let's finish up."

In Gelsey's bedroom Bob spied the little chest and decided this would be an appropriate gift for her grandson. Now I was particularly glad I had found and removed the papers and photos in the secret drawer. Wouldn't that be some kind of heirloom? Heeeeeere's . . . Grandma!

Gelsey's jewelry was in several boxes. I imagined anything of great value was in a safe deposit box—and wouldn't I like to get a look at that? But the jewelry she kept here was lovely enough to pass down, too.

As I began to go through the largest box, Bob's eyes glazed over. "Garnets, I think," I said holding up a necklace. "And maybe onyx? And look, here are earrings to go with it. Gelsey's ears were pierced, which is good for her granddaughter."

By the time I got to the second drawer, he was fanning himself with his hand, although the house was cool.

"You're not having a good time," I said.

"Why don't you take the jewelry boxes home and pick out a couple of pieces for each of the kids? The boy can give them to his wife or whatever when he's older."

"I don't want to remove jewelry from the house, Bob. But I hate to choose without seeing everything."

"Then can you stay a little while longer? I think I've seen all I need to. I'll lock up, and you can pull the door behind you when you leave."

"And you don't want any of this?" I scooped up a handful of bracelets.

"Bad memories."

"Do you want me to take everything home with me that you're giving the children? I know how to get it to their foster mom."

"That would be great. Pick out some nice pieces. I don't mind."

He really was being sweet, not murderer-ish at all. I walked him to the top of the stairs and he thanked me. He even offered to let me choose a piece of Gelsey's jewelry for myself.

"Bad memories," I mimicked, shaking my head.

He understood.

The rain had slowed enough that he could dodge raindrops outside without his golf umbrella. After he made his last trip to the car with Uncle Herb's treasures, he locked the front door behind him, and I was alone. If Gelsey's ghost was hanging around, she was feeling benevolent and didn't bother me.

I postponed the jewelry decisions and went straight for the attic. Lifting the door wasn't as easy as it had looked when Bob did it, but I finally shoved it to one side. Balanced on the top step I could just reach the box he'd mentioned. I pulled it closer and rifled through it by the light of a 50-watt bulb.

No movie.

I closed up again and climbed down. What were the chances Gelsey had kept the film anyway instead of just destroying it?

Back in her bedroom I tried to project myself into the future so I would know which pieces of jewelry would still be appealing when the children were old enough to have them. In the end I chose an opal pendant and earrings for Jennifer's daughter, and a necklace and bracelet of small sapphires and pearls for her son. I was fairly sure the stones were genuine and the pieces timeless enough to be treasured.

I placed the jewelry in the chest and tucked it under my arm. The tea set would fit inside, too, wrapped in Gelsey's flea market handkerchiefs. I was pleased since I had to bring the punch bowl home, as well.

Downstairs, as thunder rumbled in the distance, I made a half-hearted search of the garage, but gave up quickly. There were no old tires, no motor oil cans, no pots with dead plants, no coiled hoses. The walls were bare of shelves, and

Gelsey's car had already been sold. The few places worth searching were dispensed of immediately.

I could think of only one other place I hadn't tried. Last time I was here I had not pulled out all the books in the study to check behind them. At the time it had reminded me too much of my job. Besides, several shelves held old leather-bound classics, and these needed to be moved with care. I debated whether it was worth the effort, but decided I would wonder the rest of my life if I didn't.

In the study I removed the most recent books and peeked behind them with no success. Then I carefully removed five of the classics and placed them on the desk. From that point I inched five more into their place, checking hopefully behind each group. Finally when nothing appeared, I took the first five volumes off the desk and squatting, began to insert them at the end of the bottom row.

The third book I came to was *Tarzan of the Apes,* by Edgar Rice Burroughs, something I hadn't noticed before.

"Tarzan, huh?" I remembered Tarzan a.k.a. Horace and wondered if this volume had spurred that particular nick-name, not Johnny Weissmuller.

It seemed unlikely that Gorgeous Gelsey had curled up with classics in between extorting money and launching call girls. But I opened the book, and there in faded ink were the words, "G, You'll like this one." It was signed: "FXC. 1960."

"G?"

I leafed through, stopping at the first page. I'd never actu-ally read the book. A narrator explained how he'd come across the tale. Then he began to tell the story of a young nobleman, John Clayton, Lord Greystoke. I had forgotten Tarzan was of noble blood.

I closed the book, touched, despite myself. I could picture the young woman with a limited education trying to better herself by reading classic literature. The Gelsey I had known was intelligent, with a large knowledge base. She had proba-bly constructed her identity, one book at a time.

I wondered who FXC could be.

I took the time to leaf through the other books, but none

of the rest had inscriptions. There was no 8 mm movie and no place left to search. I was out of options.

While the rain held off I went to my car and delivered the chest, then came back inside with two cardboard boxes full of newspaper from our recycling bin.

I was anxious to get home, but if I returned without the punch set, the spring social committee would have conniptions. I set the cardboard boxes on the mahogany dining room table and removed the first half dozen cups. Gelsey's ghost awakened momentarily and reminded me how much the committee had paid for the set and how useless it would be if I chipped it.

I told her to go back to sleep, but I carefully wrapped each cup in two layers of paper.

I was wrapping the fifth cup when something caught my eye. I unwrapped it again and held the sheets of newspaper a little closer. I was looking at the front page of our "local news" section from about a week ago, and I recognized the service center dedication. The *Flow*'s photographer had gone all out with a photo spread. I hadn't paid any attention to it at the time, but now I scanned each photo. Something nagged at me.

Finally, just as I was separating the two pages, I realized what. On the left was a photo of Brownie Kefauver and the service center manager shaking hands. Nothing interesting there. But behind the two men a blurry Frank Carlisle lurked in the shadows talking to a constituent.

Just exactly the way he had lurked in the shadows of the Shadyside Park picnic.

I told myself to relax. Only the circumstances were similar. The man with Gelsey at the picnic could not have been Carlisle. Yet the more I stared the more certain I became. Same nose. Same chin. Same hawklike forehead. Bone structure doesn't lie and it doesn't really change. The man at the picnic had been twenty years younger, but this was the same man.

"FXC?"

It seemed preposterous. I tried to remember everything I knew about Carlisle. He wasn't from Emerald Springs. In fact I had never heard *where* he was from. He had retired from Congress to campaign as a state senator, a comedown by anyone's standards. I had guessed the demotion was related to a scandal he wanted to avoid, because that's the way politicians operate. Draw the scandal card and go back six spaces. But Bob had mentioned something about corruption, hadn't he? That day in front of Book Gems when he and Carlisle had nearly come to blows. Had Bob heard more about Carlisle than I ever had?

If any of this was true could the scandal have to do with Gelsey? Or was it even broader? Did Carlisle have mob connections? Was that why he had agreed to quietly resign from his congressional seat? Someone had discovered this and blown the whistle. Years before had he been instrumental in funding Gorgeous Girls?

The age was right. Carlisle was a little younger than Gelsey, perhaps, but not noticeably. The first and last initials matched. I wished I knew his life story. I wished I had a computer with Internet access and Lucy to operate the mouse.

Was the meeting at Shadyside Park accidental? Had Carlisle and Gelsey simply run into each other and had a political chitchat? I could almost hear Gelsey telling Carlisle that if his lungs were as corroded as his brain and heart, he would never draw another breath. And Carlisle telling Gelsey that good old Joe McCarthy had known exactly what to do with her kind.

But no, I didn't think Frank and Gelsey had discussed politics.

I didn't think they had discussed the weather, either. Or the environmental impact of Emerald Estates on the county's underground springs, or the political correctness of a major league baseball team named the Cleveland Indians. I think they discussed something personal and far-reaching, and I bet if I was looking at the missing movie, I would see a lot of anger in their faces and hand gestures.

I bet they discussed the baby they had agreed to give up together, a baby who by my calculations was on the cusp of adulthood by the day of that picnic. A baby who had not, after all, gone to a family with high ideals and love to offer.

Was Frank Carlisle Jennifer's father?

Far-fetched as it seemed, the possibility explained so much. Why the storage closet was ransacked and the movie stolen. Why Gelsey tried to extinguish my interest in the archives and possession of the materials by ridding the church of my husband. Why Jennifer was killed—because, after all, she was living proof Carlisle was not the moral beacon he claimed to be. Jennifer had discovered who her mother was. Daddy was probably shaking in his boots. And Daddy wasn't just some Joe Shmoe trying to cover up an old affair. He was an important man with everything to lose.

It *didn't* explain why Jennifer's body appeared on our front porch, or how someone knew Gelsey would be on her way to our house that morning. For that matter, it didn't explain why Gelsey had been killed when Jennifer was already out of the way.

And it didn't *prove* Frank Carlisle had been instrumental in either death or that he was now out of danger and ready to resume ruling Ohio.

I had to call Roussos anyway and turn this over to him.

My hands trembled as I dialed the station, but Roussos wasn't there. I asked for his private telephone number and the man on the other end of the line laughed and put me into voice mail.

I rambled. "It's Aggie Sloan-Wilcox, and I'm at Gelsey's house. I think maybe I've figured out who Jennifer's father was. And it's relevant. I think it was Frank Carlisle, you know, the senator? I found an old photo of him having an argument with Gelsey, and I, just, well, I put two and two together. I wasn't sure who he was at first, but I just saw this photo of him at the service center dedication plus a dedication in a book, and I realized the man standing in front of the salt dome was the same man. And . . . darn."

I hung up. It sounded absurd. Roussos would smile when he played his messages. He'd think I'd really lost my mind. And maybe I had.

Suddenly I didn't want to be in Gelsey's house speculating about her life and the reasons someone might have wanted her dead. I was one room away from the place where she had fallen lifeless to the rug. I was an intruder, an interloper, and a fraud. I wasn't a detective. I was just Aggie, Ray and Junie's daughter, Sid and Vel's sister, Ed's partner, Deena and Teddy's mother, Lucy's friend. And I wanted to go home.

I wrapped the remainder of the cups quickly and carefully, setting them in one of the boxes. I was positioning the bowl on overlapping sheets of paper when I heard tapping on the front door.

"Ed." I exhaled gratefully.

Ed's meeting was over by now, and he had decided to come and check on me. He had probably asked one of the attendees to stay with the girls while he came to bring me home. My husband, the worrier.

I left the bowl on the table, but I carried the carton with the cups to the front of the house to answer the door. It wasn't Ed. It was Harry.

I set the box on an end table and shouted to him while I fiddled with the lock. I had double-bolted the door after my trip outside to get the boxes, and now the top key was not co-operating.

"What are you doing here?" I said through the door. I jiggled the lock and tried to twist the key as I spoke. "Did you think I'd forget the punch set?"

"No, but I thought you might like some help with it. I'm on my way home."

Harry is one of those people you can always count on. In Ed's year at Tri-C, Harry has been the one to show him the ropes, to remind him of people who expect him to visit, to suggest agendas at meetings. Maybe this stop was a little over the top, even for him, but I was grateful for the company.

"You can take the whole thing if you want." Twist, turn, screech. The key only went half as far as I needed it to. "If I can get the darned door open."

"It's the rain. Our door does the same thing. Take advice from the Horace Grey Locksmith Service. Push against the door with your shoulder."

He was right. This time the key turned.

I was so glad to see him. I turned the knob and had the door open before I realized what he had said. Lightning split the sky at exactly that moment and Harry jumped, presenting me with his profile.

I had identified Frank Carlisle because two photos were similar. Now I remembered *another* profile, a much younger man caught in a compromising position at a window. A Brad Pitt look-alike.

"Hor-ace . . . !" I stepped back and gave the door a shove to close it again, but the way I said the name must have warned him. Harry put all his weight against the door just as it started to slip into place, and before I could compensate, the door was wide open and Harry was in the room.

It was too late to fake it, but I tried. "So . . . Sorry about that," I stammered. "I'm really afraid of light-ning."

"Really?" He slammed the door behind him.

"Yeah. Silly, huh? And not very . . . brave of me to leave you on the other side, was it?"

"Stupid to try."

Ray's survival training emerged. I told myself to be calm. I had to take control of the situation and fast, or I wasn't going to survive this encounter.

"Hey, somebody's not in a good mood," I said, forcing a smile. "Did the spring social committee come after you again?"

"Can it, Aggie. You got too close to the truth. You just wouldn't leave it alone."

I stopped pretending. "It was the scrapbook, wasn't it?"

"I thought I took care of *every* photo of that picnic until you showed me the scrapbook this morning. Of course, I didn't even know about the movie until last year when you mentioned you'd seen one. I never noticed anybody with a movie camera that day. I didn't know what you'd seen, but it still worried me. I went through your house a couple of times when you were gone, but I couldn't find the movies. I couldn't get to them until you so thoughtfully put them back in the closet a couple of months ago. And there was the picnic."

So much for the Women's Society checking for dust

bunnies when I wasn't around. Harry had been my phantom home inspector. I shivered and wished I'd been smarter. "I don't have a shred of proof about anything. I can't identify the man with Gelsey."

"I'll do it for you. Francis Xavier Carlucci. Better known these days as Frank Carlisle, thanks to a little name change when he was eighteen. His father was Carmine Carlucci, a major player back in Brooklyn."

It's never a good sign when the bad guy starts clearing things up. Obviously Harry thought I might as well die knowing the truth. So far he hadn't pulled a gun. There was no reason to think that advantage would last.

I tried to picture the rest of the house. A door to the backyard in the kitchen, one outside to the garage. The kitchen was my best bet. I began to back in that direction. Harry edged around me, cutting off the quickest route without giving me a clear shot at the front door, so I backed toward the dining room.

"Ed's on his way over here," I said. "He didn't want me to come."

"His meeting's not even halfway done. I was there."

"What connection do you have to this?"

"Does it matter?"

"I've spent a lot of time thinking about it. Humor me."

"You already figured out Carlisle was Jennifer's father, right?"

I shrugged.

"He was Gelsey's business partner in a little venture in Vegas. She got pregnant, he talked her into giving up the baby. Arranged the whole thing himself. Even talked her into marrying Falowell and getting out of town."

"How do you know all this?"

"Because I worked for him. Only I was Horace Greystoke in those days. I'm listed as Horace in the church directory. You've never noticed?"

Tarzan, son of Lord Greystoke . . . Tarzan, who had rated his very own page in Gelsey's book.

I had heard emotion in Harry's voice, now I tried desperately to dissect it.

"This is all so much history," I said. "Not worth protecting, Harry. You had a good life here. Friends, money from your family . . . Oh, maybe not, huh? The Wal-Mart stock and family farm?"

He smiled a little. "Wouldn't that be nice?"

"I guess it's not a coincidence you landed in Emerald Springs."

"I was in trouble in Vegas. Frankie thought I ought to get out of town. And I liked the idea of babysitting Gelsey. She was some piece of work, wasn't she?"

"You didn't like her." It wasn't a question.

"She tried to blackmail me back in the old days. She caught me with one of her Gorgeous Guys on camera. I didn't know he had any connection to her. She was going to tell Frankie I was gay, something I knew he didn't want to hear. She threatened me, but I helped her see reason the old-fashioned way. I told her if she did it, she wouldn't be so gorgeous anymore."

I tried not to react. "I can see why you were angry at her."

"So when I had to leave town I liked the idea of just sitting around, watching her for Frankie and knowing she understood why I was here. When Frankie or his friends need me, I go off and do other things, but this is as good a base as any."

"I'm surprised Carlisle didn't just have her killed." I winced at my own words. Of course he *had* eventually.

"Frankie had a soft spot for Gelsey. He never really got over it. Not even when her husband died and she asked for help finding their daughter. He should have put a stop to things then, but he didn't. That's when I came into the picture."

"So he sent you to make sure she stayed quiet?"

"Frankie told her the girl was safe and happy. He told her to leave it alone. By then it was more than his wife finding out. He was into politics. He'd always kept a low profile with his other activities. He watched his own father take the heat over and over again, so he protected himself. When it came time to run for office, there wasn't much the muckrakers could dig up."

"Except Jennifer."

"But not unless Gelsey went public."

I was almost in the dining room now. Harry didn't seem concerned. I was afraid I knew why.

I kept talking, but my mind was whirling, trying to figure out what he was going to do and how. "I bet Gelsey hated having you in town."

"She wasn't happy about it." Until this moment he hadn't looked angry. Conflicted, maybe. Even sorry to be here but resigned. Now, though, I'd hit a nerve.

I tried to sound like his friend. "She did something to you, didn't she? She tried to get back at you. Last month when we were talking about Ed, you told me she tried to get you fired, too."

The Harry I had known had never seemed menacing. Now with a muscle jumping in his clenched jaw and his eyes narrowed, I was afraid I saw the inner hit man.

"Trying to get me fired was nothing. I was indispensable. For once, nobody listened to her. No, it was bigger than that. She threatened to out me," he said, as if we were still friends and he wanted my sympathy. "Just like she had before. She said she'd already started some rumors and soon everybody in town would know, and the word would get up to Frankie."

"You must have been furious. That wasn't any of her business."

"I got back at her. I told her the truth about her daughter."

"You told her Jennifer hadn't been adopted?"

"And worse. How sick she was, how screwed up."

I wondered why he was telling me this. There was something here I didn't understand.

"She must have been beside herself." I felt the dining room table at my back. I moved around it and bumped a chair.

"She said she'd go public. That she'd tell the world, that she didn't care about her reputation. She was going to ruin Frankie's. That's why he came to town. She refused to see him, so he had to surprise her at the picnic."

"Senator Carlisle must have said something to her that day to calm her down."

"He told her he'd have Jennifer killed if Gelsey told any-body the truth."

Along the way I'd had a few moments of sympathy for Gelsey Falowell. Now I could almost feel her despair. She had made some terrible mistakes, but she probably hadn't realized until the day of that picnic how deep a hole she had dug for herself and her baby girl.

I manufactured a nod. "I guess that shut her up."

"Let's just say it gave her a compelling reason to help me get rid of every trace of Frankie's presence at that picnic. Of course, we thought we had done just that."

"Until I came along and mentioned seeing the movie."

"Uh huh. And, of course, that made us wonder what else we had missed. I guess the only way Gelsey could think of to stop you from cataloging everything and asking questions was to get your husband fired. If Ed wasn't here, you weren't here. Then she could take over the archives the way she had taken over everything else in the church and make sure there was nothing left to see."

I couldn't think about that. Just by trying to do a good deed for the church I had caused this problem for Ed. If I worried about that now, I might never have the opportunity to worry again.

I struggled to sound sympathetic. "I bet the senator was angry at you for telling Gelsey about Jennifer, though. I bet he didn't realize how she drove you to it. He probably never saw the side of her you and I did." False comradeship. I was ready to try anything.

"He got over it after a while, that and me being gay. I was too valuable to him. Valuable to everybody, that's me. Then Jennifer came to town. All ready to tell Gelsey who she was. All ready to tell the world. And she wasn't going to stop there. I knew I had to take care of things."

"You thought Jennifer might find out who her father was, too. You were afraid Gelsey might tell her. But Sax Dubin-sky killed Jennifer, Harry. Not you."

"Dubinsky was only supposed to rough her up and scare her off. I told him that. Frankie didn't want his own daughter dead. But something went wrong."

I had a revelation. "You *knew* Gelsey was coming to our house that morning. It must have been on Ed's appointment calendar. You were the one who made sure the body ended up our doorstep just before Gelsey arrived."

"Dubinsky killed her by accident in his buddy's SUV, then he called me. So I told him to take her somewhere and wait for the right moment to drop her on your porch. Gelsey would get the message, but she wouldn't be the focus of the investigation, the way she would have been if we'd dropped the body at her house."

"You knew everything that was going on in the church. You knew every event, every rumor, every appointment."

"Brilliant, huh? I took the job to keep a closer eye on Gelsey. It was kind of a joke. I wanted to show her I was watching everything she did. I thought she would quit the church, but she didn't. She was too stubborn. Then the job turned out to be a real treasure trove. Why do you think Frankie *knew* he couldn't get rid of me, even after I screwed up? How do you think I figured out who Jennifer was and what she wanted?"

"You hadn't been watching Jennifer, too?"

"I'd never seen her until she came to town. Frankie kept tabs on her through other people. But that first day she came to see Ed I could hear her shouting, even with his door closed. I figured out right away who she was and what we needed to do about her. And later I figured out how to show Gelsey what would happen if she said a word to anybody."

"But the morning we found the body Gelsey didn't know Jennifer was her daughter."

"Not then. But I knew we'd never keep it a secret. Ed was going to tell her. It was a matter of time unless I killed Ed, and I really wanted to avoid that if I could."

Something else I couldn't think about. How close my husband had come to being a victim himself. "So you told her?"

"She didn't take it well. So I didn't really have a choice. This time she wasn't going to listen to anybody, so I had to dispense with her."

"Did she threaten you? The gun probably went off when

you struggled, and that's self-defense. And Sax isn't talking. You can walk out of this with a short sentence. Don't screw this up now."

He actually looked sorry. "You've been a friend, Aggie, just like Ed. The church came to mean something to me. Nobody there tried to change me. Nobody thought twice about who I was. I don't like doing this."

"Then don't."

"I'm left with no choice. I've got to protect Frankie. That's why I'm telling you the whole thing. I want you to understand. I don't want you to think it's personal."

"It's pretty darned personal. My girls are going to take it personally, and so is my husband."

"There's no other way. You're the only one who knows the connection between Frankie and Gelsey."

"If they find me dead in this house, they'll know I opened the door to somebody, and they'll figure it must have been somebody I knew. And you left the meeting early, so you won't have an alibi."

He shook his head. "Who would suspect me?"

"Because Gelsey had a photo of you and another man together. From the days when she planned to blackmail you, I bet. That's how I finally recognized you. And she kept a book with information about a lot of men who used her services. She called you Tarzan. I broke the code today. Somebody else will break it once I'm dead."

He gave a low whistle. "You've really been doing your homework."

"Point is, I've hidden that stuff, but it will come to light after I die. Detective Roussos knows about it, and tonight I called him and told him about Carlisle being Jennifer's father. He'll go after Carlisle right away. Roussos has seen everything. He'll show it around with enthusiasm and somebody will recognize you."

He chewed his lip. "You want to tell me where the stuff is hidden?"

"You're kidding, right?"

"It won't be hard for me to get into the parsonage again

and have another look around. I'll take a casserole and a sympathy card. Maybe your girls will help."

"If you kill me, Ed's going to be suspicious of everybody. You won't get past the front porch. And besides, what makes you think the photo's in the house? That's the first place anybody would check. I'm not stupid."

"No? You don't think it was stupid to poke your nose where it didn't belong?"

"In hindsight, I'd do things differently."

His heart wasn't in our exchange. He was thinking, and I knew about what. I had edged farther around the table, and my fingers were only inches from the punch bowl. I knew he was armed, but he hadn't yet drawn his gun. He was overly confident about how defenseless I was, and maybe just as reluctant about what he had to do.

"I can't kill you here," he said.

"Tie me up then, and leave me. That will give you a chance to get out of town ahead of the cops. And it's one less murder, in case you don't make it."

"Not enough of a head start."

"Then leave me somewhere else, someplace they won't find me so quickly." I was just buying time. I didn't expect him to like my suggestion.

"I know a place like that," he said, surprising me. "A place nobody will look."

While he debated with himself he was as off guard as he was going to be. I lunged and grabbed the punch bowl, knocking over everything else in the center of the table. The spring social committee wasn't going to like this. The bowl is lead crystal. It holds gallons of punch, and it weighs a ton. I swung it for all I was worth and hit Harry squarely in the midriff.

The bowl shattered. Harry went down, and I didn't stay to see the destruction. I turned and bolted for the kitchen door.

I jiggled the key and twisted the knob for all I was worth, putting all my weight against the door. Just as the lock gave way, the world went black.

19

Through the years I've awakened from nightmares into the reassuring familiarity of my own bedroom. But rarely have I awakened in*to* a nightmare. Unfortunately, this one was a real doozy. My head felt like someone had used it for batting practice. My hands were bound behind my back and something was stuffed in my mouth, making it impossible to speak and not that easy to breathe.

I couldn't tell where I was, although I could open my eyes, so I knew I wasn't blindfolded. I tried to stretch my legs, but there was no room. I told myself not to panic, to keep breathing, while I tried to figure out what had happened.

Little by little the scene at Gelsey's house unfolded. Harry Grey. Tarzan. Reasons why Harry thought I might need to personally evaluate afterlife theories sooner than later.

But Harry hadn't killed me. I was here, wherever "here" was, and unless eternal life smelled like tires and car exhaust, I was still alive.

Once the memories returned I realized I had to be in the trunk of a car. I could feel the movement now, the not so gentle sway beneath me. I was curled around a spare tire.

The metal digging into my back was probably a jack. I had no idea how long I had been here or how long I would be. It was entirely possible Harry intended to kill me when we arrived at our destination. If the headache didn't kill me first.

I flexed my ankles and found they weren't tied. Harry had hit me so hard he'd probably figured I'd be out for the count. And I was sure he'd wanted to get me out of Gelsey's house as quickly as possible, in case Ed or Roussos arrived. So he had tied my wrists, just in case, then chucked me in here like a sack of groceries.

I could kick the trunk and alert somebody I was inside, but not until we stopped. And once we did, what were the chances we would be smack dab in the middle of a busy parking lot? We were heading to a place where no one would hear a thing. Harry wouldn't shoot me while I was still in the trunk. Too hard to remove all that nasty evidence. If he was planning to kill me, he would do it wherever he hoped to leave my lifeless body. He'd made a serious mistake by not tying my feet. But now I could only pray he didn't think to rectify that the moment he opened the trunk.

I said that prayer and others.

I made myself breathe slowly. I told myself not to panic. It was possible Harry had taken my words to heart and planned to leave me someplace where I wouldn't be found for a while. He knew there was evidence that could lead straight to him and no matter what, he had to get out of town.

He didn't know that Ed had never flipped a mattress in his life and probably wouldn't use my disappearance as an excuse to start. Gelsey's bundle of goodies would snuggle between mattress and box springs until Ed married again.

Maybe it was that last thought, or maybe just general circumstances, but by the time the car slowed, I was as furious as I was frightened.

The rumble stopped and the car was no longer moving. I heard a door open, then shut. I closed my eyes and went limp. Harry had to get me out of the trunk and take me somewhere. I was going to make that as difficult as possible.

I heard a screech, then felt a whoosh of air. Rain splattered against my cheek. I was surprised that as angry as I was, the drops didn't immediately turn to steam. Instinctively I fed on the anger, thinking of Jennifer and the way her sad life had been cut short, of Gelsey, who, at the end, wanted to do the right thing for her daughter. Of my own daughters and how they would feel if I died before they had the chance to reject me in adolescence.

I could feel Harry's breath against my face as he leaned over. His finger grazed my throat, but I told myself not to react. He probed, then his fingertip settled just under my chin. He was checking my pulse, wondering, I thought, if his work was already done.

Satisfied or "un," he abandoned my throat. I felt his arms dig their way under me, felt myself being lifted. I heard his grunt, and I was glad I hadn't joined Lucy while she spent the month of July on the South Beach Diet. I was glad for every single pound and my healthy body image.

Harry isn't a large man. He has a gaunt frame and small bones. Neither were serving him well. I remained limp and felt him stagger as he carried me. He shifted my weight in his arms and my head rolled to rest against his side, or at least that's how it felt to me. My eyes flew open and adjusted quickly. We were in a lightly wooded area. Clouds obscured whatever moon was there, and rain fell steadily, making it hard to see more than a few yards.

I heard an oath at the same moment Harry stumbled. He nearly dropped me but managed to right himself. My head bobbed face up again and I closed my eyes. But not before I'd gotten my first clue. As we had dipped together, I had seen a lone light shining on a triangular metal structure. My brain was not working as quickly or skillfully as normal, but I kept that snapshot in my mind as we stumbled along.

A playground. A swing set. I had a vision of Teddy on the same structure. But where?

The service center.

We were at the new service center, which wasn't due to be occupied until next week. Harry would know the place inside and out, since his partner had designed the entire layout and all the buildings for the city.

I doubted this boded well for me. The site might be deserted now, but it housed a public playground, a jogging and exercise trail, empty buildings that wouldn't stay empty long. Workmen would probably arrive tomorrow to attend to last-minute details. Moving companies would be arriving this week with furniture and equipment. If Harry only needed a brief head start, this site might work. But why limit himself to hours instead of days?

Unless he planned to make sure nobody was going to find me for a very long time. And when they did, it wasn't going to be pretty.

He had access to every key in the place through Greg. This was not a good thing.

My anger bloomed. Harry was going to kill me where my children had played, where my husband had given the dedication prayer, where Roussos had razzed me about my dimple.

I didn't have many chances to get out of this, and all of them would depend on one thing. At my father's knee I learned reasons for adrenaline and, even more, its uses. I learned how women are taught not to give in to anger and how men depend on that. As Harry staggered along I worked myself into a fury, visualizing exactly what I would like to do to our church secretary and how many times. I felt no guilt. This was a vision of sorts, albeit an unorthodox one. After all, God had said, "Thou shalt not kill." I was going to protect Harry from himself.

Ray would have been proud. I wasn't so sure about Moses.

Harry slowed, then stopped. He lowered me to the ground, and I heard gravel crunch as he stepped away from me. I opened my eyes just enough to see that his back was turned. The tepee-shaped dome where road salt was stored for winter maintenance, salt that probably came from Bob Knowles's family mines, loomed in front of him, and I suddenly understood what he intended. Entombment in a pillar of salt.

I rolled over and got to my feet, pushing off the ground with my elbows. I was clumsy and for a moment disoriented. I was also noisy.

Harry whirled, key to the door of the dome in hand. The key dropped as he lunged for me. I found my balance, pivoted on my left foot, raised my right knee, and the moment he was in striking range and with the precision my father had drilled into me, I slammed the side of my ankle boot just below Harry's knee.

He fell forward, but not before I slammed my foot lower and finally, stomped with all my strength right where the shin stopped and the foot began.

He howled with pain and grabbed for his foot. It was all I needed. I spun and began to run. At first I was off balance, my head throbbing so hard that the spaces between raindrops were the color of blood. Even when I recovered my balance I was disoriented and sluggish. I wasn't sure where we had come from or where I should go. I just knew I needed cover.

Lightning flashed, and I saw that the new buildings were off to my right, not far from the work yard and the dome itself. Maybe Harry thought I could find eternal rest buried under a thousand tons of salt. Maybe he hoped that someday when the salt trucks scooped deep into the pile, my desiccated body would be loaded along with salt particles, chewed up by the augers of the truck and distributed forever on the streets of Emerald Springs.

But Harry was wrong. If I died, I was going to do it right here in the open air, with the rain on my face, fighting for my life.

I heard a familiar zinging noise. I learned to shoot a pistol the year I was eleven. That summer my friends went to Camp Hiawatha and made lanyards and popsicle stick baskets. I learned to clean and load a 9 mm Glock at Camp Vigilance.

I zigged and zagged to make hitting me harder. A bullet passed entirely too close to my head. I zagged and zigged, crouching as low as I could without throwing myself off balance. Harry wouldn't be following close behind. I was fairly sure I'd broken a bone or two of the more than twenty in his foot. He would be limping and cursing and trying, through his pain, to take aim. I was going to make that as difficult as possible.

I reached the service center garage. Hugging the outside wall I followed it to the end and around the back. There was no place to hide where he wouldn't find me immediately. A set of dumpsters I couldn't climb without using my hands, a couple of portable johns that hadn't yet been hauled away, a stand of young trees that looked out of place, since they were the only trees for some distance. Harry had carried me through the only "forest" in the area. Someday the land behind me would be a rec center and swimming pool, but now it was pasture, knee-deep in dried weeds with no place to hide.

I stopped and listened. I was sure I would hear Harry coming, stumbling, because no matter how tough he was, putting weight on that foot had to be excruciating. My best bet was to circle the building away from whatever direction he chose, then, if I was lucky, make a break for the road that ran past the center. There had to be houses and people in reach. I had a chance, if I could only make it that far. And the only way to know when I could make the break was to listen.

The problem, of course, was that Harry could listen, too.

The rain was falling harder now, pinging against the metal johns, splatting against the gravel that rimmed the garage. I flattened myself against the wall and waited.

Just as I was starting to panic, I heard something scraping along the side from which I had just come. I could almost hear Harry's mental debate. *Follow her trail, or go the other way. Which would she expect?*

I skirted the building, moving as quietly as I could. As a little girl I'd had the requisite ballet lessons in some town or other. Junie had quickly determined I had no talent, but now I pulled myself high and walked on tiptoe, telling myself I was as light as a butterfly, as weightless as a moonbeam. I tried desperately to float.

Near the front, again I debated whether to flee or make another circle. If Harry was behind the building I had a few moments head start. I could dodge through the playground, cross the jogging trail, make my way out to the road. I couldn't remember exactly what was there, but surely there would be shelter somewhere. Trees or ditches or even cars to flag.

I fled.

I heard one last bullet streaking past my right ear before every floodlight on the grounds switched on. I was bathed in light, a target now with no place to hide. Then I heard a voice magnified through a bullhorn.

"Surrender your weapon. You are surrounded."

My knees began to knock. I stumbled. I saw a man with a shotgun coming toward me, another with nothing in his hands running ahead of him. I heard sirens in the distance.

I fell into Ed's arms, then all the way down as he jerked me to the ground. Roussos streaked by us, and I heard one final blast before I passed out.

20

The ER at Emerald Springs General is one notch more comfortable than the trunk of a car. I spent the rest of Monday night in a curtained cubicle being awakened periodically, poked, prodded, and asked if I remembered why I was there.

As if I was going to forget any time soon.

On Tuesday, in my own bed, I slept with only the occasional break, one of which was spent pointing out a certain package nestled under the mattress so that Ed could return it to Roussos.

When I awoke on Wednesday morning, the pain in my head was more gentle roar than screaming tirade. Teddy was cuddled beside me, frowning.

I sleepily stroked her hair. "Hello. You look worried."

"You haven't been talking."

I wondered how much she had been told. "Sometimes sleep is the only way to get better."

"Are you finally better?"

"I think I am."

"It's taking too long."

"I agree."

"I have to go to school today. Daddy says so."

"It's the right thing to do."

"Can Jimmy come home with me after?"

"Probably not today." I paused as my injured brain sifted through information. "Jimmy? The boy who was mean to you?"

"His hamster died. That's why he was so sad."

"Uh huh."

"I told him we can do a funeral. His mother threw Bucky in the trash, but we're going to pretend. It will make him feel better."

I put my arms around her and pulled her closer. "There's lots of time to think about seminary, but your father will nudge you toward Harvard."

"I probably have to finish first grade."

" 'Fraid so."

I was sitting up, testing what serious movement would do to the day's prognosis, when Deena came in. She was dressed in her usual jeans and a leaf green fleece pullover. Her lovely hair was bare. I was encouraged.

"Hey, you're sitting up." She smiled.

"And doing it very well, I might add."

"Daddy's making you breakfast in bed."

"That almost makes getting hit in the head worth it."

"Did you know Harry was a bad person? Before, I mean?"

I considered my answer. I wanted to tell her yes, that people were predictable, and I had spotted Harry's dark side the first time I laid eyes on him. I wanted her to feel safe with the people she knows, not worried that they, too, might turn into killers.

But I couldn't lie. Deena would need the truth to make her way through life.

"I didn't know. I saw a different man. Maybe the one I saw was at least partly real, and that's why the other part was so well hidden." I wondered what had happened to Harry, but Deena wasn't the person to ask.

"Can people really be that bad and still be partly good?" she asked.

Where was Ed when I needed him?

"Never mind." She knelt carefully on the bed and hugged me. "I know the answer."

"Great. What is it?"

"Nobody really knows."

I kissed her hair. "There's some good news. Most of the people you meet will only be a little bit bad."

"Did you really break Harry's foot?"

"I don't know. Did I?"

"He's in a cast. How did you learn that?"

"Your grandpa thought I might need to know how to protect myself someday."

I didn't want to tell her now, but in the not so distant future, Deena was going to be learning self-defense techniques of her own. I was definitely going to see to it. I could see an entire karate class of Green Meanies working on their black belts. I was terrified imagining such a thing.

She left, and I pondered the image of my captor in a cast. Harry must have lived through Roussos's shotgun blast.

I thought Ed would be my next visitor, but instead Lucy arrived with a tray of scrambled eggs, toast, coffee, and, from her voluminous Coach satchel, an order of crisp bacon in Styrofoam. She was dressed in black, as if she had anticipated worse than me sitting up. Her expression was surprisingly somber.

"Shhh . . ." she said, looking around furtively. "I got the bacon at Lana's Lunch and it's still warm. If you eat it fast, Ed will never know. The eggs and toast are from him."

I dug right in, scruples temporarily on the wane. "How did you know bacon's what I miss the most?"

"When we eat breakfast together, you look like you're going to snatch it off my plate."

"The bedroom smells like a smokehouse. Ed will know."

"I'll crack a window, but don't worry, he won't toss you out. He's been absolutely beside himself."

"You could fool me. Where *is* the guy?"

She opened the window beside my bed. From outside I could hear the call of a cardinal. "There's some kind of committee meeting downstairs."

"Charming. They'll probably fire Ed because I crippled our secretary instead of coming to a peaceful consensus on the best way to handle his aggression." I looked up. "What happened to Harry, Luce?"

She carefully lowered herself to the side of the bed. "He's in jail. Broken foot, injured arm, cracked ribs."

"The ribs are probably a punch bowl injury. It must have nearly killed him to lift me in and out of the trunk. Stay away from punch bowls on general principles, Luce. They're lethal."

She shook her head. "Detective Sergeant Roussos did some damage. Enough that Harry surrendered. How did Roussos only manage to hit him in the arm? With a shotgun of all things?"

"Cops shoot to kill. Anything else is too dangerous. But I guess Harry was too far away to be a good target. He just lucked out. I bet Roussos is a sharpshooter."

"*You* lucked out." She put her hand on mine. "Aggie, are you out of your mind?"

"What? For trusting a guy with a collection of handblown paperweights? For not thinking that the man who bought doll clothes for Teddy at the last rummage sale could be a murderer?"

"No, for not waiting until I got back into town!"

I grinned, and my head didn't split wide open. Another very good sign. "Trust me, this was one gig you were lucky to miss."

She was pouting, prettily, of course. "Well, I do have one piece of gossip. Good news and bad news."

"Uh huh?"

"But you don't sound interested enough."

"Have I ever described my first labor to you? Starting with my doctor's visit that morning?"

She held up her hand. "Okay, but only because you're semi-incapacitated."

"And . . . ?"

"I talked to Bob Knowles yesterday." Another pause.

"Luce, it's hard to keep with the 'uh huhs' and 'tell me mores.' Give me a break, okay? Just this once."

"He's decided to start a trust fund for Gelsey's grandchildren. Nice sized, too."

Maybe I'm just an emotional mess. Or maybe recovery from a head injury strips off all protective layers. But I teared up. Lucy rose and got me a box of tissues, usually my job.

"For a while I thought he was Gelsey's murderer." I sniffed and blew my nose.

"Don't get too sentimental. When probate ends he'll have more money than he'll know what to do with," Lucy said. "He can probably write it off somehow, since he's vaguely related. But still, it's a nice thing."

"Now the family that wants to adopt them can afford to. The fund can pay for college."

"That was the good news."

"Oh, great."

"Bad news next. He's selling Book Gems."

"What?"

"Bob's moving to Cleveland. He wants to put this whole episode behind him. A family named Giovanni approached him. They already have their money on the table, but they have enough kids and cousins to staff the store. It'll be a real mom and pop enterprise."

At least Emerald Springs still had a bookstore, even if I was out a job.

Lucy read my mind. "You didn't love working there. You know you didn't. Business was too slow. You didn't have enough say in what you were doing."

"Maybe not, but I'm going to be looking for work again."

"Well, I don't think so."

I looked up from my eggs. The bacon was history. "Why not?"

"Here's the thing." She touched her nose, as if it were some weird sort of totem. "I've bought the house across the street."

"You did what? You already have a house."

"Not for me. Good grief. You don't think I'd want to live that close to you, do you?" She winked. "We'd never get anything done."

"Then what for?"

"You and I are starting a business. This first house is on me. I bought it, but we'll split the profits once we sell. Then we'll buy the next one together. I'll be on the lookout for houses that need TLC but not major overhauls."

I wasn't following this. "Buy, sell, buy? My head hurts. Take pity."

"Aggie, you know how to make a house a home. You've done it a million times. You know what to fix up and what to repair and what to camouflage. We'll haul out the junk, replace the countertops, paint the cupboards, buy new hardware . . ." She went on, regurgitating the points I'd made on the morning poor Jennifer showed up on my porch.

She finished at last. "We'll hire somebody to do the work we can't do ourselves. And when it's all ready, I'll sell the house at a good profit. And it will sell. There's a market for houses buyers can move right into. You can work in your spare time. It's a cinch."

It made a crazy kind of sense. And already I could feel myself getting excited at the prospects. I love houses. I love seeing them come to life. I could work while the girls were in school. Heck, they could help me do some of the work themselves to earn spending money. If something came up, no problem. And, if we were really lucky, no one would stage a protest because I painted a bedroom yellow or planted landscape roses instead of rhododendrons.

There was only one problem. I was pretty sure I was going to be living in Boston.

I wasn't ready to tell Lucy. Besides, she was busy taking my tray and folding back the bedcovers. "Time for a shower. Think you can manage? I'll stay here to be sure you're okay."

"Can I change into real clothes?"

"Something comfortable."

The shower felt good, although washing my hair wasn't fun. I gently towel dried it and slipped into a black jogging suit and wool socks.

When I emerged Roussos was standing by the window talking to Lucy.

"Look what you've got," Lucy said, holding out a bouquet of gold-tipped spider mums. "From the policeman's own garden."

"You look pale," he said. Roussos looked uncomfortable, as if I might sink to the ground again and require some action on his part.

There was something about getting back between the sheets with Roussos standing there that bothered me. I chose a chair in the corner and lowered myself demurely.

I closed my eyes a moment. "My stars are aligned today. My horoscope says I will be popular beyond measure."

He smiled. "We're just glad you're around to visit.

"You're not going to start in on me, are you?"

"About what? Tampering with my case? Narrowly avoiding getting killed?"

"Just tell me you arrested Frank Carlisle. Or do I have to spell out his connection to Harry?"

"I'll need to take your statement later today. But Harry's been obliging. He's hoping for some favors. Like us taking the death penalty off the table."

"I'm opposed to capital punishment."

"I more or less figured you were."

"He told you he murdered Gelsey?"

"Said she put up a struggle. Called it self-defense."

"He's lying, and by the way, I'm not opposed to life in prison without parole. Not even for old friends. Harry killed Gelsey because she was going to tell the world Frank Carlisle had their daughter murdered. That was apparently a mistake, by the way. Jennifer's murder, I mean. Sax was just supposed to scare her away."

"Dubinsky is still going away for a long, long time, mistake or no."

"What about Carlisle?"

"We're making the case. When we're done, he won't be around to bother you or anybody else again."

Lucy looked at her watch. "I've got to get going." She held up the flowers, six huge, perfect specimens. "I'll take these down and put them in water. If I can find out what's going on downstairs, I'll call you and let you know. I'll ring once and hang up first."

"I thrive on secret codes."

Lucy bent over and kissed my cheek. "Don't stay too long," she told Roussos.

I looked up after she left, and Roussos was towering over me.

"The flowers are lovely," I said.

He squatted beside the chair, so we were eye to eye. "You're doing okay?"

"I feel better today."

"You went through a lot. I think you should see somebody a couple of times, just to talk things out."

I was touched. "Maybe I will."

"Don't try to tough it out. Work through it and get it over with."

I managed a smile. "Thank you for coming to my rescue. You and Ed."

"It was too close for comfort."

"I'm glad you listened to your voice mail. I'm glad you took me seriously. I thought you'd roll your eyes and think I was a complete idiot."

"I might have rolled my eyes. I don't remember." He smiled, too. It was an extraordinary sight.

"I . . . well, a lot of what happened is still kind of blurry. And maybe I'm not thinking too clearly yet. But I can't quite figure out how you knew where to look for me."

"You made it easy. If it hadn't been for the clues you left, we might not have figured it out."

"Oh. The clues." I tried to think. My headache crescendoed.

"I don't know how you had the presence of mind to knock over the salt shaker right on top of the newspaper photo of Carlisle. But it clicked big-time for me. I saw that little mound of salt right on Carlisle's face, your husband saw the shattered punch bowl Harry was so worried about. He knew Harry's roommate designed the service center complex. I realized you were leading us to the salt dome. It all made sense."

"Sense . . ." I closed my eyes. "Good. Right."

He squeezed my hand. When I opened my eyes, he was gone.

✦ ✦ ✦

I had to go downstairs sometime. Lucy and Roussos had been gone awhile when I decided to chase away everybody with the bad manners to confront my husband while I was still recovering. I wasn't sure what I had to lose. If I behaved badly, we could claim it was my poor injured brain. Or better, we could explain if our visitors didn't like it, they could fire Ed—which was most likely why they were here in the first place.

It was a no-lose situation.

As I carefully descended I detected the scent of roses. I caught sight of the first bouquet on the table at the foot of the stairs. One degree at a time I turned my head and saw that the living room was filled with flowers.

I heard the kitchen door slam, then Ed came into the hallway.

"What are you doing up?"

"Where is everybody?"

"They just left. Out the back way. That seems to be the preferred route these days."

He came over and wrapped his arms around me. I slumped against him. "It smells like somebody died," I said. "It smells like a funeral in here."

"You have a lot of friends. The Meanie moms sent a gift certificate to the Emerald Spa. May suggests a massage. Crystal O'Grady suggests Botox."

I sniffed. That brain injury thing again.

"The sofa for you," he said.

He dragged me to the sofa and tucked me in with one of Junie's afghans. "Tea, coffee?"

"Just you." I patted the sofa, and he perched on the edge facing me. He looked worse for wear. His eyes were puffy from lack of sleep. His beard looked even scragglier than usual. It was probably going to be history soon.

He smoothed my hair back from my forehead. "Your head's better?"

"Uh huh. What did the doctor say?"

"That you'll need to take it easy for the rest of the week. No stress."

"Gosh, is he sending me to the Caribbean?"

He smiled and touched my cheek with the back of his fingers. My eyelids drifted closed. "There were moments Monday night when I wondered if I'd ever feel you do that again," I said.

"Damn it, I would have shot Harry myself if I'd had the gun."

I opened my eyes. "You're a pacifist."

"We can safely say I'm not."

"Wouldn't it have been funny if at the very end of my life, I finally had *something* in common with Gelsey? Harry."

He lifted my hand to his lips and kissed it. "Don't even joke about it."

"You might as well tell me."

"What?"

"Why that committee was here."

"It's going to complicate your life."

"Oh, my poor simple life. How can I cope?"

"That was Tom and Yvonne and about six others from the board."

"Well, there's always Boston."

"That's the complication. Everybody wants me. The Tri-C board wants me to stay here. They've given me a full vote of confidence. They delivered dozens of letters in support from people in the congregation."

"Wow."

"And Boston says an offer's in the making."

"Oh . . ." For a moment I couldn't wrap my mind around this. "Oh. We could stay here if we wanted? Or we can go?"

"The board's proposed a raise to go with their offer— now that they can count on Gelsey's addition to the endowment. How's that for irony? And they sweetened the deal with a new floor for the kitchen. They think we deserve it after everything."

"Bargain for a new sink while you're at it."

"What do you think?"

Boston was a wonderful city, but it wasn't the life we had chosen for ourselves. Ed had wanted time to breathe, time to pursue his beloved research. Despite the pleasures of a large city, I guess now I wanted to raise our daughters somewhere less intense. Maybe I'd had some reservations about Emerald Springs, but I'd made friends here and so had our children.

I tried to feel my way through an explanation. "This whole thing had to be an aberration. This is a quiet town, an easy place to live. Nothing else could go wrong, could it?"

"I'm inclined to stay, if you're willing."

There was plenty of time to tell him about Lucy's plan for my future.

"Let's," I said.

"Then it's a done deal."

"Before you leave me so I can take the next nap of the day, I just have a quick question."

"Sure. What?"

"You being the real moral compass of the family."

"Uh huh. What do I need to point to?"

I pictured an overturned salt shaker on Gelsey's dining room table, and a sheet of newspaper from our recycling bin. I pictured a shattered punch bowl—and boy, did I hate to tell the spring social committee about that.

"Let's just say there's this woman I know. And she was very brave, even remarkably daring one night. But she did not, in fact, lead a certain police detective and her husband to the place where a murderer intended to kill her. Let's just say that as she grabbed something off a certain table to throw at her attacker, she probably knocked over everything else in sight."

"And the dilemma?"

"Well, does she take credit where none is due? Or does she make a painful confession and admit it was purely accidental?"

"Well, is she absolutely sure it was an accident? Remember what Freud said? Or could her unconscious have sensed the murderer's intentions and triggered her actions to save herself? Or was this some entity outside herself taking action? Some mysterious force in the universe acting for her good? The answer to a prayer she doesn't even remember praying?"

"You had to complicate this, didn't you?"

"That's what a good moral compass does." He kissed me. I put my arms around his neck and kept him there for a long moment. I never wanted to let him go.

"So I don't have to tell Roussos?" I said after he sat back up.

"I didn't say that."

"He won't buy the unconscious, mysterious force, answer to a prayer explanation."

"He doesn't have time to think like that. He has to act and act fast."

"So maybe I shouldn't complicate his life. You know? Besides, it doesn't really matter. Our paths won't even cross again. Right?"

"Promise me this was your one and only stab at solving a murder."

"Promise me nobody will bring another case right to our doorstep."

"Aggie . . ."

I closed my eyes. Nap time. Nothing beats a concussion for closing off a conversation.